Grayslake Area Public Library District
Grayslake, Illinois

1. A fine will be charged on each book which is not returned when it is due.

2. All injuries to books beyond reasonable wear and all losses shall be made good to the satisfaction of the Librarian.

3. Each borrower is held responsible for all books drawn on his card and for all fines accruing on the same.

DEMCO

THE ★★★★ BETRAYAL

A PRECINCT 11 NOVEL

JERRY B. JENKINS

TYNDALE HOUSE PUBLISHERS, INC.
CAROL STREAM, ILLINOIS

Visit Tyndale online at www.tyndale.com.

Visit Jerry B. Jenkins's website at www.jerryjenkins.com.

TYNDALE and Tyndale's quill logo are registered trademarks of Tyndale House Publishers, Inc.

The Betrayal

Designed by Erik M. Peterson

Some Scripture taken from the New King James Version.® Copyright © 1982 by Thomas Nelson, Inc. Used by permission. All rights reserved.

Some Scripture quotations are taken from the *Holy Bible*, New Living Translation, copyright © 1996, 2004, 2007 by Tyndale House Foundation. Used by permission of Tyndale House Publishers, Inc., Carol Stream, Illinois 60188. All rights reserved.

Library of Congress Cataloging-in-Publication Data

Jenkins, Jerry B.
    The betrayal : a Precinct 11 novel / Jerry B. Jenkins.
      p. cm.
    ISBN 978-1-4143-0908-8 (hc)
    1. Police—Illinois—Chicago—Fiction. 2. Police corruption—Fiction. 3. Chicago (Ill.)—Fiction. I. Title.
    PS3560.E485B48 2011
    813'.54—dc22   2011020854

Printed in the United States of America

17 16 15 14 13 12 11
 7   6   5   4   3   2   1

To my brothers
Jim, Jeoff, and Jay

Chicago Police Department
Organized Crime Division

Chief: Fletcher Galloway

Deputy Chief: Jack Keller

Gang Enforcement Section Commander: Pete Wade

Gang Investigation Section Commander: Boone Drake

Division Secretary: Haeley Lamonica

1

★★★★

DISSONANCE

Boone Drake awoke before sunup with little recollection of the previous two days.

Oh, he knew the basics—where he was, that he was fortunate to be alive. Two uniformed officers still guarded his door. The noises and odors invaded his room at what everyone still called Cook County Hospital. And slowly, it all began to come back.

Boone, a detective in the Gang Enforcement Section of the Chicago Police Department, had masterminded the most massive sting in CPD history, bringing down the heads of not only the biggest street gangs in the city but also the Outfit—the old crime syndicate.

Key to the operation had been the secret spiritual conversion of gang kingpin Pascual Candelario—and his becoming an informant.

Candelario had been processed at central booking, then spirited to a secure location until he was due to testify before the grand jury. The story became the biggest in Chicago in decades, and the priority of the CPD became to protect Pascual at all costs until he was transferred to begin his testimony.

Two nights before, Boone and four undercover cops had ushered PC out and made their way to an unmarked van. As the group passed a security guard, Boone glanced back to find the man in full crouch, reaching behind his back. Boone had bellowed, "Gun!" and moved between the shooter and Candelario.

The man produced a .45 caliber Glock and squeezed off one deafening round from fifteen feet away. The slug hammered into Boone just below his left clavicle and knocked him to the floor. He felt his left lung collapse.

Two officers emptied their service revolvers into the man while the other two hustled Pascual into the van. Boone lay there knowing Pascual was safe and that every Chicago cop in the vicinity would respond to an officer-down call.

Boone had felt himself go woozy and fought to remain conscious. "Suicide shooter?" he rasped. "Had to be an inside job."

And he felt himself drifting, drifting. An injection. Floating. Then roughly slid into the back of an ambulance for the trip to John H. Stroger Jr. Hospital. Being bathed for an operation, anesthetic drip, the sweet relief of unconsciousness.

Boone had awakened midmorning the next day, screaming pain in the shoulder, exhausted, achy all over, his mouth cottony. His former partner and now boss, Jack Keller, leaned close. "You got questions?"

"We got a traitor?"

Jack whispered, "That or a real smart gangbanger."

Boone had had another miserable night, and not only because of the constant interruptions to check his vitals. He had been nearly shot dead, and to the best of his recollection he was on heavy doses of Percocet and OxyContin, not to mention a morphine drip. Maybe that's why the activity in his private room the day before now ran together in his mind, a jumble of incomprehensible images—including one he would never forget.

Boone had so looked forward to seeing Pastor Francisco Sosa, but now he could dredge not one memory of his visit. He had intended to tell Sosa something—something about him and Haeley. Their first kiss. The prospect of a second gave him something else to look forward to.

Today's dawn brought a male nurse who seemed terminally cheerful and insisted on turning on the local news. "I wouldn't normally do this," the man said, "but Indian summer doesn't often hit us in February, does it?"

Boone squinted at the TV. A few minutes after sunrise the temperature was already pushing fifty, with the possibility of sixty by midafternoon. And of all things, not snow but rain. Thundershowers.

Would anything in Boone's life be normal ever again?

"Don't get too comfortable," the nurse said, opening the drapes. "After breakfast a physical therapist will get you up and walking."

"I'm high," Boone slurred. "Remind me what comfortable means."

"After that your surgeon should visit, but I don't even try to predict timing for those guys. You wanna go potty before all the fun begins?"

"I do, but do we really have to call it that?"

The nurse laughed. "Just trying to be delicate, Detective. You know you're on the front page of the *Trib* this morning?"

"You don't say."

"I'll bring you one later. Now let's do this."

The nurse removed the wrappings from Boone's shins that inflated and deflated every few seconds to prevent blood clots, then slipped an anklet with rubber traction onto each foot. He helped Boone sit up and slide his legs off the edge of the bed, advising him to stay seated and get his bearings before trying to stand with his IVs attached.

Days before, Boone had been in the best shape of his life, but wobbling toward the bathroom in his cursed, open-backed gown, aided by a nurse and hissing against pain that pushed past his drug-induced haze, he felt disjointed and twice his age.

He had always hated immobility and dependence, but he knew they would be his lot until he could rehabilitate himself. Boone would be obsessive about that. He was already determined to snap back faster than any patient his caregivers had ever seen. And yet he couldn't deny that his bed, which had been miraculously changed during the moments he had relieved himself, appealed to him like an oasis.

As the nurse got him situated again, Boone pressed back against the cool sheets and felt as close to comfortable as he had since being wheeled in from surgery. Something told him that wouldn't last. Unique as this experience was, something else was off. Boone couldn't put a finger on it yet, but that would be his project for the day. He would eat what they told him to, ingest what they prescribed, start with as much physical therapy as he could abide, ask every question that came to mind . . . and try to get a handle on what had gone wrong.

The beacon that beckoned him was Haeley's next visit at the end of the day. Or might she sneak over on her lunch break? How great would that be? Maybe he could text her, ask her plans. Had she been there when Pastor Sosa was? Could she help him recall any of that visit?

But when Boone asked for his cell phone, intending to also text an apology to Sosa for anything he might have said or done, he was informed there was zero reception in Stroger Hospital. "Interferes with our equipment."

Fine. He'd call her from a landline. But first came breakfast. Swallowing was torture. Breathing remained a chore. And then came the physical therapist, who referred to herself as the PT. "You shouldn't need walker, crutches, or cane," she said. "You're unaffected from the belly down. I'll be right here if you need a hand."

She was half his size, yet Boone did find himself less steady than he expected. The trip to the bathroom should have been a harbinger, but food and more meds had made him overconfident. He shuffled down the hall—greeting and thanking the uniformed cops, rolling his IV stand with his good arm, and keeping his slinged other immobile. His recoup had only just begun, and already it seemed a life sentence.

At the end of the corridor, just past a waiting room, Boone

espied a covered balcony outside a sliding glass door. As he padded past he noted that it overlooked a parking lot. "What are the odds I could sit out there this afternoon?"

"Up to your doctor," the PT said. "You'll likely have to be in a wheelchair, in case we need to get you back inside quickly."

She told him he had done fine "for a first outing" and that she would be back midafternoon for another round.

Dr. Robert Duffey visited late morning, wearing surgical scrubs. "If you saw me on the news," he said, "we can keep this short."

"Missed it," Boone said. "Sorry."

Duffey sighed. "MRI shows your shoulder is a mess. That'll have to be rebuilt by an ortho guy. The clavicle, though painful, is the least of your problems. It'll mend itself. A bullet fragment caught the pleura and—"

"Sorry," Boone said. "I'm a layman."

"That's the double-layer membrane that surrounds the lungs and the chest wall. You were born with it airtight. It was compromised by the bullet, causing a pneumothorax, a collapsed lung. If it had been small it might have resolved on its own, but yours was total, so we had to get in there."

"What'd you do?"

"Aspirated it. Released the air with a needle. Then drained it with a chest tube and a water seal bottle. That was supposed to allow air in the chest to move into the bottle but keep air in the room from entering the pleural space, and the pressure balance should have reinflated the lung."

"Should have?"

Dr. Duffey nodded. "Didn't work. So I scraped the surface

of the pleura to cause scar tissue, which makes the two layers stick together."

"You've lost me, but you sound like you know what you're talking about."

The doctor smiled and looked weary. "That's half the battle. You're going to be okay, but you need to know that shoulder will never be the same—regardless who does the work, and I'll refer you to the best. Rehab will make you wish you'd never been born."

Boone had already been through days like that. A destroyed shoulder hardly compared to losing a wife and baby. But now, with Haeley's kiss, he had more than enough to live for. He was reaching for the phone when Pastor Sosa poked his head in.

"Francisco! Do I need to talk to you!"

Sosa pulled a chair next to the bed. "This time I plan to take notes."

"So you *were* here yesterday."

"Doesn't surprise me that you don't remember. You made no sense, Boone."

"Sorry."

"You know what you said?"

"All I remember is that you were coming."

"You asked me how many shoulders were in the human body! I assured you there was one per arm."

Laughing made Boone grimace. "Man, sometimes it hurts even to think."

Sosa read Scripture and prayed for Boone, then promised to try to make contact with Pascual Candelario if Boone could get the pastor approved through the powers that be.

"Obviously, it'll be a while before I can get back to see him," Boone said.

Boone decided against telling Sosa about the latest step in his relationship with Haeley. He found himself suddenly exhausted and was embarrassed several minutes later to awaken, realizing he had fallen asleep before Pastor Sosa had left.

By lunchtime he was ravenous and had still not called Haeley. She wouldn't visit him during her break without his having asked. Anyway, he knew she didn't get a lot of time. He resolved to call her after his afternoon PT. She would have to make arrangements for her son, Max. No way the nurses would allow the boy in.

After eating, Boone was drowsy again, wondering what the PT would do if she found him sleeping. Actually, he knew. Physical therapy took precedence.

Still something niggled at the back of his mind. Why had he heard from no one in Organized Crime? They'd been all over him the day before. At least Jack Keller should have called.

Where was Boone's brain? He had forgotten to ask Dr. Duffey about sitting outside if the weather permitted.

The PT awakened him, and Boone proved only slightly steadier this time. She got him to go twice as far, and he noticed on his way past the small patio that there seemed no trick to opening the sliding door. Who needed permission anyway?

Back in the room he phoned Haeley, but a temp answered. "She's in meetings," he was told. And when he asked for Keller, he was told the same.

"Pete Wade?" Boone tried.

"The same, sir. Sorry. There's actually no one here right now."

"Not even the big boss?"

She paused. "You haven't heard? Chief Galloway announced his retirement today."

Wasn't that just like Fletcher? The man had perfect timing. The OCD busts up all the gangs in Chicago, including the Outfit; how does one top that?

"Do me a favor. Tell Haeley I really hope to see her at the end of the day."

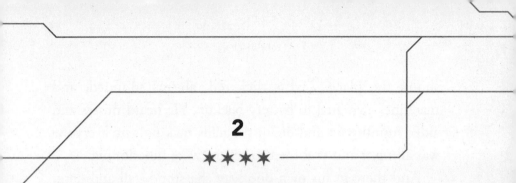

2

★ ★ ★ ★

THE OMEN

BOONE FOUND HIMSELF so antsy all afternoon that he could not sleep, despite his exhaustion from therapy and the prodding and poking of nurses.

Temperatures skyrocketed past sixty, though the sun was soon hidden by foreboding clouds. Still no word from anyone in OCD. Boone called again after four o'clock, only to find Haeley's substitute still manning the phones.

He imagined the brass hunkering down and regrouping in light of the fiasco, but what would any of that have to do with Haeley?

By five thirty, the sun had been down for half an hour, and a steady rain became a violent storm complete with long, rumbling thunder. Boone had given up on seeing Haeley when a blinding streak lit up his window and a deafening explosion shook the place. Lights flickered, alarms sounded, and machines switched to battery backup. He heard nurses and aides running up and down the halls making sure everyone was all right and that their monitors were functioning.

And there in his own doorway she stood, tall and dark, high cheekbones pronounced by flashing security lights. Haeley's business suit made her look like she could succeed Fletcher Galloway.

Warmth as soothing as morphine surged through him as she approached. He expected a smile, something, anything that would tell him their last encounter had been no dream nor drug-induced fantasy. She gathered him in her arms, clearly careful to avoid his devastated shoulder, but something was obviously wrong.

Haeley sat next to Boone's bed and forced a smile.

"You need to check on Max? Who's got him?"

"Florence. The woman from church. He's fine."

"And you?"

She shrugged.

"What's going on, Haeley?"

"Is there somewhere we can talk?"

"Is there ever. But I'll need your help with logistics."

She smirked and stood. "Everything's an operation with you."

Boone triggered a shot of morphine and talked Haeley through getting his shin dressings off, his antislip socks on, wrapping him in a blanket, arranging his IV stand, and getting him moving down the hall.

"Where to, Detective?" one of the cops said.

"Promise you won't tell anybody?" Boone said. "The staff will frown on it."

"Anything happens to you and it's our jobs."

"Florence Nightingale here will accept all responsibility." Boone told him they were going to sit out on the patio.

Haeley blurted, "Boone, no."

"Don't deny me," he said. "Nothing I love more than sitting as close as I can to a good thunderstorm."

"Not sure that's a good idea," the cop said.

"That's why it appeals so much. You guys can watch me down there as easily as you can here."

The cops shrugged and headed to the sliding door, setting up on either side of it.

Haeley held up a finger and moved to the window, peering out. "It's blowing the other way. At least you're not going to get wet."

The corridor was clear when one of the cops slid open the door, but a nurse materialized just as Haeley was helping Boone move out.

"Where do you think you're going?" the nurse said.

"When he's in his room," one cop said, "he's yours. Out here, he's ours."

"Idiots," she hissed as she hurried off.

Haeley guided Boone out and sat next to him on a wrought-iron bench. She leaned close and gingerly put an arm around his back.

"Talk to me, Haeley."

She stood and moved in front of him, her back to him as she seemed to study the roiling black sky. Boone loved just looking at her. Finally she turned to face him, her expression dark as the horizon. "Jack smells a rat."

"Well, duh. Who doesn't? What's his guess?"

"He won't tell me. It scares me."

Boone raised a brow. "He's worried it was an inside job."

She nodded. "'Fraid so. And I think he thinks Galloway is too."

Boone shook his head, trying to follow that through his anesthetic high. "That's the real reason Fletch is stepping down? Not because this should have been the capstone to his career?"

Haeley sat back down and leaned on Boone's good side.

"So where's Pete Wade in all this?" Boone said.

"He just seemed angry all day. Doesn't seem to want to look inside. He's saying we shouldn't assume the shooter had to be tipped off. Maybe the guy was just lucky, or maybe all those gangbangers are smarter than we give 'em credit for."

Boone carefully sat forward, Haeley steadying him. "I trust Pete. He's been around forever."

"He's wrong on this, Boone. First thing you asked me was whether everyone agreed it was an inside job. Jack said you asked him if we had a traitor. Galloway retires in what looks like shame. Come on."

They sat in silence for several minutes, Boone trying to enjoy the storm. He was warmed by Haeley's being so close. He loved this stage of the relationship, where they got comfortable with each other. They were going to be good together.

Finally Boone said, "Pete probably thinks we need somebody to believe in the team."

"Maybe," she said. "But that's naive for a veteran, isn't it? Blind faith at the expense of truth?"

"Listen to you," Boone said, hoping his admiration came through.

She pulled back and cupped his face in her hands.

"Haven't shaved," he said.

She shushed him. "I got to talk to your Dr. Duffey, you know. He says not to trust a thing you say and not to expect you to remember much of this."

Boone chuckled. "Even now? I'm remembering more every day."

"Just sayin'. It hasn't been two full days, Boone."

"Well, I won't forget how troubled you seem."

"Sorry. But you've got to admit it's sobering to think there's someone inside we can't trust."

"Terrifying."

Haeley folded her hands in her lap, gazing out at the storm. "Just concentrate on getting better," she said quietly.

Boone shivered, which caused a twinge deep in his shoulder and a piercing pain in his clavicle. Despite his damaged body, he couldn't recall a more satisfying moment since before he had lost his family.

Everything from then till now had been about enduring. He had grown, sure, had somehow come through grief and despair. Now his pain was physical and not psychological.

Boone was suddenly overcome with feelings long forgotten. He loved the rain, the chill, the coziness of the blanket, the presence of his new love. Despite this setback that would make him virtually have to start over physically, all he could think about was the future.

Boone pictured their wedding, living together, raising Max together. And he knew that if he mustered the courage to mention one word about any of that, she would either run or chalk it up to his meds. Besides, she was clearly preoccupied with the crisis that had nearly cost him his life.

Part of him wanted to do or say something to pull Haeley from her funk. But at the same time a resolve began to build in him. He wanted to get healthy fast, get back in the game, get back to being the cop, the person he knew he could be. It wouldn't be easy. But that had never stood in his way.

There would be those, he knew, who would encourage him to take advantage of this jackpot—full salary for the rest of his life with disability benefits. Others would say he should take a desk job and stay out of the line of fire.

Boone would have none of that. Life was not jackpots, payoffs, ships coming in. He would settle for nothing less than full recovery, evidenced by his return to active duty.

"Nice that you can have the shoulder work done just up the block," Haeley said.

"Sorry?"

"Valdez is at Presbyterian St. Luke's. You could walk there from here."

"Valdez?"

"The shoulder guy Duffey's referring you to."

Boone squinted against a chilling wind. "He told you something he hasn't told me?"

"You really don't recall?"

"Think I would remember something like that."

"Nothing like good drugs," she said. "Dr. Duffey said he walked you through the whole thing. Said you seemed pleased with being able to have the surgery at St. Luke's."

"I'm completely blank, but I can't imagine being pleased about anything associated with St. Luke's. Hard memories there."

She nodded, looking as if she wished she hadn't brought

it up. "Duffey says it's going to have to be an open-shoulder operation, a total rebuild. And no guarantees."

"The guarantees are going to come from me. Whatever they leave me with, I'll make it work."

"I know. And I'll have to compete with your mom for nursing duties. Lucy's an interesting woman."

"You've talked with my mom, too?"

"So have you."

"Uh-oh."

"They were here within hours of your lung procedure. Ambrose was quiet. Lucy wasn't."

"There's a shock. And you're telling me she and I talked?"

Haeley nodded. "She says you weren't making much sense, but you were clear about not wanting them to visit you again until you were out of here."

"I wondered why I hadn't heard from them. Was I awful?"

"According to her, yes. They're staying at your apartment and keeping in touch with your doctors every day."

"Oh, grief. How'd they get into my apartment?"

"You gave them the key, apparently with lots of caveats. They have to be gone within a few days of your getting home."

"She's going to want to stay and take care of me after the shoulder work."

"What mother wouldn't? I was hoping to help too."

"Not sure I want that either, Hael. I'm kinda independent."

"Tell me about it. You told her Jack Keller was going to be taking care of you."

Boone snorted. "Even unconscious I was making some sense."

"You don't want me there at all?"

"Of course, but not to take care of me."

"You're going to be a piece of work. But give your mother a break. Imagine what she's going through. She nearly lost you. You of all people know about that."

Lightning slammed a high-tension wire not two blocks away, and the resounding thunder made Boone instinctively raise both hands to cover his ears. His left didn't get close, of course, as piercing agony shot through his body.

Haeley leapt to her feet as the cops slid open the door. "Back inside," one said. "Now."

Boone was shaken and couldn't rid himself of the feeling that yet another close call had been an omen. Something was telling him he still had a tortuous road ahead.

3

★★★★

CONFUSED

BOONE DID NOT KNOW what to make of Haeley's departure without a kiss. Had he only dreamed their first? Or had she meant it only as encouragement to a fallen colleague? But she had called him "love." Or had that been only in his mind too?

He had forgotten the first visits from his pastor and his own parents and important stuff from his doctor. But Boone would not allow himself to entertain that he might have invented this next step in his relationship with Haeley.

They had left it that she would return at the end of the next day for a meeting with Dr. Duffey and Boone's parents. It would be time to adjust his meds and confirm when he could go home, how much help he would need, and when his shoulder surgery could be scheduled. Boone looked forward to that meeting. For one thing, it would allow him to establish that he did not want his parents' help. He appreciated their concern and their sacrifice to come and be with him. But he had one perfectly good arm, and he needed to learn to do things for himself.

Neither did he want Haeley in the role of caregiver. That would be unfair to his own mother—if he sent her home on the basis that he didn't need help.

Boone couldn't stand having heard nothing from his former partner and mentor. Three calls to Jack Keller's cell in an hour resulted in Boone's leaving messages. Finally he called Jack's apartment and reached Margaret, Jack's live-in girlfriend.

"I'll have him to call you, Mr. Drake. He's sure worried about y'all."

"Something wrong with his phone?"

"I think he's shut it off is all. You know he's in line for the chief's job."

"Doesn't surprise me."

"The press is all over that, and I don't think he wants to talk to 'em."

"I need to see him."

"I'll tell him, Boone. You sound good. You feelin' better?"

"Just frustrated. Jack used to keep me up on everything."

Margaret reiterated her promise to have Jack call, but Boone wondered. Something was going on.

WEDNESDAY, FEBRUARY 3

Boone was surprised at how much better he felt the next day. The phone, however, remained silent. And no visitors.

Finally, late in the afternoon, Boone left another message

on Keller's cell. "If you care a whit about me, I need to hear from you. I'm in the desert here."

Boone hated to sound so needy, but what was the deal? The press treated him like a hero, his friends like a pariah, and his loved ones like a victim. All he wanted was to get home, get strong enough for surgery, then get back on the job as fast as he could. If Keller was really in line for Galloway's job, surely there had to be something good in that for Boone.

As much as Boone dreaded dealing with his overbearing mother and passive father, he couldn't wait to see Haeley. And he was eager to talk with Dr. Duffey in a more rational frame of mind.

Boone recognized the male nurse who had tended to him early on. He squinted at the name badge. "George," he said, "I need a favor."

"Don't we all? You know I'm programmed to say no to just about anything you ask for."

"I just want my stuff. We both know I didn't show up in this stylish gown. Where are my clothes?"

With a flourish, George opened a closet door below the TV. On the top shelf was a plastic bag, bulging taut. Boone's parka hung beneath the bag. "That's not pretty," George said.

"Never was a fashion plate," Boone said.

"I mean this." George turned the coat so Boone could see a jagged tear and a mass of clotted blood. "You're lucky to be alive, Detective."

"My stuff in that bag? Watch, ring, wallet?"

George shook his head. "Lockbox at the nurses' station. You get them when you check out."

"I need 'em now."

"Sorry, it's against protocol, and—"

"There are things I need in my wallet. I haven't lost the rights to my own things, have I?"

George lifted both hands. "I surrender, Officer. You just have to sign a form."

"So go get it."

Determined to change into street clothes before his visitors arrived, while George was gone Boone laboriously made his way to the closet. The smell of dried blood nauseated him. The parka was a mess, not worth keeping.

Reaching for the plastic bag made him recoil in pain. And now he was dizzy. He tried reaching again, but his bad side convulsed and he yelped. And now he felt himself blacking out.

His spine pressed back against the closet doorframe, and as Boone began to slide to the floor, he heard something fall and then felt George's hands under each of his arms, moving damaged tissue on that left side.

Boone grunted as George guided him back to his bed.

"That wasn't too smart now, was it?" the nurse said.

"Can't blame a guy for trying."

"I get back ten seconds later and your head hits the floor. Then where are we?"

George got him situated, then retrieved the fallen envelope. "Hope your watch survived, but it seemed more important to keep you from falling."

"Thanks."

"And if your clothes are so important, here." He yanked the bag off the shelf and plopped it between Boone's legs. "You expect to find anything in there you can change into? Get real."

Boone pulled the plastic apart, revealing a black-red ball, stiff with blood. It proved to be his shirt and undershirt. George quickly donned rubber gloves and took them. "May I dispose of these, or did you want a souvenir?"

Boone pointed to the trash and dug his jeans from the bag. They too were a wrinkled mess, and a patch of blood covered the belt and reached the bottom of the front pocket.

"These are salvageable. I'm going to rinse them out and change into them before my guests arrive."

"And how are you going to do that? Balance over the sink next to your IV pole and work with one hand?"

"Nothing worthwhile is easy."

George shook his head. "Incorrigible. Listen, we're about the same size. Okay, so I'm fat and you're not. But I've got a couple of sets of clean work clothes if you're so determined to get out of that gown."

"I accept."

"You're going to look like a nurse in scrubs."

"Better than this."

"Give me half an hour. You're not my only patient, you know."

"I appreciate this, George," Boone said, handing the man his bloody jeans.

"I'll deep-six those shoes, too."

When George returned, he brought everything—slippers, socks, underwear, undershirt, and scrubs. He even produced a large sheet of clear plastic with adhesive on the edges.

"This'll allow you to take a shower if you want, and believe me, you want. You're getting gamy."

"Tell me about it."

"The IVs, all that, are waterproof. We tape this over your wound, you sit on the fold-down bench in there, and you can use the flexible hose and nozzle. Don't rush. You want to shave too?"

"Do I!"

"You're going to be exhausted after all this, but you'll be glad you did it. And so will your visitors. Especially the one."

Boone shot George a double take.

"I've got eyes," the nurse said.

A few minutes later Boone sat in the shower with his chin on his chest, catching his breath. With the plastic protecting his ugly wound and stitches, he lifted the nozzle over his head and let the steaming water cascade over him. This was as good as he'd felt since hitting the concrete floor with a .45 caliber hole ripped through him.

Shampooing with one hand was a new experience, and Boone knew it would be his lot for months. When he finally turned off the tap he felt as if he could sit in the steam for an hour.

George reached in with a razor and shaving cream, and Boone slowly managed that task. When he finally emerged, George helped him towel off and dress, deftly disconnecting the IVs long enough to get the scrub top over his head.

The nurse appeared unable to suppress a smile.

"What?"

"You look like a nurse who's been shot."

"Thank you, Dale Carnegie."

Boone carefully rolled his IV pole next to a side chair and sat, crossing his legs. He tipped an envelope, and out slid his watch, ring, wallet, and the leather bracelet he had fashioned with buttons salvaged from his late wife Nikki's top the day she died. "I believe I'm ready to entertain," he said somberly. "If I can just keep my eyes open. George, thanks. This was above and beyond the call."

The nurse waved him off as he left.

As the sunlight through the window changed colors and muted, Boone noted that the Indian summer had gone as quickly as it had come. The thermometer had plummeted again, and the temperature was forecasted to hit as low as twenty overnight.

Soon he was nodding, then dozing, yet ever aware that Haeley would soon be there.

4

★ ★ ★ ★

AGITATED

No surprise, Ambrose and Lucy Drake were the first to arrive. "You're looking good, Son," Boone's father said. "A lot better."

"Where are your own clothes?" his mother said. "Is that even a man's outfit?"

"I don't know," Boone deadpanned, watching her adjust the blinds and drapes. "I got it from a man."

"We could have brought your clothes."

"You could bring me my car."

"You're not able to drive. We'll handle that."

"You won't be here when I'm released."

She stopped and faced him with a sigh. "Your father blamed your nastiness the other day on your condition."

"I'm sorry, Mom. Really. I don't even remember your being here."

"You were pretty articulate."

"Not really," Ambrose said. "Doesn't surprise me he remembers nothing. Now, Boone, what do you need your car for?"

"It doesn't take two hands to drive. I want to drive myself. And as much as I appreciate that this has to be hard on you too, I really want to recuperate on my own."

"With shoulder surgery looming?" Lucy said.

"Again, I'm sorry, Mom, but I don't want caretakers."

"Care*givers*."

"Whatever. I *would* like you to bring me a set of my own clothes and my car. Can you do that?"

"Of course," Mr. Drake said. "Whatever you want."

"Ambrose!"

"He's a grown man, Lucy."

His mother stalked into the hall, calling back, "How many are we expecting?"

"The doctor and Haeley Lamonica."

From somewhere she found enough chairs. "We met her, your coworker. Was she named after Hayley Mills?"

"Not likely. It's H-A-E-L-E-Y."

"Why is she coming anyway?"

Boone hesitated. "Same reason you and Dad are here. She loves me."

"She seemed very nice," Ambrose said.

"Oh, honey," Lucy whispered. "We only talked with her for five minutes."

"Boone seems to care for her. She must have something on the ball."

Lucy looked away. "Well, where is she?"

"She'll be here," Boone said, looking at his watch. It wasn't like her to be late and not call. "Might be looking for someone to watch her son."

"Her son?" Lucy said, shooting Ambrose a look.

Boone shrugged. "She's a single mom. Precious little guy."

When Dr. Duffey arrived carrying a large envelope, Ambrose and Lucy immediately rose for greetings and pleasantries. Boone asked if the doctor would mind waiting a few moments for Haeley to arrive.

Dr. Duffey looked at his watch. "How about I continue my rounds and you buzz the nurses' station when she arrives?"

He left the envelope, which bore the name of a local imaging company. "Pull that out of there, Dad," Boone said. "Let's have a look."

Ambrose slid it out and held it up to the light. Boone had no clue what to look for, but what he could make out made his shoulder look like goulash.

Boone's mother leaned in. "Oh, my," she said. "What are they going to do with that?"

"All they need to do is give me something to work with," Boone said. "Trust me, this is just a temporary setback."

When Haeley had still not arrived fifteen minutes later, Boone called her cell and got an immediate voice mail. He called her office. Strangely, the recorded after-hours message was from her stand-in. He couldn't make that compute.

Half an hour later Dr. Duffey poked his head back in. "Do you want to put this off till tomorrow?"

Boone shrugged. "You did already talk with Ms. Lamonica anyway, didn't you?"

"I did," Dr. Duffey said. "She hasn't seen the MRI, but I told her what I told you about Dr. Valdez at Presbyterian St. Luke's down the street—but you remember none of that, do you?"

Boone smiled and shook his head.

"He's a fellow at the Rush Arthritis and Orthopedics Institute," Duffey said.

"When can he do this?"

Duffey pulled out his BlackBerry. "He's opened a slot at dawn on Monday the fifteenth. Neither of us wants to wait any longer than that."

"When can I be done with all this?" Boone nodded toward the IV pole.

Duffey rose and squinted at the hanging bags. "We can get you off the saline now. How often are you hitting the morphine?"

"Not at all today."

"Really? You're not just playing macho?"

"No, it's okay. I'd just as soon be off it."

"That's easy enough," the doctor said, shutting off the feeds and detaching the tubes. "It's been too long since I've removed a port from the hand, so I'll let the nurses do that. You're still on the oral meds, right?" He checked his notes. "Perc and Oxy? You're going to need those, especially after surgery. You've got to be able to push through the pain to regain your strength and range of motion. That's no time to be a hero."

"I'm going to be obsessive about therapy and rehab."

"That's good. I can't tell you how many patients don't complete their physical therapy because it hurts. They wind up with chronic pain and immobility."

"You won't have to worry about that with me."

"Doctor," Lucy said, "Boone has this idea that he won't need any help at home after surgery."

"Well, he'll need a ride home. We won't want him driving while on hallucinogenic narcotics. But once he's home, he needs to learn to function with one arm on his own as soon as possible. Then, with therapy, he can get back the use of the shoulder."

Lucy fell silent.

"When can I get out of here?" Boone said.

Dr. Duffey cocked his head and shrugged. "Give it a day or two and then you tell us. You're off the drips, so now you just need to stabilize."

"I'm ready."

"No, you're not. I can see from looking at you that you'd rather be in bed than sitting here. But it won't be long."

Dr. Duffey held up the MRI film. "The shattered bone and ripped tendons and ligaments can be repaired or even replaced." He pointed with his little finger. "But these blood vessels were cauterized in the ER to stop the internal bleeding. Those need to be repaired so you get proper blood flow." He tucked the film back into the envelope and stood. "Tell Ms. Lamonica I'm sorry I missed her."

As soon as he was gone, Mrs. Drake said, "You and your coworker are an item now? Does everyone know about this but us?"

"You know about it now too."

"Boone! There are so many good girls in our church, the church you grew up in."

"Mom, Haeley is a wonderful Christian girl."

Lucy was quiet a moment. Then, "She's a churchgoer?"

"She's on the worship team."

She raised a brow. "Maybe we should stay around and get to know her."

"All in good time, Mom. I'm getting to know her myself. Let's not get ahead of ourselves. You and Dad bring me some clothes and my car in the morning and say good-bye. I promise when I'm doing better after surgery I'll invite you back up and we can all get acquainted."

"But don't you need us here, honey? You're not well."

"I am, and I'll be better. I just need time. Now, I appreciate you and love you and need you to do this for me."

Bone weary as he was, Boone wouldn't even try to nap until he had located Haeley. After calling her cell several more times, he called the pastor of her church.

"Haven't heard a thing, Boone. If I do hear from her, I'll sure tell her to call you. It's been fun seeing you all over the news. That was some deal you were involved in. How you feeling?"

Boone gave him enough to not be rude, then asked for Florence's phone number. "Maybe she knows something."

Florence was a single working woman, but Boone expected her to be home during the evening. Yet he got another answering machine and left another message.

He tried Jack a few more times, then reached Margaret at Jack's apartment again.

"He workin' late, hon," she said. "But he told me to tell you he'd come by in the morning. All right?"

"Has he said anything about Haeley?"

"No, nothin' to speak of."

If Boone had a car, he would have driven right then to Haeley's to find out what was up. But he was so tired he could hardly move. A nurse came in to remove the IV port from his hand. She proved either new or uncaring, because she didn't even come close to George's bedside manner. Everything stung when she yanked off the tape and pulled out the needle. She did, however, steady Boone as he lay back in bed.

Worried and puzzled, Boone slept till dawn, rousing only when nurses came to check his vitals.

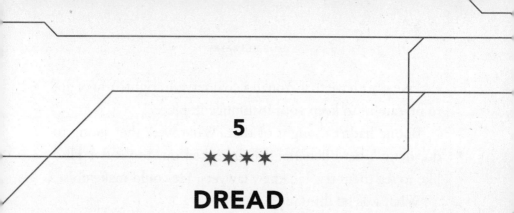

5

✷✷✷✷

DREAD

THURSDAY, FEBRUARY 4

Boone awoke with such a sense of foreboding that he had to force himself to eat breakfast. He was not in the least hungry but knew he needed nourishment. When the physical therapist came by, he moved quickly out of bed and marched up and down the hall, despite her cautioning him to take it easy.

"You said yourself I was unaffected from the torso down, so unless you want me to play volleyball, this is a piece of cake."

"Slow but sure," she said.

"Yeah, well, my patience is in short supply," he said. "Ignore me. It's not your fault."

"Being focused is good," she said. "It's what we look for before discharging people."

"I'm about to discharge myself," he said.

"We can't have that. You're a civil servant, right? You've got to be careful to keep your insurance in place."

Boone hadn't thought of that. What were they going to do, deny a hero benefits if he checked out too early? He'd like to see them try. He knew lawyers. He could make noise.

What was he thinking?

He wasn't back in his room long when his parents showed up, his mother finally seemingly resigned to leaving. "You know I'm willing and want to stay and help you," she said.

"I know this is hard for you, Mom. But it's the right thing. Thanks for understanding."

His dad hung Boone's coat, shirt, and pants in the closet and also set a pair of shoes in there. He put underwear and a T-shirt in a drawer, along with Boone's car keys, telling his son where his car was parked.

Boone felt guilty that he couldn't be rid of his parents soon enough. He found himself pacing, aching, and looking forward to his once-every-four-hour meds. As soon as they were delivered, he called the office. Again he reached Haeley's substitute.

"What's going on over there?" he said. "Where's Haeley?"

"Not in today, Detective. May I take a message?"

"Where is she?"

"I'm not sure, exactly. I was asked to fill in. That's all I know."

"Really? Why is the after-hours message in your voice and not hers?"

Silence.

"Is she still even working there?"

"I'm not at liberty to speak to that, sir. I'm sorry."

"You've replaced her permanently?"

"I didn't say that."

"Is she still an employee of the CPD or not?"

"I'm sorry, Detective, but I can't—"

"Is Jack Keller in?"

"He's unavailable to come to the phone just now—"

"Tell him I need to talk with him immediately."

"Hold, please."

Boone was ready to throw the phone against the wall. He paced to the end of the cord and back.

"Sir, Deputy Chief Keller told me to tell you he is still planning on visiting you this morning and to please wait until then to talk with him."

"Tell him I need just thirty seconds."

"Sir, I have other calls coming in."

"Listen, you tell Jack that if he doesn't call me back in ten minutes, I'm checking myself out of here and finding Haeley myself. And I'm not kidding."

Boone set his watch, shut the door, and changed into his street clothes, tears streaming as he gingerly worked the sling off, the shirts on, and then the sling back on. He sat, one knee bouncing.

Thirty seconds after ten minutes had passed, he stood and drew his coat on, draping the left side over the sling. There would be no zipping it. He peered outside. Ice everywhere. Terrific.

Boone could not be mad at Haeley. She'd call if she could. He was mad at Jack. Leaving him in the dark after all they had been through, after all Boone had suffered? Unforgivable.

He peeked out the door, and the uniformed cops raised their brows at him. "Goin' somewhere?" the big one said.

"Getting out today, Ferguson."

"No kidding? We hadn't heard."

"You're hearing now."

"We supposed to walk you out?"

"Yeah. Soon." Boone hesitated only because he saw Francisco Sosa get off the elevator.

"You know this guy, right? He okay?"

Boone nodded and backed into the room.

Sosa knocked and entered. "What're you doing, Boone? You know better than this."

"What're you talking about?"

"C'mon, man, don't play me. Jack Keller called and asked if I was on my way. Wanted me to be sure to keep you—"

Boone slammed his fist on a rolling tray. "Keller calls you and won't talk to me? What's going on?"

"They're not telling me anything, Boone, but Keller will see you this morning. He promised."

Boone sat, shaking his head. "Do you know how hard this is?" He told Francisco about Haeley's not showing the night before and now being unreachable. "I'm about to go crazy."

Sosa shrugged. "I know nothing except that they really don't want you checking yourself out."

"I wasn't checking out. I was just leaving."

"Jack said something about jeopardizing the integrity of your insurance."

"Scare talk. They're not gonna leave me out in the cold after what I've done. And somebody'd better tell me something or they're going to be sorry. How do I know Haeley's not in danger? Do they think I'm going to sit here and do nothing?"

"I don't get the impression she's in trouble."

"How would you know?"

"I don't. But I'd be surprised if she was in danger and they weren't telling you."

"They're keeping *something* from me."

"You'll find out this morning. Jack will tell you. How can he not?"

"Francisco, I'm sorry I got you in the middle of this."

"I'm here to help. Just tell me what I can do."

Before Boone could answer, Jack Keller swept in wearing his dress blues, something Boone hadn't seen in a long time. Boone stood and took a breath to start in with his questions, but Jack stopped him with a gesture, then shook Sosa's hand as the pastor stood.

"I appreciate your getting here so quickly, sir," Jack said. "Now, I'm sorry to have to ask you to leave us, as we have confidential business. Forgive me."

"Not at all," Sosa said. "I'll be in touch, Boone."

"Wait," Boone said. "As long as you're both here—Jack, Pastor Sosa needs to be cleared to meet with Candelario. I was making some progress with PC, and—"

"Way ahead of you, Boone," Francisco said. "Chief Keller already set that up, and I've already been there. Pascual remains very moved that you were willing to take a bullet for him. Believe me, it gave him a living picture of the sacrificial love of—"

"Where is he?"

Sosa glanced at Keller as if for permission. "I've been sworn to secrecy within an inch of my life."

"Not secrecy from me!" Boone said. "What in the world, Jack?"

"Sit down, Boones," Keller said. "Push that door shut, would you, Pastor?"

As Sosa grabbed a chair, Boone said, "I don't want to sit down. I want out of here. I want to find Haeley and then I want to visit Pascual."

"You're going to sit down or I'm not gonna tell you anything. You looked in a mirror lately? All dressed up but lookin' like Shinola. I'm no doctor, but you look to me like if you don't sit down you're gonna be on the floor in sixty seconds."

Boone reluctantly sat.

Keller dragged over a chair and leaned forward, speaking softly. "I got to say, CPD bought the best safe house we've ever had. Because it's in DuPage County rather than Cook—Addison, actually—nobody with a brain suspects it. It's an old junkyard with a Quonset hut and a couple of mangy dogs. Twelve-foot-high fence with razor wire along the top. Junk all over. Old guy who put it up for sale had it overpriced. All he wanted was to cash in and move back to the South. CPD paid cash through a dummy buyer, and the old guy was gone the next day, no questions asked and everything left just the way it was—dogs and all.

"Took us about a week to make the place impenetrable and redo the inside. We ferried Candelario and his mother and baby in there after midnight in a couple of impounded cars and a beat-up old pickup. Place is stocked like a hotel and comfortable.

"It's at the end of a long, unpaved drive, and nobody gets in there except on purpose. We have all kinds of signs that say the junkyard is closed, and we've had only a couple of cars that got that far and U-turned out of there. It's perfect."

"It is," Pastor Sosa said. "I couldn't believe it."

"Great," Boone said. "I'm going to want to get there at least once before surgery. Now tell me that for some reason you've got Haeley there too."

Keller pressed his lips together and Boone went cold. Finally Jack turned to Sosa. "Now I really do have to excuse you, sir. Sorry."

The pastor rose. "I'm going to get out to see Pascual before heading back to church, Boone. Any message or anything?"

Boone waved him off. "Just tell him I'll see him soon."

As soon as the door was shut again, Boone said, "Jack, this had better be good."

"It's not so good, Boones."

"Tell me she's okay."

"As far as I know, she's all right."

"So spill it."

"She's in Cook County Jail."

"What the—?"

Boone started to rise, but Keller put a hand on his knee. "We have really got to keep it down, Boones; now I mean it." He looked over his shoulder as if to be sure the door was shut and lowered his voice even more. "I'm not even sure what the charge is, but you know I'm convinced we have a rat inside."

"You can't possibly suspect her."

Jack hesitated. "Tell you the truth, I'd sooner suspect Garrett Fox."

Garrett Fox? Boone's onetime partner had left the force in disgrace after lying during Boone's misconduct hearing the year before. "Fox isn't even CPD anymore!"

"He was close enough to us that he could have picked up information he shouldn't have had. That would give him the means, and we all know he had a motive to see you hurt."

"I'm not buying that. But even if it's true, what's that got to do with Haeley?"

Jack spoke deliberately. "There are some who think she was, at the very least, careless with classified information."

"C'mon! I've never seen anyone more careful."

Jack shrugged. "Apparently there was enough to get her on violating the public trust, breaching her oath of loyalty—"

"Jack, who's behind this? Galloway didn't have her arrested and then quit, did he?"

Keller shook his head. "You don't want to know."

"Of course I do!"

"It was Pete."

"Wade? You've got to be kidding! Wasn't he the one who didn't want to even suspect anyone inside? Anyway, he loves Haeley!"

"That's what I thought. He's not happy about all this. In fact, I get the impression he's really conflicted over it. But he studied everything himself—and you know he's always been tops as an investigator—"

"Sure, but—"

"He's even hoping it will come out that if she somehow inadvertently leaked information, it was a mistake and that she won't take a real hit for it."

"She's already taking a hit if she's in County, Jack! That

pit breaks the worst gangbangers. Imagine what it'll do to an innocent, someone with no record, no history . . ."

"If she *did* have anything to do with this, she's regretting it now."

"Why didn't you stop it? You know it can't be true, and you're Pete's boss."

"I'd have to have cause to stand in the way of an arrest like that. I'd have to be dead sure. . . ."

"Jack, it makes no sense. Don't people know Haeley and I are seeing each other? What possible motive would she have for putting me in danger?"

"Having a relationship with you would be a good cover."

Boone shook his head. "What's happening with Max? Tell me Child and Family Services doesn't have him."

"You kiddin'? Haeley would have killed herself before she let that happen. She got some woman from her church to take him, and her mother is driving up from South Carolina to take over, today or tomorrow, I think."

"How's Haeley doing? I've got to get over to see her."

"No one's heard from her that I know of, but I wouldn't advise that. She used her one phone call to make arrangements for her son. Far as I know, she doesn't even have a lawyer yet."

"And you don't advise my getting over there? You'd have to put one between my eyes to keep me away. You think I'm going to let her sit there alone—?"

"Boones, slow down. Don't make things worse for her. Get her a lawyer, but don't make it look like you're conspiring."

"Conspiring? What, I was in cahoots with her to get myself shot? Anybody who hears about my visit will know I don't believe for a second that she was behind any of this. What're you worried about, Jack? If I get too noisy now, is that going to affect your angling for Galloway's job?"

Keller recoiled. "How can you even say that?"

"Well, what are you all gussied up for?"

"Downtown is doing a little press conference tribute to Fletch. I have to be there."

"Naturally."

"Don't start with me, Boones. You know I'm not political."

"This is a pretty good job."

Keller stood and turned away. "I don't deserve this, from you of all people. You know me."

"I thought I knew you, Jack. But tell me: why wouldn't you get back to me? You knew I was desperate to know where Haeley was. What was that about?"

Jack sat again. "I got to shoot straight with you, Boones. Pete's no slouch. There could be something there. Now don't look at me like that. I can't be going behind his back, filling you in, knowing full well you're going to hit the roof, check yourself out, go see her, all that."

"And I will."

"That's what I'm afraid of. Why don't you just get her a lawyer and send him in there with a message from you. It gets out that you visited her, what's that going to do to the investigation, to her, to Max . . . ?"

"To your future."

"I don't want to hear that again, Boones. This has nothing to do with me and my future. And in case you haven't noticed, your career has been in step with mine all along. If I do happen to get the OCD chief's job, that only helps you."

"Like I care about that right now. You know the department is going to push me to take full disability or a desk job. And that's not happening. I'll take a civilian job before I give in to that."

"If you must know, I don't see that in your future either. I have something way juicier in mind."

"Don't do this right now, Jack. You know I'm curious and I want to stay with you whatever happens, but how can I think about myself when Haeley's in County? I can't believe I'm even saying that! And you seem to think it's okay, a woman like that locked up with all those lowlifes."

"You want to do something for her? Get her a lawyer and get her out of there. Surely she can be bonded out. I wouldn't have my name associated with the bail, though, if I were you. It's going to complicate things. I can just see your mug on some TV gossip show. 'She sets him up and he bails her out!'"

"Don't even kid about that, Jack. Tell me you know as well as I do that she's innocent."

Jack looked miserable, as if Boone had raised an issue he didn't want to face. "I learned a long time ago not to jump to conclusions. I've been a Pete Wade fan a long time."

"Who hasn't?"

"Spotless career. Smart, savvy, good investigator, good manager, cop's cop."

"So what's he up to? This looks like a misdirection play to me. Taking the spotlight off where it needs to be. I mean, the department secretary is the culprit? Please."

Jack looked at his watch. "I've got to get downtown, but listen: Garrett Fox was in line for your job. You know that. Maybe he shouldn't have been, and maybe he would have been a disaster. But he had a motive to get in the way of all this, to get you and embarrass us. He must have had help. That's the only way I can make this make sense."

"That's a stretch, Jack," Boone said as Keller rose. "Haeley helping Fox?"

"Do me a favor, Boones. Hard as this is, stay here a couple more days; let me come and get you when it's time to go home. Find Haeley a lawyer and get her out of there, but don't do anything stupid. Stay under the radar. And I'll get you out to see PC before your surgery. Okay?"

"No promises."

"How about if I make it an order?"

Boone shook his head. "Still no promises. You know I don't want to do anything that could hurt you, but I've already lost one family. I'm not about to let anything happen to my next one."

11:00 A.M.

As soon as Keller was gone, Boone began planning the most inconspicuous time to make his break. He needed a lawyer for Haeley, but he also needed to get out of the hospital. He wasn't doing her any good here.

Money would be no object. Fritz Zappolo was the most impressive criminal defense attorney Boone had ever come across. He'd try to get an appointment with him, then have lunch in his hospital room. Then, before his tray was removed, he'd have the uniformed cops escort him to his car. With luck, no one would even question them.

While his cell did not work within the hospital, Boone was able to access his contacts and find a phone number for Zappolo. But as he was reaching for the landline phone, it rang.

"This is Boone."

"Mr. Drake. This is Brigita Velna. Remember me?"

"Of course." How could he forget the CPD counselor he'd had to meet with after losing his family?

"You can't seem to keep yourself out of trouble, can you?"

Boone appreciated the humor in her voice. "No, ma'am. If it's not one thing, it's another."

"I've drawn the short straw again and have been assigned to meet with you. When's convenient for you?"

He told her of his upcoming surgery. She suggested that as soon as he was mobile after that he should make an appointment with her.

"Will do. But you're not going to try to talk me into full disability, are you?"

"Frankly, Officer, you'd be crazy not to take it. But no, that is not my role. My job is to protect the interests of the department. If I determine that that means reassigning you, that will be my recommendation. I look forward to meeting with you again. Everyone is most proud of you, and I must say, you have gone from a terrible low to a most impressive high. I hope you're well."

Low to high to low was the truth, but he wasn't about to get into it. He promised to call Ms. Velna after surgery. Before he was able to call Zappolo, however, a nurse breezed in to check on him.

"You ought to be watching the news," she said. "Just saw it on channel 9. Your shooter turned out to be a member of some funny-named coalition of street gangs. Dee-something."

"The DiLoKi Brotherhood?"

"That's it!" she said. "Mean anything to you?"

"Means everything. No surprise, but it is telling."

6

★ ★ ★ ★

FRITZ

BOONE CALLED FRIEDRICH ZAPPOLO'S office just before lunch was to be delivered and insisted on talking with the man himself. The receptionist went into a long riff about how that was not the way things worked, that one of the legal assistants evaluated potential clients and determined whether Mr. Zappolo would become personally involved. "And then—and only then—you might land an appointment with him."

Boone wanted to ask why it seemed easier to get an audience with God, but rather he said, "He knows me. Please tell him my name."

"He knows everybody, sir."

That was hard to argue. Most cops had been cross-examined by Fritz Zappolo at least once. Boone had squared off with him three times.

"Tell him I'm on the front page of the *Trib* again this morning and that I need him."

"Sir, I—"

"I'll take the blame, admit I made a nuisance of myself, whatever you need. And if he still won't speak to me, I'll surrender."

"Hold, please."

The next voice was Zappolo's. In typical fashion, he dived in with no preliminaries. "You don't need a lawyer, Drake. You need an agent. You could parlay all this publicity into a comfortable living. Reality show, you name it."

"Good to talk to you too, Fritz."

"You're usually looking sideways at me because I'm representing somebody you thought you had dead to rights. And now you need me?"

"I'm calling for a friend."

"No doubt one who can't afford me."

"Of course. She's in—"

"Don't tell me anything over the phone, Boone, please. Can you get to my office within the hour?"

"I'm sure your palatial suites will be easy to find, but I wasn't kidding about . . . you know . . . the matter of—"

"C'mon, you know I don't need the money anymore. But I can always use the press. Just tell me this is related to why you're all over the news."

"It is."

"Get here as soon as you can."

Boone had to force himself to relax and stay with the plan. He wanted to rush out to his car right then, but he would have his lunch first, then stroll out with the uniforms.

Problem was—little shock—lunch was late. And cold. And institutional. For some reason the hospital had deigned to treat its constituents to a turkey dinner, with, as the folded paper menu bragged, "all the fixin's."

Two thin slices of dry turkey breast had been laid across a scoop of sticky instant mashed potatoes, accompanied by those fixin's: a clump of dressing from a box and a jiggling hockey puck of cranberry surprise next to what appeared to be a sample slice of pumpkin pie.

"Getting out today?" the candy striper delivery girl said, eyeing Boone in street clothes. "Lucky you."

"What's this?" he said. "Thanksgiving leftovers?"

"Sir, Thanksgiving was more than two months ago."

"Really? Where've I been?"

"Enjoy!"

Boone gulped a couple of bites of each offering, thinking fuel rather than enjoyment, then gathered his stuff and invited the two officers in. "I'm taking off, but I don't want to get you guys in trouble." He snapped off his wristband and handed it to Ferguson. "Once you've seen me to my car, check me out at the main desk. Then you're free to get back to headquarters."

"Oh, sure. And if something happens to you before you get home?"

"Your assignment was to protect me here, right? Well, I won't be here long."

"Sorry, bro, but if you're leaving our jurisdiction, I gotta call it in. You know that."

Boone pressed his lips together and shook his head. He'd been in uniform. He couldn't argue. "Do what you've got to do, Fergie, but walk me out."

1:00 P.M.

As the three started down the hall, Ferguson began radioing in that their charge was about to leave.

"Could you do that by phone? I don't need everybody in the place knowing my business."

The cop switched to his cell but didn't talk much softer.

When they reached the first floor and were heading toward the exit, Ferguson handed his phone to Boone. "For you. Commander Lang."

Great.

"Hey, Commander."

"Drake, what're you pulling? I know you're a celebrity now, but when you're under the protection of the 11th precinct, you got to watch out for us too."

"I'll take full responsibility."

"You sure as fire will. Can my guys take you somewhere, follow you somewhere, make sure you don't go from their custody into some kind of a trap?"

"I'm in no danger, Commander."

"Yeah, nobody's tried to kill you lately. You don't have an enemy in the world, let alone the city, let alone every gang-banger who hasn't been arrested yet. Now where you going? Home? At least let them see you in and check the place."

"I've got an appointment not four miles from here. I'm going to park in a garage. They can tail me and make sure I get into the elevator if they want, but as far as I know, I haven't been assigned twenty-four-hour security."

Lang sighed. "All right. But I'm going to be in touch with downtown about this, and if they don't want us to release you, don't be trying to shake us."

That was all Boone needed. It wouldn't be long before everyone—including Jack Keller and, worse, Pete Wade—would be aware of his every move. He could only hope they wouldn't restrict him.

Outside, Boone fought to keep his coat covering his exposed left hand. Unable to zip it over the sling, he felt the attack of frigid air and wanted to hurry to his car. But speed meant agony.

Ferguson helped Boone into his car while the other officer went to get the squad. Boone had not fully settled when the man began to shut his door, and Boone had to lean far to the right to keep from getting a slam to his fragile left side. As it was, the door nudged his elbow, sending a current of torture up his arm and causing him to cry out.

"Sorry, man!" Ferguson said. "Forgot."

Boone gingerly reached across his body for the seat belt, which caused the officer to open the door again and help.

"I really need to do this myself, because there's not always going to be someone with me."

"Suit yourself." And he shut the door on Boone again.

With his coat bunching, his shoulder throbbing, and his vision blurring, Boone had to wrench around in the seat to snag the belt with his finger and slowly maneuver it into place. By the time he got it clicked, the squad had pulled up.

"Lang tells us we're with you all day, sir," Ferguson said. "Sorry. And someone will be patrolling your street day and night too."

Terrific.

The cops followed at a discreet distance as Boone drove slowly, hoping the heater would eventually catch up with the icy gusts that rocked his car. The Loop was heavy, slow stop-and-go, as the traffic reporters liked to say. When he finally pulled into a parking garage and up to the automatic ticket dispenser, Boone realized he would not be able to reach it. He unfastened his belt, turned until he could reach the door handle with his right hand, pushed the door open with his foot, and slid out to where he was able to grab the ticket. By the time he parked he was ready for a nap. Or at least a Percocet or OxyContin.

But that would have to wait. He couldn't be floating while meeting with the attorney.

The cops rode the elevator with him to the sixteenth floor, which was entirely occupied by Zappolo and Associates, Attorneys-at-Law. He told the officers they could wait in the hall.

Boone recognized the receptionist's name. "Didn't I tell you I'd keep you out of trouble?" he said as she carefully took his coat.

"You didn't tell me you were a celebrity. Congratulations, by the way."

Was that how it was going to be? Strangers thanking him for his part in breaking up the gangs and taking a bullet for the star witness? That would get old quick.

Boone had been in lawyers' offices before and knew the routine. Normally he would be asked to wait until some-one's assistant fetched him and schlepped him to a conference room, where he would wait for counsel.

Admittedly, he had not been in a suite of law offices quite like this. Nothing had been left to chance, not a corner cut. Everything looked of old movies and TV shows, lots of dark wood and leather.

And to Boone's surprise, no lackey delivered him to a conference room. Zappolo himself breezed out and motioned to Boone to follow. "Better we talk in my office," Fritz said.

Friedrich Zappolo looked like he had been put together with a kit. Tall, trim, late fifties, tanned, and with short, bristly white hair, he was clearly a fitness buff and a connoisseur of fine suits.

Boone took in the cavernous office with an expansive view of the Loop and Lake Michigan. "Nice."

Zappolo grabbed a leather-bound legal pad from his desk and pointed to a round side table. Boone had never had a powerful lawyer come out from behind the desk and sit with him. He had to wonder if Fritz would have done that if Boone weren't in the news.

Regardless, Haeley needed the best.

Boone cleared his throat as he sat. "You take this case and your client is a civil service clerical worker, currently unemployed. That makes me the payer."

Zappolo snorted. "You couldn't afford me if you were the superintendent of police. Find me five grand for incidentals and consider the rest pro bono."

"You serious?"

"That's if the case is worthy and interests me." He pulled a Montblanc from his pocket. "Shoot."

Over the next half hour Boone spilled the story.

Zappolo wrote quickly in neat, compact lines. Finally he sat back and stretched his legs, crossing his feet at the ankles. With his hands behind his head, he seemed to study the ceiling. "I know all these people," he said. "Except Ms. Lamonica, of course, and I may have even met her. I've been in and out of those offices a lot."

"You know Fox?"

Zappolo chuckled. "Everybody knows Garrett. I half expect him to try to hire me. Thankfully this precludes that."

"You mean you'll take Haeley's case?"

"Of course. That she's in County is an outrage. Let's get her out of there."

As Zappolo was pulling on his coat, he pressed a button on his desk. "I need the car, and bring Detective Drake his coat."

"We're going now?" Boone said.

"It's less than ten miles, Drake, and she shouldn't be there a minute longer than necessary, should she?"

2:15 P.M.

By the time Boone and the lawyer reached the street, a sleek Town Car was waiting, the driver standing by the back door.

"Are they necessary?" Zappolo said, nodding at the uniformed cops who had followed them out.

"'Fraid so," Boone said. "And we need to give them a minute to get their squad."

"Tell them to hurry. And they don't have to come inside the jail, do they? Can they wait outside?"

"I'll make it happen."

But when they were on their way, Boone's cell phone rang. Jack Keller.

"Where you goin', Boones?"

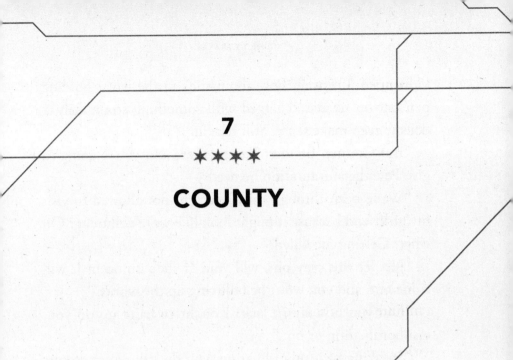

7

★★★★

COUNTY

Boone heard Fritz Zappolo on his own cell tracking down Haeley's location and disposition while Jack Keller was bleating at Boone on his.

"Do I have to spell this out for you?" Jack said. "Every gangbanger in the city, in or out of jail, wants your head. You were safe where you were."

"So if it was you, Jack, what would you do? You're a target, you're wounded, you're in a cozy hospital, and Margaret is in trouble." It wasn't often Boone found Jack Keller stumped. "Puts a different spin on things, doesn't it? I'm listening, boss. I need my mentor, my champion, to tell me what I ought to do."

"You should've sat tight," Keller muttered, plainly with zero conviction.

"That's what you would have done? Margaret's missing. Or

kidnapped. Or, wait, how about she's in the worst holding pen known to man, charged with something so unlikely it doesn't even make sense. Still relaxing?"

"But County, Boones? You go there and you're going to give Pete the ammunition he needs—"

"We've been through this, Jack. I'm not allowed to visit my girlfriend because it might look like we're colluding? On what? Getting me killed?"

"Just let this play out, will you? If she's innocent it will come out, and you won't be bollixing up the works."

"Did you just say *if*, Jack? I ought to hang up on you, insubordination or not."

"Speaking of insubordination, you do still report to me, and I'm telling you I want you—"

"Pete Wade works for you too, and you're not giving him orders. Don't do this, Jack. You're not going to keep me from Haeley any more than anyone could keep you from Margaret."

Keller swore. Boone had won this round.

"I'm not on speaker, am I, Boones?"

"No."

"Zappolo, really?"

"You know he's the best."

Keller paused. "Yeah, but . . ."

"You're surprised the Mob hasn't engaged him?"

"I know he doesn't stoop that low. But he's defended guys you and I have caught red-handed."

"And did a good job for them."

"Too good."

"Imagine how he'll do with a client who's innocent," Boone said.

"How you gonna pay him, anyway?"

"None of your business."

"Fair enough. Listen, as long as you're out running around, you want to see Candelario?"

"'Course."

"I'd sure feel better if we put you out there too. Talk about safe. That place is—"

"I'm not staying there."

Keller sighed. "You don't mind costing the city thousands to keep an eye on your place?"

"I didn't ask for any of that."

"What's the option, Boones? What're you gonna do, sit in your window with an M4, defending yourself one-handed?"

"The guy who shot me is dead and everybody else who wants me is locked up."

Zappolo motioned to Boone to get off the phone.

"The naiveté of youth," Keller said. "You think we arrested tens of thousands? Every junior gangbanger sees this as his opportunity to rise in the ranks. Any one of them would take you out without blinking."

"I gotta go, Jack."

"Get back to me and I'll run you out to . . . you know, where you can see PC."

2:45 P.M.

Zappolo's driver pulled into the Cook County Jail parking facility, and the two clambered out.

"Boss giving you a hard time?" the lawyer said.

"Nothing I can't handle."

"You should've asked him if he wanted to talk with your attorney."

"You're *my* attorney now too?"

"Whatever you need."

"I hope I don't need a lawyer to communicate with my own boss."

"Never know. Without counsel, you may be bound by protocol to obey his every order."

"I'll keep that in mind."

"Don't get me wrong, Drake. Keller's a good egg. Lot of respect for him, though I doubt that goes both ways. I'm just saying that I wouldn't stand for his getting between you and doing the right thing for Ms. Lamonica. Now, the people downtown tell me she's to be arraigned tomorrow morning—"

"Tomorrow!"

Zappolo held up a hand. "Hang on. That's why we're here. I've already called in some favors. No way we're letting her stay here another night. If I'm successful, she can be arraigned in a nearby precinct station house with a gaggle of hookers and drunks. It's our best chance of getting her out on bond immediately. You don't want her in there another night. Anyway, we wait till tomorrow and it's done downtown, the press will be all over it. Nobody will expect this."

Zappolo never seemed to announce when he was finished talking. He just moved on, striding toward the entrance, and Boone had to rush to keep up. He'd almost forgotten how exhausted and tender he was. It was all he could do to manage the door and hurry along, trying to keep his coat draped over his bad wing.

"What happens now?" he called out, hoping to slow Zappolo.

Fritz turned and looked surprised at how far behind Boone was, but he never broke stride. "You're going to see her. I don't need to. I need to talk to the brass about being sure she makes the next squadrol so she doesn't miss this arraignment. There's not another until tomorrow, and we don't want that."

Boone had been to Cook County Jail before, of course, but it never failed to overwhelm him. Covering ninety-six acres on Chicago's west side, it was the largest single-site jail in the United States. As he and Zappolo moved past Division 5—Receiving—he saw a long line of cuffed prisoners waiting to be processed.

"More'n three hundred new detainees a day," Zappolo said as they entered. "Don't know where they put them all."

Boone recoiled from the stench and was surprised anew at the sheer din. He wondered how long it would have taken him to get in, had it not been for Fritz. The lawyer seemed to know everyone and was directed further and further up the chain of command until he finally motioned Boone to join him. A supervisor summoned a corrections officer, who checked Boone's ID, wanded him, confiscated all contraband, including his cell phone, and walked him through a metal detector. He affixed a security tag to Boone's shirt and escorted him through several checkpoints, finally delivering him to a long line of others waiting to visit inmates.

The officer whispered, "She's been informed she has a visitor, and when you show your pass up there—" he pointed— "they'll tell you which booth to go to, and she'll be on the other side of the glass. You talk to her by phone."

Boone kept glancing at his watch. More important than even seeing Haeley now—while he could hardly stand the wait—was her making the local arraignment and getting bailed out as soon as possible. He didn't want to be responsible for her missing that opportunity.

The line crept as the clock sped, and the pain in Boone's shoulder reminded him he had missed his last dose of meds. And these were not pills one took on an empty stomach.

To keep his mind off the pain, Boone filled his mind with images of Haeley. Since the day he met her he had never seen her other than impeccably dressed. Even after hours—once when she had called him to change a tire for her—it was plain she had touched up anticipating his arrival.

At work she never wore anything but smart business suits that flattered her. And off the job she clearly never just threw on something comfortable. The woman knew how to dress, for church, for dates, even for playing in the park with Max.

Boone knew she would need encouragement, given that she would be sitting across from him in a county-issue orange jumpsuit. Maybe he could muster a joke, something lighthearted. As early in the conversation as possible, he wanted to give her the good news—that if Zappolo was successful and she was able to make the arraignment, she would be out before she knew it.

3:30 P.M.

When it was finally Boone's turn, he showed his badge to what appeared a terminally bored civil servant and was pointed around the corner to booth nine. "If she's not there," he was told, "she will be in a few seconds."

Any inkling of banter disappeared when Boone approached and saw the squinting woman sitting across from him. He would not have recognized her.

Haeley's long dark hair—normally flowing—was greasy and flat and had been pulled into a ponytail. She wore no makeup or jewelry, and the jumper was a couple of sizes too big, making her look like a child.

She sat, eyes dark and darting, face pale. Haeley covered her mouth with one fluttering hand and tears came.

Boone picked up the receiver and forced a smile. "Expecting someone else?"

She nodded and mouthed, "My mother."

He pointed to her phone and she picked up.

"She's coming?"

"I don't know," she said, voice quavery. "I figured she'd come see me before taking over Max from Florence. I don't even know if Florence got hold of her."

"You okay?"

Haeley laid the phone on the counter and buried her face in her hands. She shook her head and sobbed.

Boone knocked on the window and pointed at the phone. "Don't, Haeley! I have good news."

She peeked up at him, looking miserable. He read her lips. "You've got to get me out of here."

He nodded and pointed to his watch, mouthing, "I got you a lawyer."

She finally picked up again. "I already have a lawyer, some public defender who talks to me like I'm a number. Some kind of hearing downtown tomorrow and he wants to know how much money I have. When I told him, he said I should expect to be in here a few more weeks. Boone, I'll kill myself before I do that."

"Don't say that. Too many people need you and love you. Think of Max."

"You don't understand. I don't belong here—"

"I know."

"—and that's obvious to everybody who does belong here. If I have to stay here overnight again . . ."

"You won't." Boone told her about Zappolo and the local arraignment.

For the first time he saw a flicker of hope in her eyes. "Now? Today?"

"This afternoon," Boone said. "Zappolo will meet you there."

"And you'll be there?"

"Of course."

"Oh, Boone! I prayed and prayed that you would do something."

"Did you even imagine I wouldn't?"

"I didn't know. For all I knew, they had you drugged for a reason and wouldn't even let you know where I was! Boone, why is Pete doing this? He has to know I would never—"

Boone shushed her. "All in due time," he said. "I'm going to put the phone down for a second so I can put my hand on the glass."

Haeley winced and pressed her hand up to his. "Grimy," she mouthed.

He shrugged and picked up the phone. "I can't wait to touch you for real."

"Me either."

Haeley flinched at footsteps behind her. A female officer handed her a manila envelope and a plastic bag and reached for the phone.

"Sir," the officer said, "this missy has a squadrol waitin', and it leaves at four, so you got to let her go."

"Gladly."

Boone hung up and pressed two fingers to his lips. Haeley followed the officer out. When Boone returned to Receiving and retrieved his cell phone, he found a text from Zappolo.

"Car. Now."

8

★★★★

EXPOSED

Boone couldn't stand the pain anymore and downed his pills, then slipped into a back bench in the dank, crowded underbelly of a local police station and waited for them—and the nausea—to kick in.

Haeley was the only detainee in line awaiting arraignment wearing county orange. The rest were ladies of the evening and drunk-and-disorderlies who had apparently spent their nights in local lockups.

The judge, a swarthy, sweating man whose double chin covered his collar, was apparently used to dealing with repeat neighborhood offenders represented by public defenders. He seemed to rouse when the nattily dressed Friedrich Zappolo rose and announced he represented Haeley Lamonica.

The judge studied the charge sheet, then looked over the top of his glasses. "What's a case like this doing in my court? Your client also a hooker?"

"Your Honor would be advised not to verge on slandering an upstanding Chicago civil servant, a mother, and a woman with not even a hint of a record."

The judge leveled his gaze at Zappolo. "And counsel would be advised not to lecture the court. This may not be Mahogany Row, but the same rules apply."

"Begging Your Honor's pardon, may I suggest that my client be released on her own recognizance until this misunderstanding can be sorted out? She poses no flight risk and is eager to be reunited with her young son."

"Maybe she should have thought of that before she—" the judge pursed his lips as he again perused the charge sheet— "violated the public trust and her oath of—"

"As I say, Your Honor, a misunderstanding. I pledge personal responsibility for the custody of Ms. Lamonica and—"

"Oh, come now, counsel. I'm not going to just let you walk out of here with a fugitive. Your client may well be innocent of these charges, but if she's not, she's at least indirectly responsible for a Chicago Police Department hero being gravely wounded in the line of duty. This man was almost single-handedly responsible for ridding our streets of the worst sort of—"

"Would it aid the court to know that the very victim you speak of is present in support of the defendant, clearly persuaded that she bears no responsibility?"

Boone had just started to feel better, the anesthetic beginning to dull his pain. Now he wanted to hide. He knew

Zappolo would make up for his minuscule fee by riding the publicity, but did Fritz have to use him in the process? Jack Keller would be spitting bullets.

The announcement of Boone's presence seemed to catch the attention of every lowlife in the room. The judge asked that Boone rise and introduce himself, and when he hesitated, Zappolo whirled and glared at him.

The judge said, "Where is our phantom hero, counselor?"

Boone stood. "Detective Boone Drake, sir. Gang Enforcement Section, Organized Crime Division, Chicago PD."

Over a smattering of applause the judge said, "Allow me to thank you on behalf of a grateful city."

"May I speak, Your Honor?"

Zappolo shook his head, but the judge said, "The court would be honored to hear from you."

"It happens that Ms. Lamonica and I care deeply for each other, and so it makes no sense that she would have had anything to do with endangering my life."

"Thank you, sir," the judge said. "Bail is set at one hundred thousand dollars, which I assume counsel has in his wallet."

Zappolo sprung to his feet. "A hundred thousand?"

"Sit down, counselor. Can't a judge have a little fun? You realize how long it's been since I've set *any* bond, let alone six figures? Make it ten grand, final offer."

Twenty minutes later, when Haeley emerged from the women's locker room, she looked like a different woman. Her suit was wrinkled, and while she had done nothing more with her hair, she had apparently found her makeup. She still looked exhausted and pale, but nothing like at Cook County.

She laid her head gently on Boone's good shoulder and sighed.

In the back of the Town Car she thanked Zappolo profusely and said she wanted to be driven to her car so she could rush to her son. "That's fine," the lawyer said, "as long as you know I am going to need a chunk of your time tomorrow."

It was after seven when Boone retrieved his own car and followed Haeley to her apartment—his department escorts not far behind. They waited out front.

Max hugged his mother like he'd never let go and sat in her lap as Florence brought her up to date. "He's not been happy," the woman said. "Naturally. I love him, but I'm no substitute for the real thing. I just got off the phone with your mama, Haeley. She can't leave until tomorrow morning."

Haeley immediately called her. "Yes, I still need you. I don't want to drag Max downtown to lawyer meetings, and Florence has used up her days off. . . . I'll tell you all about it later. . . . Of course it's not true. I'll talk to you when you get here."

"Back to work tomorrow," Florence said. "I was kinda liking the break."

"This couldn't have been much of a break," Haeley said. "How will I ever thank you?"

"Hush. It was a privilege." As Florence retrieved her coat, she said, "He didn't sleep much last night and there was no nap today. Lord knows I tried."

"I'm sorry."

"I woulda been the same way, his age," she said as Boone and Haeley walked her to the door. "He was just scared and wanted you."

Max, cheek pressed against his mother's shoulder, peered at Boone. The boy's eyes looked heavy and he blinked slowly. "You could probably put him down, Haeley. He's about to go."

"I will. In about a year." She settled on the couch, arms wrapped around her son, whose breathing was soon even and deep. "Boone, what in the world is going on?"

"I wish I knew. And I will as soon as I can get after it. So now Wade thinks it's an inside job? He's going to have me turning everything inside out until I know the truth. Anyway, how bad was County?"

Haeley looked away and shook her head.

"Did the noise ever die down? I can't imagine how anybody sleeps in there."

"I don't want to talk about it."

"Maybe later?"

"Never, Boone. Please."

"You sure it won't help?"

She shook her head.

"Did somebody try something? Hurt you? Threaten you?"

"You're not going to leave this alone, even when I'm begging you?"

Boone rose and paced. "Haeley, if someone—"

"Listen to me. You know that most of the women in there are the worst of the worst, right?"

"Of course," he said.

"They target the weak, pick on the newbies. Even the younger gangbangers have no chance. Fortunately for me, most of the women are mothers. In fact, most of the ones I talked to had two or three kids. When they found out I was a mother, they told me who to stay away from and what to do or say if one of the leaders tried anything."

Boone sat and leaned forward. "Good. So you had some protection."

"Just a little moral support."

"And so did anyone try any—"

"Do you believe me when I talk to you?"

"Sure! What do you mean?"

"You're on the edge, Boone. Now I've already said way more than I intended to, and I'm finished. I'm not going to say another word about it, and if you ask you'll regret it. Do I need to be clearer?"

Boone shook his head. "That was clear enough. I'm sure glad you're out."

Haeley's voice grew thick. "You and me both. Would you mind staying with Max while I take a shower, and then till I fall asleep?"

"You know you don't have to ask twice."

But she seemed in no hurry, and for nearly the next hour they chatted, and he filled her in on how hard it had been for him to get any information on where she was. She seemed impressed by his idea to hire Zappolo.

Finally she laid Max on the couch next to Boone, then took a long shower. When she returned in a floor-length terry robe, she was in tears again.

"Imagine my mother having to hear all this. She said she was prepared to stay with Max as long as I needed, even if I had to go back in. Can you believe it?"

"She loves you."

"She works, and time off counts against her."

"Like you wouldn't do the same for Max."

Haeley nodded. "I've got to go to bed."

She carried Max into her bedroom and lay next to him, the door cracked an inch. "I should be asleep within twenty minutes."

"Don't rush on my account."

For the first time that day he saw a hint of a smile.

Boone sat in the living room, whispering on his cell phone, arranging where he and Keller would meet. "And can you tell the coppers at the 11th that you'll take over watching me?"

"They're still going to need to know when you leave me and head home, Boones."

"No, they aren't. Come on."

"Don't be naive. I wouldn't want it any other way. Unless you want to stay at the safe house with PC and his mom, let these guys do their jobs."

Boone and Jack agreed to meet at the 11th at 10 p.m. The tail squad would pass off responsibility to Jack, and Boone would leave his car there while riding with Keller to the safe house.

"You sure you're up to this?" Jack said. "It's got to be way past your bedtime. You're supposed to still be in the hospital. And rest is the best thing for—"

"Thanks, Mom, but I can handle my own energy level from here. Okay?"

"Hang a guy for tryin'. Just get to the 11th, will you?"

Boone tiptoed to the bedroom and pushed the door a couple of inches further open. Haeley lay cradling Max, and both were clearly gone. He was tempted to kiss her on the cheek, but he didn't want to wake her—or worse, scare her.

He pulled the door shut, killed all the lights in the living room, and quietly made his way down to the street.

The squad sat idling as his protectors drank coffee. The driver rolled down his window when Boone approached.

"Got the call from 11," Ferguson said from the passenger seat. "Once you're in Deputy Chief Keller's car, we're out of your hair."

9

★ ★ ★ ★

THE OFFER

BOONE FOUND JACK KELLER behind the wheel in an idling, unmarked squad parked at the rear of the 11th precinct station house. Jack leaned over and pushed open the passenger-side door, but it took Boone a while to extricate himself from his own car.

As Boone made his way to the squad, he felt Jack's eyes on him and tried to add energy to his gait, anything to hide his exhaustion and pain. This little outing was a bad idea, but he wanted to see it through. He poked his head in the car and said, "Got any water? Behind on my meds again, but I didn't want to drive under the influence."

"Half a bottle, if you're not afraid of my germs."

Boone thought about using the water fountain in the station, but the thirty-foot walk looked like a mile. "You don't have cooties, do you?"

Keller flashed an obscene gesture as Boone slipped into the car. It was a lot easier with his good arm on the door side. He fished for his pills, popped them into his mouth, then took the bottle, which Jack had cleaned with a shirtsleeve.

"This is an eighteen-mile ride," Keller said. "You still gonna be with me when we get there?"

"I'll be with you, but will I remember? That's the mystery."

"Those drugs make this the best injury you've ever had, eh? Maybe it's better you don't remember tonight."

"You want to put a bag over my head so I can never tell anyone where this is?"

Jack pulled out. "I don't care who knows; they'll never get in. But no one does know."

About ten miles into the ride, the combination of the heater, Boone's thick coat, and the pills made him logy. "How cold is it?" he slurred.

"Single digits. Hey, don't leave me, Boones. We've got to talk."

"I'm okay. What's up?"

"I want you to meet with Pete when you're up to it."

Boone yawned and looked out his window. He shook his head. "Believe me, I'd love to talk to him, but I wouldn't trust myself just yet. I'd want to give him a piece of my mind, but that's not going to help. I want to talk to him after I've persuaded myself that he's really thought this through."

Traffic was light, but it was clear Keller was in no hurry. He cruised along under the speed limit. "I've always looked up to Wade," he said.

"Who hasn't?"

"No, I mean he's a model. Concrete investigative reasoning

76

is a hallmark of his, just like we were all taught. I'd love to think he's going off half-cocked on this deal—for Haeley's sake and yours—but when a guy like him takes a stand, I've got to listen."

Warmth had spread from Boone's chest. He could feel it all the way to his fingers and toes, and though a dull ache remained in his shoulder, it was tolerable. He was, however, fighting sleep. "You sound as if Pete's convinced you of something."

When Jack didn't respond immediately, Boone shot him a look. "What, he's got something on her? Something real?"

"That's not my call; you know that."

"It's not his call either, Jack, but you brought it up. What's he got?"

"You know you're the last person I should be talking to about this."

"So you were just going to throw that out and leave it lying there? C'mon. You brought it up for a reason."

"You can't tell Zappolo, and you can't act on it."

Boone wrenched in his seat to face Keller. "I'm making no promises, but you'd better tell me."

"Can't do that."

"Then why'd you start?"

"Can't tell you without assurances, is what I'm saying. You know I'm on thin ice here."

"And I know you intend to tell me or you wouldn't have brought it up."

"Listen, Boones, I do want you to know, but I'm way off the reservation here. You're a friend and the best partner I ever had. And we both know you're not going to be allowed anywhere near a case that involves your girlfriend, not to mention you. I have to know this won't get out, because if it does, everybody will know where it came from."

Boone settled back in his seat. "You're worried I'll rat you out? Really?"

"That's how big this is."

"You wouldn't want it to get in the way of your shot at Galloway's job."

"Now, see, Boones? You know better than to go there. You know *me* better'n that. This isn't about me. It's about you. Nothing I say or do is going to keep you from nosing around and trying to prove Haeley's innocent. But you can't let on you know anything."

They sat at a red light, the defroster trying to keep up with the cloud on the windshield. "You want to prick fingers and mingle our blood?" Boone said. "Want me to cross my heart and hope to die, stick a needle—"

"Just give me some hint you realize how dicey this is for me. And a little gratitude wouldn't hurt."

Boone fell silent. This was a different side of Keller. Talk about a model. Pete Wade may have been an interesting veteran and dramatic looking, always natty in his dress blues, the sky of his shirt playing off the navy of his trousers and jacket, and the gold star and brass buttons setting off his tight snow-white Afro and ebony face. And though Pete's diction and delivery were as crisp as the crease in his pants, Jack Keller had always been Boone's ideal.

Jack looked good in uniform too, but there was something earthy, something accessible about him. He looked the part, no question. Ruddy-faced with short, gray hair, he was wiry and rugged. You got the impression he had seen it all.

Boone had always counted on Jack's being transparent, honest, direct. No bull. He opened his mouth, truth came out. If it hurt, it hurt, but you never had to wonder where he stood.

And now he was hedging? Even through his Percocet and OxyContin fog, Boone felt on high alert. This was so out of character for Jack that the man seemed almost needy. Boone was desperate to know what Pete had on Haeley, if anything. But he never wanted to owe a thing to Jack Keller.

"Okay, so you're going to make me do this," Boone said, "this vulnerable man thing where I tell you what you really mean to me? Do I have to convince you I'm still trustworthy?"

Jack stared straight ahead as he drove. Boone let the question hang there, and it clearly embarrassed his boss. That was all right. The man didn't have to answer. Not saying anything was answer enough.

"Because I'm willing, Jack. Listen, you've been the best mentor a cop could have. You taught me everything I know. I would no more do or say anything to hurt you than I would surrender my badge. If anything, I'm hurt that you even have to ask for assurances, but if that's what you need, that's what you've got."

Keller cleared his throat. "I appreciate that, Boones, and I only asked to be dead sure *you* appreciate how dangerous this is."

"Got it. Now we okay?"

"'Course. We'll always be okay, no matter what happens."

"What's going to happen, Jack?"

Again the boss hesitated and Boone felt it in his gut. "It doesn't look good, Boones."

"For Haeley, you mean?"

Jack nodded.

Boone tensed. His legs felt tingly and his good hand was balled into a fist. "I'm listening."

"Jazzy Villalobos is cutting a deal."

Boone went blank. "I've got to tell you, Jack, that was the last thing I expected to come out of your mouth. What in blazes does Jazzy Villalobos have to do with Haeley? And how can he cut a deal? Candelario had to have spilled so much on him before the grand jury that—"

"Villalobos is already out."

"You serious?"

Jack nodded. "He's turning state's evidence."

"Who's he going to rat on? PC nailed him along with all the rest of 'em."

"His nephew was your shooter."

"That kid was a Villalobos? I mean, we all knew he had to be DiLoKi, but—"

"And Jazzy is willing to tell where the kid got inside information, enough to almost kill PC. You were just in the way."

"And what, he's going to claim some connection with Haeley?"

"Indirectly."

"I'm lost."

"We all are, Boones. But doesn't it make sense that this kid being in exactly the right place at the right time and almost taking down the biggest canary the Chicago PD ever had means he had inside information? How many people knew where Pascual was and when he would be moved?"

"Precious few."

"How many, Boones?"

"I guess just the five of us. You and me, Pete and Fletch, and Haeley."

"Even the undercovers who went with you that night didn't know where they were going. They just followed you."

"It doesn't make sense that any of the five of us would leak that information, but least of all Haeley. What's in it for her?"

"I have no idea, Boones. But on some log sheet for the file, she wrote just enough information for the wrong people to have, and they got it."

"And we know this how?"

"I saw the copy Jazzy gave to Pete."

"A copy?"

"Claims it was shot with a cell phone, right off her desk."

"By . . . ?"

"He's dangling that tidbit. Before he gives up too much he's parlaying it into getting out of jail, getting immunity, all that."

"And he's going to rat on his own nephew, who's already dead?"

"No, he's going to rat on the insider who gave up PC."

As they neared their destination, Boone tried to make it all make sense. "Let's say someone copied—or shot—confidential information from files in Haeley's control. At worst she was careless. Is that a crime? Does it breach her loyalty oath? It's not like she handed over the info."

"According to Jazzy—and this is Pete's version—she was in league with a former employee, who paid her."

"Garrett Fox?"

"That would be my guess, but Jazzy hasn't given that up yet."

"Haeley taking money from Fox? No way."

"Boones, I'm afraid there's some incriminating evidence."

"Such as?"

"A deposit to her checking account the same day the information leaked."

"And we know which day that was how?"

"Time stamp on the photo."

"Some phone. And how much was deposited in her account?"

"Five grand."

Boone exhaled loudly. "That would be a lot of money for her. But there has to be an explanation."

"Here's the thing. You can't go trying to find out."

"Someone will."

"Of course. But not you."

"Why?"

"Conflict of interest. You're a principal in the case. The victim."

"All the more reason she wouldn't have done it."

"Anyway, you don't want to jeopardize your future."

"I've got no future without her, Jack."

"Not so fast."

"She's given me a reason to go on, man."

"I know that. But I also know you thought your life was over after the fire."

"It was."

"But here you are, Boones. And on the brink of a real future."

"What's that mean?"

"I've been told to keep you off this case."

"Naturally."

"But there's a real reason, Boones. You're visible, a hero, a victim. People are watching, seeing what your future holds."

"It holds retirement with full benefits or a desk job, if it's up to the brass."

"Wrong."

"I'm all ears."

"There's a plum down the road," Jack said. "An incentive for you to come back to full strength."

"I already have an incentive. Haeley."

"But this is in play regardless what happens to her."

10:40 P.M.

Jack pulled onto a gravel road and approached a rusty pickup truck. The driver rolled down his window and greeted Keller.

"Any traffic tonight, Quincy?"

The man looked at a clipboard. "Some pastor from Chicago. Sosa. Here ninety minutes and gone."

"That's all?"

Quincy nodded.

"Not sure how long we'll be. Anybody else expected tonight?"

"Nope. See you on your way out."

As Jack started down the road and pulled out of sight of the pickup, Boone asked him to pull over. "We've got to finish this before I see PC. Otherwise, I'm going to be too distracted. What're you telling me?"

"You notice the construction going on at the 11th?"

"Yeah, but I didn't pay any attention. Downtown is always sprucing something up in some precinct."

"They're adding a suite of offices."

"For?"

"The Major Case Squad."

"Seriously, like New York and St. Louis?"

"Our aim is to be better than both. It would fall under OCD but would be pretty much autonomous."

"Some goal."

"You want in, Boones?"

"Me?"

"Chief detective."

"Get out."

"Dead serious. But you have to be healthy. And I mean totally. No residual damage, no little things you can't do in the heat of battle."

"Talk about incentive. That job is every cop's dream."

"You bet it is."

"But I can scotch it by getting involved in Haeley's case."

"Exactly."

"Jack, are you bribing me to stay out of it?"

"*I'm* not. Somebody might be."

Boone shook his head and sighed. "I can't imagine anything else in the world that would even turn my head. I was born for that job."

"Tell me about it."

"I'll tell you something, all right. If Haeley turns out to be dirty in this—and I cannot fathom that—I won't even want to be a cop anymore, let alone chief detective in the Major Case Squad."

10

★★★★

THE SAFE HOUSE

The Chicago PD had added a couple of K-9 units to the old dogs the previous owner of the junkyard included in the sale. They came with human officers, of course, or they might have torn to pieces anyone who breached the twelve-foot-high razor-wired gate.

While the old dogs were apparently asleep, the young and muscular German shepherds assigned from downtown rushed the fence and stood ready to pounce when Boone and Jack emerged from the squad. Interestingly, they made not a sound, clearly waiting for a cue from their trainer.

"Hey, Chief," the buff plainclothes trainer said, then said something in German. The dogs immediately lost interest in the newcomers and settled in at their master's feet. "Officer Williams here."

"Nice to meet you, Williams," Jack said. "Say nice things to your dogs about us, hear?"

Another officer—also in plainclothes—opened the gate, locking it behind the visitors as soon as they were inside.

Boone was mellow from the drugs, though the late-night air stung. He also found himself distracted by the plum Jack had dangled. He thought it naive of Jack to think the job might be attractive to Boone even if everything he was sure he knew about Haeley proved false. But he wasn't even entertaining that possibility.

Chief detective of the Major Case Squad, Chicago PD. Now that had a ring to it.

The dilapidated Quonset hut that had been fashioned into a safe house for Pascual Candelario and his mother and son had been left untouched on the outside. It looked for all the world like a storage unit for a junkyard. Rusty. Paint peeling. There was even a snowdrift that hid a shoveled walkway. Boone and Jack had to find their way around it to reach navigable ground.

The two cops who met Boone and Jack inside the building were also dressed like anything but police officers. It was unlikely anyone would ever breach security that far, but if they did, they would find two scruffy-looking characters on plastic-covered chairs behind a disintegrating counter under two hanging bare bulbs. The wall behind them was cluttered with dusty bric-a-brac no one would want.

But that proved the extent of the ruse. Once the inside guys had identified Boone and Jack, one of them, who introduced himself as Officer Unger, pressed a button under the counter. A section of the shelving behind them spun on its axis, just like in an old horror film, and opened to a short, dim, cavernous passageway with sheets of cloudy plastic hanging at both ends.

Unger held the plastic back, and as soon as Boone and Jack stepped inside, the wall closed behind them. When they pushed aside the plastic drape on the other end, it emptied into a large room that had been turned into a dining area. Tables, chairs, refrigerator, sink, everything.

Then, through a normal door, they came upon a corridor that led to several other doors. "PC knows you're coming," Jack said. "We'll stay clear of the family's living quarters. He hangs out down here after hours."

At the end of the hall Jack knocked twice and the door immediately swung open to reveal the man mountain who was Pascual Candelario. Boone had to stifle a laugh. Every other time he had seen the man, he had been dressed the way you'd expect the most powerful gang leader in the US to look. Besides the requisite prison tattoos, PC had always worn a lot of bling, the latest basketball shoes, high white socks, oversize athletic shorts and jersey—variously White Sox, Blackhawks, or Bears.

Now here he stood, with no jewelry, a baggy sweatshirt, blue jeans, slippers, and all covered by a massive, open, white terry-cloth robe. Except for his huge size and the tats, one of the scariest men on the planet looked like a middle-ager about to watch the news—though it was probably too late for that. Somehow the gangbanger responsible for multiple murders and countless other crimes looked—Boone searched his mind—cuddly.

In a move way out of character, PC opened his arms and

gathered Boone in. Just as it seemed he was about to complete the bear hug, Boone said, "Careful of the shoulder!"

Pascual immediately backed off and raised his hands. "Sorry, bro!" he said with his thick Spanish accent. "Come in, come in. Sit."

What the CPD had done to this space was nothing short of miraculous. How they had turned the place into comfortable living quarters in such a short time was incomprehensible to Boone. It wasn't palatial, but it was new and more than adequate.

"This is where I hang out when my *madre* and my son are asleep. Bored out of my mind, man."

"I can only imagine."

"No, you can't. I mean, I'm done with that life and have been a long time. But that kinda work gets a man up in the morning. Now I play with the kid, read, watch TV, talk to lawyers, work with your pastor—thanks for that, by the way. He and I speak the same language, and I don't mean just Spanish. But then, all I got is time on my hands."

"I'm glad Francisco's taken over for me," Boone said, as PC took their coats and led them to a long couch. "I don't really know enough to be trying to teach anybody the Bible."

PC held up a hand as if he had something to say and needed silence to get it framed in his mind. "I got to tell you something. The more I think about this whole thing, the more I realize what you did for me and my family. You took a bullet for me, man. You coulda been killed."

"Doing my job," Boone said. "Something happens to you, our case is out the window."

"Yeah, but you didn't have time to think about that. You

just got between me and the shooter." Suddenly the big man stood and went and got his Bible. "Listen to this," he said on the way back, picking through the Post-it-noted pages. "I mean, you probably know this already, but your pastor showed me this verse and I been trying to memorize it. John 15:13. 'There is no greater love than to lay down one's life for one's friends.'"

"Of course, that's what Jesus did. I'm sure Francisco told you that."

"Sure, but you know what that means? You were like Jesus to me when you did that. I mean, you didn't die, but you could have. That makes us friends."

"We were friends before that."

"Yeah, maybe, but not really. We were working together, that's all."

"We were brothers in Christ, PC."

"I know. But I got a lot of brothers and sisters in Christ, and I don't know too many of 'em I would call my friends. And I only know one who was willing to die for me."

Boone was certain his action had been trained into him, that he had responded out of instinct. But he didn't want to spoil the moment by assuring Pascual that he would have done the same for anyone he was charged with protecting.

"There's something I got to admit to you, Boone," PC said. "I feel really bad about it. It even makes me emotional sometimes, like when I think about what you did for me."

"Admit to me?"

"Yeah. I had a funny feeling when I saw the guy, the shooter. Something didn't feel right, and I should have said something."

"You recognized him?"

"Sorta, but not really. I just knew something was up. And I know that if I say something right away, like, 'Check that guy,' he never gets off even one round, you know?"

"That's me too," Boone said. "That's what made me turn and give him one more look. If I hadn't, neither of us might still be here."

"What'd you notice?" PC said. "You didn't know he was Jazzy's nephew, did you?"

"No, I just noticed he was out of dress code. Cornrows. *Did* you recognize him?"

PC shook his head. "I don't think I ever met him, but he looked familiar. When I see pictures of him now in the paper and on the news, I can see Jazzy. My instincts used to be real good like that. I could see stuff before it went down. Maybe it's good I'm out of the game."

"Maybe?" Jack said.

PC laughed. "You know what I mean."

Boone leaned forward. "Pascual, I've got to ask you something."

"Boones," Jack said, "careful where you're going now. I don't want to hear stuff I might have to testify to later."

Boone sat back. "I think this is a logical question under the circumstances. You want to leave the room to protect yourself?"

"Just proceed with caution is all I'm saying."

"What's up?" Candelario said.

"I'm wondering," Boone said, "from your perspective, where did Jazzy's nephew get his information? How was it that he was in the right place at the right time when we were keeping such a tight lid on it? I mean, if Jazzy told him, how did Jazzy know?"

"You thinking I said something?"

"No! You'd have been writing your own death warrant. Anyway, you're way past trusting Jazzy, even if you were cohorts for a lot of years."

"You got that right. Plus, if you remember, you didn't even tell me all the details. I couldn't have told anybody even if I wanted to."

"Then what do you make of it?"

"I'm no cop, but you gotta go back to square one and figure out who knew. Couldn't have been too many people, right?"

Boone nodded and glanced at Jack, who was shaking his head. "Let's not start listing the only people we know of who had inside information. There's no future in that."

"I'm already getting the drift," PC said. "Had to be a leak, eh? Inside job? But why? Who would do that to a case like this and to somebody like you?"

"Exactly."

"If I'm you," Pascual said, "I'm wanting to get to the bottom of that, and right now."

11:30 P.M.

On their way out, Boone was dragging and couldn't hide it from Jack. Keller stopped him before they got to the secret exit. "Let me suggest something," he said. "This place has a lot of room—"

"No."

"Hear me out. You give me your apartment key, tell me

everything you need, and I bring it back. You're about to drop where you stand."

"Jack, I want to get back to my own place, really."

"You know I have to call the 11th and trigger the block patrol for your apartment 24-7."

"Not on my account."

"Regardless, it has to be done."

"I need my own car and I need to be close enough to help Haeley and Zappolo, maybe even Haeley's mom."

"You're about to collapse."

"So let's go."

"I'm going to have to follow you home to make sure you make it."

"Isn't that what friends are for?"

"Don't flatter yourself, Boones. Besides, PC is your new best friend."

"Then let him follow me home."

"Just get going."

11

★ ★ ★ ★

GARRETT FOX

Despite his pain and exhaustion, not to mention the heavy meds he took before retiring, Boone found sleep elusive. His mind roiled with questions, puzzles, leads.

For more than an hour, as he struggled to find a position where the raging pain didn't push through the anesthetics, Boone racked his brain for any hints from his history with Garrett Fox.

Garrett was the kind of cop that other cops largely couldn't stand. Oh, he was built for the job and had the requisite tools. Squat and muscular, he was about five years older than Boone. He had worked undercover for the Organized Crime Division while Boone was learning the ropes on the streets of the 11th precinct.

Long before they met, Boone had formed an opinion of the man. He was known as a big talker—largely about himself. That was not a prescription for success as an undercover cop. Jack Keller had once been undercover, and for a lot longer than Fox. He'd planted seeds still being harvested years later. And yet Boone had been Jack's partner and protégé for a long time before he knew Jack had ever been undercover.

That's how it was supposed to be. A cop infiltrating bad guys for a living was on the edge every minute and was expected to keep that from even his loved ones. Jack eventually told Boone that he had gone through "my second and third wives during that time, and they still don't know I was undercover. I left the house in suit and tie, had a place where I changed into street clothes, and changed back before getting home. 'Course, the hours were so lousy and unpredictable that no woman in her right mind would believe paperwork kept me at the office till the wee hours."

Garrett Fox, though he seemed to relish the undercover role, talked his way right out of his assignment. Those in the know said that Pete Wade finally had enough of him and told him that if he heard one more story of Garrett blabbing about his work—even just to other cops—he'd put him back in uniform in the toughest district in the city, the 11th.

When it happened, Garrett told everyone it was his own choice—that he was burned out and wanted a normal life again. No one bought it, particularly Boone. After his own personal crisis and Jack's reassignment, Boone found himself temporarily with a new partner: Fox himself.

From the first day, he found Garrett so obnoxious and mouthy that he wished he could say the man wasn't a good cop. Trouble was, in many ways he was very good. He was one of those by-the-book guys you could trust to have your back. He never backed down, never took any guff from punks, and he was good about doing his own paperwork.

That, however, didn't stop him from talking constantly. He seemed to never take a breath, even to let his partner get a word in. Not only did he regale Boone with all his heroic exploits—some so embellished that they couldn't stand the light of scrutiny—but he also bragged of all his prowess with, and conquests of, females.

Boone's memory of the months riding with Garrett had to do with endurance. He tried tuning out the constant din— not only all the stories, but also Fox's penchant for reviewing and critiquing every move Boone made. It was common knowledge that, though young and inexperienced, Boone was already a better cop than Garrett Fox would ever be. But that didn't stop Garrett from exhorting, counseling, advising, criticizing.

Rather than cause a rift that would make for even more horrible eight-hour shifts, Boone would look out the window and offer a few grunts and uh-huhs. But when Fox would ask what he thought and Boone hadn't been listening, he had to fake it.

Boone had to admit, despite all that, he and Garrett had also had some choice moments on duty. Even in the middle of the night, wishing he could turn off his brain and rest his ravaged body, Boone found himself chuckling aloud at the memories.

One snowy night they had been called to a liquor store to break up a domestic disturbance. "That's a new one," Boone said. "They brought their fight out in public?"

Fox shook his head when the name of the couple was announced. The two cops glanced at each other. They had been called to Barry and Barbara's home for the same reason more than once. But now at a liquor store?

Barry was a skinny little unemployed man known to have girlfriends on the side, while Barbara—the breadwinner—looked like a walking fire hydrant. She wasn't more than five feet tall but weighed more than two hundred pounds and was a long way from pretty. Both were known drinkers and substance abusers. No cops ever knew which to take to jail after one of these calls, because while Barbara would call to report he had hit her, Barry always looked like he had taken the worst of it.

So Boone and Garrett pulled into the parking lot of the liquor store, only to find Barbara ranting about her husband being "in there with some whore!"

Garrett told Boone, "Let me talk to her. You find hubby and whoever."

As Boone headed for the door, he could hear Barbara raging about what she was going to do "to both those dirtbags!" Garrett was trying to calm her.

To Boone's surprise, he found Barry and a nice-looking young woman casually perusing the shelves. "Hey, Barry. Can I talk to you for a minute?"

"I know she's out there, Officer. I heard the man call you guys."

"Then can we get this sorted out? We can't have her disturbing the peace."

The young woman said, "Tell her to get herself gone."

"Ma'am," Boone said, "you'd be advised to stay out of this."

"Stay out of it? I'm the reason for it."

"That may be, but we're here to calm the situation, and that's what we intend to do."

"With her out there? Good luck with that."

Barry said, "If you were me, would you want to go out there?"

Boone fought a smile. "My partner should have her calmed down by now. It's only fair to this establishment that we take the discussion elsewhere, don't you think?"

"Can I at least buy my hooch?"

"You probably owe it to this guy."

Boone noticed that the cash for the alcohol came from the girl's purse. When the two followed him out, a crowd had gathered, and it was obvious Garrett Fox had had little success mollifying Barbara. As soon as she saw them walking between the cars she spun away from Fox and charged, screaming, "I'll kill both y'all!"

Boone extended both arms like a safety patrol officer and said, "No, Barbara! Stop!"

With that she punched Boone square in the mouth.

"Barbara! Don't make me cuff you!"

And she slugged him again. Barbara, two; Boone, zero.

Though he knew he could knock her into the middle of next week, Boone was not inclined to hit a woman—though just then her resemblance to one was not clear.

Fox was rightly trying to control the crowd, and Boone was worried that Barry might suddenly come to Barbara's aid. That made no sense but happened often in such situations. Boone pulled his cuffs from his belt, hoping to simply get Barbara subdued and into the back of the squad without giving anyone cause to charge police brutality.

Barbara was having none of it. She came right out of her shoes in the snow, attacking Boone as he tried to grab her flailing arms. She scratched his face, gouged an eye, ripped his shirt, and somehow her blouse tore open. Not a pretty sight.

Fox finally decided that the crowd was just there for show and that Barry was not going to be a problem, so he moved in to help. Boone was slipping and about to go down when Garrett grabbed Barbara by her hair, only to have her wig come off in his hands.

Barbara spun like a dervish, ripped Fox's shirt, and scratched his face as the two cops fought to drag her closer and closer to the squad. Boone had wrestled fifty-five-gallon drums with more success. Fox got the back door open, but now all three were thrashing and slipping.

Boone reached the transmitter at his shoulder and radioed for backup. For several minutes it was all Boone and Garrett could do to just keep Barbara contained. She never quit struggling.

Finally three more squads pulled up and four cops leaped out.

"Throw her in the car," Boone said.

They did, and as soon as her door was shut, one of the cops said, "Who's next, Drake?"

"That's it," Boone said.

"What?"

"That's it, thanks."

The cop looked at the mess Barbara had made of Boone

and Garrett. He fell to his knees in the snow, laughing so hard he could hardly breathe. "She did that to you?"

Boone had still not lived that one down.

To cap it off, as they were about to get back into the squad, a tall, mean-looking guy emerged from the crowd pulling off his parka, pointed at Boone, and said, "I'll take you on right now all by myself."

Boone squinted at him. "Ronnie, is that you?"

"That's my name. Ask me again and I'll tell you the same."

"You didn't just say that."

"Put up or shut up, pig!"

"Ronnie Hibbard, right?"

That stopped him.

"Yeah! What of it?"

"Didn't I just see a warrant for you yesterday?"

Ronnie's shoulders slumped. "Yeah, that's me." His picked up his parka and put it on as he approached one of the other officers, hands before him and ready to be cuffed. "No sense gettin' all excited about it."

2:20 A.M.

Boone decided to give up trying to sleep for a while. He wanted to see Haeley in the morning and meet her mother later in the day, but she would understand if he had to sleep in. He gingerly rolled over and worked his way to a sitting position on the side of the bed.

Garrett. Where was he? He just had to know. Fox was the one guy with a motive.

Boone's career had almost ended prematurely when he slipped on the ice putting a drunk-and-disorderly into the back of the squad, grabbed the door to keep from falling, and nearly crushed the arrestee to death. Fox claimed to have seen the whole thing, while confiding to Boone that he knew he had lost his cool and done it on purpose. In some act of blind loyalty to a partner, Garrett lied under oath, only to have the truth exposed in the end by the victim himself.

Boone was conflicted. Here the guy had tried to stand up for him, misguided as he was. Boone had certainly not asked Fox to lie. Lying under oath to a police investigative panel had cost Fox his job. And Boone's acquittal had freed him to take the new role under Jack Keller in the Organized Crime Division.

To Boone's amazement, he discovered that Jack and the rest of the brass in OCD had been fully prepared to go another route if Boone had been convicted and dismissed from the force. They had another candidate in the wings. None other than Garrett Fox.

It made zero sense. With Fox's background and reputation, why would anyone think he would fit back into OCD, this time in a leadership role?

Maybe he was a pet of Fletcher Galloway, the OCD chief. Jack sure knew everything about Fox. Pete Wade had busted him back to uniform. Even Haeley had had her run-ins with him. He was one of many who had come on to her, and she had told Boone that he was the most egregious, the most inappropriate, the one who had made her feel the most uncomfortable.

Boone had seen Fox around the office now and then, and he was largely ignored. He liked to pretend he had just moved on, but when he lost his job, that seemed the end of him.

Boone knew he had landed some kind of security gig. But was it possible he was still able to get past personnel on other floors after hours and nose around in OCD?

It didn't seem likely. But he had to still be upset with Boone for not appreciating that he was willing to lie for him. He had to be devastated at not getting the job that had gone to Boone. And he was humiliated—or should have been—by Haeley's continual rejections.

If there was a disgruntled former employee with more of a motive for screwing up a major case, Boone had no idea who it would be.

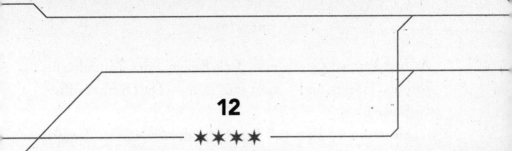

12

★★★★

MRS. LAMONICA

Boone finally drifted off in the wee hours of the morning and slept till noon, rising famished and in need of a shower. He had not thought to ask for a supply of the plastic coverings for his shoulder, so after lunch he fashioned his own. Working one-handed made it slow, and the drape turned into a mess, but he made it work.

His entire routine took him twice as long as usual, and Boone wondered if he had been wise to dismiss his parents. It was way too soon in his relationship with Haeley to even consider involving her in his care. Post–shoulder surgery was bound to be even worse.

Boone turned on his cell phone and found messages from virtually everyone in his life. Pastor Francisco Sosa had called.

As had Pascual Candelario, Jack Keller, Fritz Zappolo, his parents, Haeley, and—most intriguing—Dr. Duffey's office.

Busted.

He returned that call first. The doctor was in surgery, but the receptionist read Boone a strongly worded statement from him, scolding him for leaving the hospital without informing the doctor, listing things to do and not do, symptoms to watch for, and how to get in touch with Dr. Valdez in advance of his surgery. Boone asked the receptionist to pass on to the doctor his thanks and assurances that he would behave.

And yet one of the instructions from the doctor was to not venture out into the weather. As Boone planned to accompany Haeley to Zappolo's office, he would not be obeying that one.

Sosa and Boone's parents and PC had been just checking in on him, though the pastor had spent more than two minutes reading Bible verses into the phone. That made Boone feel guilty. As faithful as God had been to him in the lowest valley of his life, Boone felt he had regressed again spiritually. It was as if he hardly gave God a thought. Sosa added, "Remember the survival of the spiritual life. It needs to be fed. That means Bible reading and prayer."

Zappolo's message confirmed his appointment with Haeley and Boone for late that afternoon, after Haeley reported that her mother would arrive from South Carolina to watch Max.

Jack's message was an invitation to a farewell party for Fletcher Galloway on Monday, the eighth. Boone immediately returned that call.

"Wouldn't miss it," he said. "I don't suppose Haeley is invited."

"Hilarious."

"Just sayin'."

"Yeah, very funny."

"You sure you want *me* there?" Boone said.

"'Course. Fletch loves you."

"He might not when he finds out I'm all over this case."

"Just don't spoil the party by talking about it, huh? There'll be plenty of time to—"

"You think I'm not going to try to get a minute with Pete?"

"That's not the time or place."

"Then when?"

"Boones, I got to think Pete wants to talk to you too, to assure you it's not personal and to advise you to stay out of it."

"Fat chance."

"You want me to arrange a meeting?"

"I'll let you know."

"Just promise you won't complicate the party. That wouldn't be fair to Fletch."

"That's going to be one weird party with one of our own conspicuously absent."

"Well, it will be a little awkward because significant others are invited. Margaret will be there, and so will Fletch and Pete's wives."

"I suppose Haeley's replacement will be there. I'll be the odd one out."

"It's not going to be a big deal. Cake and stuff and a few words. Fletch just wants to clear out."

The last thing Boone wanted was a CPD tail when he went to meet Mrs. Lamonica and take Haeley to Zappolo's office.

Though freshly mellow from his meds, he stood by his upstairs window for ninety minutes to get a read on when and how often a squad cruised the block to keep an eye on the place. Seeing them come around only twice in an hour and a half told him when he could slip out late in the afternoon.

He called Haeley. She sounded miserable.

"I thought you'd be perkier today, considering."

"I'm scared to death this is temporary, Boone. You know the US Attorney wants to make this a federal case. I might wish I'd stayed at County rather than get sent to a federal facility."

"Zappolo will never let that happen."

"Is that a guarantee?"

Boone hesitated. The Metropolitan Correctional Center (MCC) at Clark and Van Buren was newer and had to be better than County, but he didn't want to see her sent there any more than she did. It had been a stupid thing to say. "I mean, Fritz'll do everything possible to keep you and Max together."

Haeley did not sound reassured. She told him her mother had left South Carolina at about three that morning, and she expected her at about three in the afternoon. "Come around four so you can get acquainted before we go."

At about three Boone returned to the upstairs window to watch for the patrolling squad. As soon as it had left the neighborhood, he slipped out the back to his car in the alley. Again the frigid air pierced his damaged lung and slowed him.

Several minutes later, when he pulled to within a few blocks of Haeley's apartment, he parked on a side street in a long line of cars. Someone would have to be specifically checking every license plate to find him.

Boone covered his mouth for the walk to Haeley's, longing

for the day when breathing would be second nature again. Seeing Mrs. Lamonica's car with its South Carolina license plate gave him an idea. That was the car they should take downtown.

Haeley's mother was pleasant looking with short dark hair and medium build, plain compared to her striking daughter. She greeted him politely and seemed shy, but that soon proved a mistaken impression. As soon as Haeley excused herself to get ready, Mrs. Lamonica said, "Max will be up from his nap soon, but we have time to talk."

"Good," Boone said, but her tone had been such that he wasn't so sure.

"Haeley tells me you're a Christian man."

"I am."

"That's good. And what does that mean?"

"Mean, ma'am? I thought she told me you and your husband were believers too."

"That's true."

"So you just want to be sure I know what it really means to be a Christian?"

"Tell you the truth, Mr. Drake, I want to know it means you're not sleeping with my daughter."

"Wow."

"Is that an answer?"

"No, sorry—you deserve an answer. I appreciate someone who gets to the point. You know Haeley and I have just begun to get serious."

She sat gazing at him with raised eyebrows, as if to say she still hadn't heard an answer.

"Rest assured I respect her too much to be sleeping with her. I believe that's wrong for a Christian outside of marriage."

"I wish she'd always felt that way," Haeley's mother said, "though I do love what came of that sin."

Boone flinched.

"That's what it was, you know."

He nodded. "She has said as much herself."

"Her father and I raised her right. 'Least we tried to. Maybe we were a little too strict; I don't know. She knew better is all I can say."

"Well, if it makes you feel any better, she seems to be a whole different person now, but of course I didn't know her back then."

"Then how do you know?"

"She tells me she was away from God, away from church. Rebelling."

"Against God or against us?"

"I don't think she was ever that specific."

"Well, I took it personally."

"She knows that."

"I guess I should be more forgiving."

"You haven't forgiven her?"

Mrs. Lamonica pressed her lips together. "Sometimes I think I have. Maybe I haven't forgiven myself. If we were too hard on her, too strict, you know . . ."

"She was an adult. And like you both say, she knew better."

"It's just such a heartache. And that young man . . ."

"Did you meet him?"

She shook her head. "Just what she said about him, and him leaving before he even saw his own son. I just hope she never sees him again."

"I can't imagine."

"Well, with people like that you never know. Families keep secrets and have histories, and sure enough someday, sometime, somebody comes out of the woodwork."

"From what she tells me, he has no interest."

Mrs. Lamonica sighed and looked away. "Sure, now. But when it suits him . . ."

"Let me pledge to you, ma'am, that if I'm in the picture and he shows up again, he's going to wish he hadn't."

Suddenly the woman who had appeared weary from her long drive seemed to sit straighter and life came to her eyes. "I might come to like you after all."

"I hope so!"

She offered a weak smile. "I know you've had your share of tragedy."

Boone hadn't been sure how much Haeley had said about him. "Yes, ma'am."

"If it means anything coming from me, I approve of you and Haeley—and Max—getting to know each other better."

"It means everything. And excuse me if I'm out of bounds, but I do think Haeley really wants and needs your forgiveness and approval."

"I know. I'll try."

They both stood when Haeley emerged. "There was one other thing I was going to ask you," Boone said. "Might we be able to borrow your car? No one will be looking for us in that model car with an out-of-state plate."

Haeley said, "Good idea. And my car's here, Mom, if you have an emergency."

"I'd feel better if the one of you with two good arms did the driving," Mrs. Lamonica said.

"Me too," Boone said.

On their way downtown Haeley said, "So how did you two get on?"

"Okay, I think. She liked that I promised to take care of your ex if he ever shows up again."

"Don't call him that."

"Sorry. Anything else I call him you might not want to hear."

"I can't believe you got that far with her already."

"She brought it up. The woman speaks her mind."

"Daddy's even worse. And they wonder why I was so eager to get out on my own."

"I'm sure they mean well."

Haeley squinted at Boone. "That's easy to say from a distance. I still feel judged."

"She loves you is all I know."

"Conditional love is painful."

"Believe me," he said, "I know. Our mothers have completely different looks and styles, but I'm overparented too."

Haeley parked in the garage in Zappolo's building, but before she got out she reached across Boone to take his good hand. She was shaking. "I need you," she said.

"I know. I'm here."

"Mr. Zappolo said to be prepared for a long session and lots of questions."

"You'll do fine."

"I hope I can remember everything. I don't even know what he wants to know."

"Don't worry until he asks."

"I have a feeling he knows stuff I don't even know yet."

"We'll find out soon enough."

"Will you pray for me, Boone?"

"Of course."

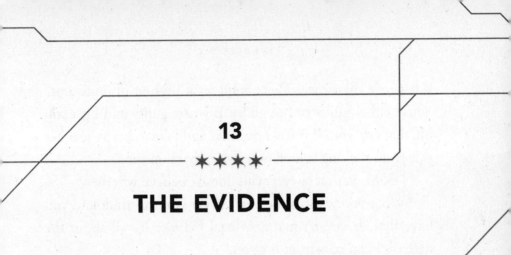

13

★ ★ ★ ★

THE EVIDENCE

Despite being known for playing his cards close to the vest, Friedrich Zappolo appeared to have trouble hiding his unease. He didn't look either Boone or Haeley in the eye and seemed distracted even as he hung their coats.

They sat at his side table, and the attorney stacked next to him his notes and an overstuffed envelope. He tapped it. "Disclosure from the other side."

"Disclosure of what?" Haeley said.

"We'll get to that. Now, Ms. Lamonica, I want you to know that it makes zero difference to me whether or not you are guilty."

"I assure you I am innocent—"

Zappolo held up a hand. "I don't want to hear it. It's irrelevant. My job is to defend you in every way possible and make the other side prove their case. There is no legal finding of 'innocent.' You're either guilty or not guilty. If you're guilty and I get you off, that's on you. If you're not guilty and I fail to keep the other side from making it look otherwise, that's on me."

"I don't want a lawyer who doesn't believe whether—"

"What you want is the best lawyer you can find, and you have that. It doesn't matter what I believe. It's all about the defense I can construct for you."

Haeley stood. "I want another lawyer."

"No, you don't," Zappolo said. "Another lawyer won't know how to work around the evidence the other side has against you. Please, sit down. If you decide after we chat that you would be more comfortable with other counsel, of course I can't stand in your way."

"Fritz," Boone said, "just tell her what you've found."

Haeley turned to Boone. "You know what he's found?"

"No, but it obviously doesn't look good or he wouldn't have had to give you the guilty-or-not-guilty speech."

Haeley sat. "Is that true? Something makes you doubt me?"

Zappolo sat back and sighed. "Let's just say they have a case, and we have a problem. But I like a challenge."

"Just get it all on the table," Boone said.

Zappolo opened the envelope and slid out documents and two photos.

"This is a copy of a cell phone photo of a classified document entrusted to you and which bears notes written by you in code, revealing the location and timing of the transfer of Pascual Candelario from the original safe house to a lockup near where the grand jury was to be seated. Is that your handwriting?"

Haeley leaned forward. "Yes. And after the last meeting, that went into a locked file."

"The question will be asked, how was an outsider able to photograph this?"

"Well, I—"

"No need to answer now. This other photo is of you making a deposit at your bank on the same date stamped on the other photo."

Haeley studied it, pulled a tiny calendar and her checkbook from her purse, and leafed through both. "That was payday. I deposited my check." She turned her check ledger so Zappolo could see it.

"Mm-hm. When do you get your bank statement?"

"The end of the month in the mail, but I can see it online anytime."

"Checked it lately?"

"No."

"I have been given a copy of your current balance."

"And?"

"It shows the deposit of your check."

"Of course."

"And a separate deposit the same day."

"To my account?"

"Yes."

"Not by me."

"And yet it appears in your new balance. Five thousand dollars."

"Well, the deposit slip won't have my signature on it. How does someone deposit money into my account without my knowledge?"

Zappolo raised a brow. "You tell me. The deposits were both processed by the same teller."

"I'm telling you I made one deposit," Haeley said. "So what is all this?"

"Here's their case," Zappolo said. "Only someone familiar with CPD lingo would understand your notes. Former detective Garrett Fox has an acrimonious relationship with Mr. Drake due to a previous Internal Affairs investigation that cost him his job. Plus he had been in line for the job Mr. Drake was awarded. He had a personal relationship with you, Haeley, that went sour—"

"Absolutely untrue!"

"Ms. Lamonica, I'm telling you what the US Attorney believes, based on his staff's discovery, which included lengthy interviews with all the subjects."

"Except me."

"Except you, of course. That will happen in court."

"I never so much as even ran into Garrett Fox outside the office. I couldn't tell you where he lives, and we never, ever, socialized."

"He's claiming an intimate relationship."

"A lie."

"His testimony is that it went south and you expressed a desperate wish that knowledge of it never reach Mr. Drake. Your new relationship becomes another motive for Mr. Fox."

Haeley shook her head, and her voice grew quavery. "They'll never be able to prove something so far from the truth."

"Fox's testimony will be that he assured you he would never reveal the truth of your relationship if you would merely leave on your desk the file in question, just for the duration of your afternoon break."

"And five thousand dollars?"

"Exactly."

"I never took money. I never would."

"Naturally it will need to be retrieved from your account."

Haeley looked as if she were about to explode. "What did I ever do to Garrett Fox?"

"It was more likely what you wouldn't do with him," Boone said. "Didn't you tell me he was always after you?"

"Yes, but how will that look now? Like he wore me down? My own lawyer doesn't believe me, so—"

"Please, ma'am," Zappolo said, "we need to be clear about this. It isn't that I don't believe you. It's that what I believe is wholly irrelevant."

"I need you to believe me."

The lawyer shrugged. "I've never liked Garrett Fox. So I'm willing to give you the benefit of the doubt, if that makes you feel better."

"That's all?"

"That's more than most of my clients get. 'Course most of them *are* guilty."

Haeley shook her head. "Boone swears by you, but let me ask you something. If you're known for defending guilty people, doesn't that make me look guilty?"

"He gets most of them off," Boone said.

"I want to be acquitted because I'm innocent, not because of a tricky lawyer."

"You don't mean 'innocent,'" Zappolo said. You mean 'not guilty.' Big difference. But it's your call. Let me tell you where I think things stand. You're going to have a tough time explaining away the deposit."

"Keller has been trying to talk me into direct-depositing my check as it is. This sure makes that an easy decision. If I ever get my job back."

"That's my goal. But then there's the matter of explaining the relationship."

"I've told you, there's never been a relationship."

"He's claiming otherwise and may come up with corroborating witnesses."

"They'll have to be lying."

"If we can prove that, and if you'll let me, I'd like to sue the City of Chicago for false arrest and myriad other things, which may result in a settlement that would keep you from ever having to work again."

"Oh, no you don't. That's not me."

"Don't be silly. There are all kinds of reasons to accept a settlement."

"Because someone tried to make me look bad?"

"Because if you're right, the CPD didn't determine you were somehow set up."

"So now you believe me, when a settlement would get you a hefty fee?"

"Whether I believe you or not—"

"Yeah, I got that."

"If I can get you a settlement, provided they don't prove their case, let me have my percentage and you can give away the rest, if that'll make you feel better."

"And what's your percentage?"

"A third is standard, though if the settlement were in the

high seven figures, I might reduce that to a quarter after a certain level."

Haeley looked gobsmacked. "*Seven* figures?"

"Potentially high seven figures."

"Hold on," Boone said. "Where is Fox in all this? Out on bond?"

"Yes, awaiting trial. But he's in deep trouble and he knows it. He's ready to tell of his involvement with Ms. Lamonica in exchange for a lighter sentence."

"Something's not adding up," Boone said. "Haeley never left that file out, which means Fox had to be working with someone else inside. And what was in this for him, anyway? Just getting our star witness killed to ruin the case and my major collar? He had to be getting big bucks."

"Want to know what I think?" Zappolo said. "I think he takes a reduced sentence, trying to take down anyone he can in the process, serves his time, and then still gets a big payday on the other end. The one hole in your sting case is that you have not rounded up all the cash the gangs have hoarded over the years. Millions? Billions? You realize they brought in so much cash it was easier to weigh it than count it to know how much they had? Anyway, we know why Jazzy wanted Pascual dead. That had to be worth quite an offer. The question is, how did Fox get connected with people like that?"

"He was undercover for a few years," Boone said.

"Well, there you go."

Haeley said, "How do I prove Fox is lying about a relationship with me?"

"The burden of proof is on him," Zappolo said. "But be

prepared. Your reputation is going to be dragged through the mud. Do I understand you have a child out of wedlock?"

"Tell me Max won't figure into this."

"I can keep his name out of it, but no, I can't get that fact excluded. It speaks to your character and lifestyle, which will be under attack."

"What it speaks to is a period of my life that is long past."

"That may be, but the other side will try to make you look like a bed hopper. Sorry."

Haeley buried her head in her hands.

"Rethinking the idea of a settlement when this is all over?"

"Maybe," she said quietly. "If they really do this to Max and me."

"Before you decide you're dead set against profiting from a debacle like this," Zappolo said, "think of your son. You could set him up for life: college, the whole thing."

"You're pretty confident you can win."

"I'd better be. If I just get you off, Boone's five grand pays a few of my expenses. We take it to the next step, my third can more than pay off my boat."

Haeley stood and paced. "How ugly can this get?"

Zappolo shrugged. "Everything's fair game. It wouldn't surprise me if they called the father of your son to testify."

"You have got to be kidding."

"And if they're smart, they'll get him to paint you in a pretty bad light."

"Meaning?"

"You sure you want to hear this?"

"Better from you than in court for the first time. I can't believe I might have to face him again."

"Maybe they won't want to go to the expense of flying him in. Where does he live?"

"He works in a casino in Hammond."

"Then you can bet he'll be here. If I were on their side, I'd get him to portray you as a loose woman."

"It won't be hard for you to impugn his character, Fritz," Boone said. "He's still never seen his own son."

Zappolo shrugged. "They'll get him to say it was because he wasn't allowed and that he isn't even sure the baby was his."

Haeley shot him a double take.

"I'm just telling you what you're facing."

6:00 P.M.

As they headed back to Haeley's mother's car, Boone was exhausted. At times like this he was reminded of the trauma done to his body and how much worse he was bound to feel ten days hence when he would come out of surgery. He had the feeling he had a lot to accomplish before rehab.

The parking garage was cold and drafty, and Boone was eager to get in the car. But as he stood there with his good hand on the door handle, Haeley seemed paralyzed on the other side of the car. "I can't leave it like this," she said.

"What?"

"I need to tell him."

"Zappolo? What?"

She marched off toward the elevator.

"Could you leave me the keys?" Boone said.

"You're not going with me?"

"I guess I am."

They met Friedrich Zappolo in the foyer of his law firm, dressed for the weather. "Forget something?" he said.

"You need to hear this from me," Haeley said. "That's all."

"I'm listening."

She got in his face. "I don't care about the legal mumbo jumbo, whether I'm innocent or not guilty or whatever you want to call it. And I don't care whether it's relevant or you want or need to hear it, but I need you to. I never had any kind of a relationship with Garrett Fox, and I never would. I never left any classified documents out where anyone could see them, least of all an outsider. And I never took money to do anything wrong."

"Okay."

"Okay? That's all?"

"I've got it," Zappolo said. "Feel better?"

"No. Because you're not buying it, and I need you to. I have to have a lawyer who believes in me."

"I have the capacity to believe whatever you tell me to believe."

Haeley caught Boone's eye and set her jaw, shaking her head as if she were so angry she couldn't even speak.

"Ms. Lamonica," Zappolo said, "your odds of success are better with me than with anyone else you could choose. The other side, even if it's the US Attorney, is going to have to perform miracles to make any of this stick against you. You need to trust me."

"I'll let you know," Haeley said through clenched teeth, spinning to head back to the elevator.

Zappolo nodded to Boone as if he wanted him to lag for a moment. "Meet you at the car," he told Haeley. She looked surprised but left.

Zappolo led Boone around the corner and leaned back against the wall, clearly out of earshot of anyone else. "You need to tread very carefully with this woman."

"What're you saying? You believe the other side's discovery?"

"I didn't show all of it."

"How much more is there?"

"Plenty. There *was* some kind of a relationship, probably closer to what Fox maintains than Ms. Lamonica says."

Boone felt a stab in his lung, indoors for the first time. "What evidence?"

"E-mails."

"From her?"

"Both."

"From what computer?"

"His laptop and her office unit."

"Get out. How stupid do you think she is?"

"Hard to argue with the evidence, Drake."

"C'mon, Fritz. It's got setup written all over it."

"The techies will spend a good deal of time on the stand, is my guess."

"Why didn't you hit her with this?"

"Oh, I will. She won't hear it first in court, you may rest assured."

"What else?"

"Her signature is not on either deposit. You don't sign a deposit slip unless you're taking some of the money as cash."

Boone shrugged. "They still have to prove she deposited the payoff, if there was one."

"Don't be naive. The money's in her account and Fox

corroborates the amount. Hey, you don't look so good, Drake. You all right?"

"A little short of breath."

"Need to sit?"

Boone shook his head. "You're telling me this woman I believe I know is loose, a liar, and a criminal?"

"I'm telling you to tread carefully, and I'm also reminding you that she has the best lawyer money can buy."

"Who believes she's guilty."

"Give me a break, Boone. It doesn't matter. I know my job, and I'll do it to the best of my ability."

"She's going to want to know what you wanted."

"That's on you. Tell her or don't tell her; I'm okay either way."

"She'll probably fire you."

"That would be a mistake."

"I hate to say I agree, Fritz. But I also want to prove everyone wrong, especially you."

"That would be most helpful. Nobody's restricted you from the case, have they? I can't afford a private investigator on what you're paying. You want to handle it?"

Boone snorted. "It would only be my career."

"Your career? That's as good as over anyway, isn't it?"

"Hardly."

"Admirable. If you want to risk it by digging into some of this stuff for me, I'll be all ears."

Boone was grateful to climb into a warm car, but naturally he dreaded the questions from Haeley. Her look said it all. She didn't even have to ask.

"I may have a new part-time job," Boone said. "'Course it doesn't pay."

"What?"

"I'm gonna act as PI on your case."

"If I keep Zappolo, you mean?"

"Haeley, you really need to decide that right now. With the US Attorney nosing around, you could wind up at MCC and lose Max to DCFS."

"Don't even say that. I'd die first."

"Zappolo can make sure he stays with your mom, but this is the wrong time to be switching lawyers."

"I don't like him, Boone."

"You don't have to. But I'm telling you, he's the best."

"Even if he doesn't believe in me."

"Maybe especially because of that. He has no illusions. What if you had someone who totally believed you but couldn't mount an effective defense? The result is all we care about."

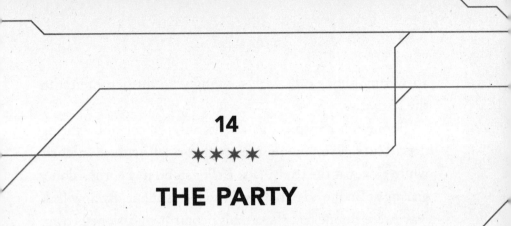

14

★★★★

THE PARTY

Boone felt silly pulling Mrs. Lamonica's out-of-state car into a parking garage a block from his office. He didn't want to be so obvious as to park at the CPD, but really, how much difference would a block make?

Boone reached the Organized Crime Division's suite of offices a tick before 11 a.m., when Fletcher Galloway's party was to start. Everybody was there except the guest of honor and his wife and several of the upper brass. Even the mayor was there, but he surprisingly kept to himself and his entourage and seemed eager to speak his piece and get going.

Haeley's replacement proved to be a married woman in her midthirties who apologetically got herself a piece of cake and a cup of coffee and ferried them to her station. There she sat answering phone calls with seemingly no further interest in the festivities.

Boone felt conspicuous as the only officer not wearing dress blues. Everyone else looked formal, with even their white gloves at the ready. Jack Keller stood in a corner alone, glaring at Boone. He knew what that was about. By now Jack was aware Boone had shaken his department-assigned cover.

When Jack finally approached and shook his hand, he said, "You don't *have* to accept protection, but I have to live with it if something happens to you."

"Let me make it official, Boss. I exonerate you."

"Oh, that makes it all better. That'll help me sleep if you wind up on a slab."

"I can't live in fear, Jack."

"No, you'll leave that to me."

"So, where's Margaret?"

"My office. A little shy, you know."

"That'll be the day." Everyone who had met Jack's girl-friend loved her.

"I'm kidding. Just touching up her makeup. Here she comes now."

Margaret was the epitome of the Southern belle, somehow maintaining a tan, not even attempting to hide her freckles or the streaks of gray in her chestnut hair. She was ten years too old for the length of her skirt, but somehow she made it work.

She kissed Boone on the cheek, then stepped back and seemed to study him. "Where's your honey?"

"Not invited."

"Oh, I knew that. Forgive me, sugar. Me and my big mouth. Well, I'll let you make the rounds."

No one Boone had ever seen wore a dress uniform like Pete Wade. The Gang Enforcement Section commander may have been a bit thicker than in his prime, but he was still a dramatic-looking man with deep chocolate coloring and pure white hair.

Boone tried to hide his unease when Pete approached and warmly shook his hand. "How's our hero?" he said. "Coming along?"

"Hanging on for dear life, Commander," Boone said.

Pete introduced Boone to his wife, Thelma, a small woman who offered her pleasantries just above a whisper. She showed a shy smile and was perfectly manicured and coiffed. She wore diamond earrings, a pendant, and a ring that looked like a set, and each stone was huge and radiant. Boone decided it must be nice to have as many years on the job as Pete Wade.

Pete put a hand on Boone's good arm and gently tugged him a few feet away. "Excuse us a moment, dear," he said in his crisp baritone. "If we get a minute later, Boone, I'd like a chat."

"Me too, Commander."

At that moment, Fletcher Galloway, the man of the hour, breezed in. He helped his wife remove her floor-length coat, and she helped him with his. Finally the secretary emerged from behind her desk to hang up their coats and apologized for having already partaken of the cake and coffee.

"But someone has to run this place," she said, giggling.

Galloway looked as if he would rather have been anywhere else. It struck Boone that if the day ever came when he was feted after decades of impeccable service, he planned to enjoy it.

The former chief of the division appeared to paste on a

smile when the mayor approached, and it seemed clear that the boss of the city was suggesting that he had another obligation and needed to move things along. Someone let the press in, and Boone immediately retreated behind Jack and Margaret. "I've had enough publicity for the rest of my life," he said.

"So you do still have a modicum of common sense," Jack said.

When the rest of the CPD brass arrived, the mayor did his thing, seeming to make every effort to take credit for the mammoth gang sting but finally praising the career of Fletcher Galloway.

Galloway mentioned everyone on his senior staff, including Boone. When the formalities were over, the press came looking for Boone, but Jack headed them off. Margaret and Mrs. Wade wound up together as Pete pulled Boone into his office.

"We can kill two birds with one stone," Wade said. "Get you out of the spotlight and have our talk."

Boone sat before Pete's ornate desk, another perk after so many years on the job. While they were both officers in an elite division, Boone's office was a concrete block chamber with gray steel institutional furniture and antiseptic-green walls. He was young and new and didn't expect anything else. But Pete's office was like Jack's, which wasn't that different from what Fletcher Galloway had enjoyed.

A handsomely appointed office wasn't the point of being on the job, but Boone could look ahead. It would be nice. Someday. Even if he took the Major Case Squad assignment, though the bank of offices in the 11th precinct station house would be new, they certainly wouldn't be opulent.

Boone expected nothing else from the appropriately self-possessed Wade, but the man made no attempt to level the playing field and join Boone at a side table or even in a chair next to him. Rather, the commander of the Gang Enforcement Section strode behind his desk and made a show of unfastening the row of gold buttons on his dress coat before settling in the tall leather judge's chair.

"You carrying a Glock, Commander?" Boone said. "That's new, isn't it? Thought you had a Beretta like mine."

"This? Yeah. It's the 30." He stood and deftly removed it from his holster, popping out the magazine. "Compact and takes the .45 GAP hollow-point ammo."

"Nice."

As quickly as he had removed and showed it, Pete snapped it all back together, holstered it, and sat. "We need to talk, Boone," he said slowly and precisely, as was his style. "You need to know how proud I am of you and how deeply grateful I am for your personal sacrifice. We could not have asked more from you in this whole operation, and I'm just sorry I haven't had the opportunity to express myself till now."

"Thank you, sir."

Wade shifted in his seat, causing his leather Sam Browne belt to squeak. To Boone it was one of the sweetest sounds in the world. He knew that made him weird. He also knew that others who shared the love of that sound were usually described as all cop.

Pete folded his hands before him and seemed to be at a loss for words. That was out of character. His eyes darted and he cleared his throat. "Hey, I've got something else to show you. Have you seen the new M4?"

"There's a new one?"

Pete stood again and moved to his gun safe, briskly spinning the dial. "It's a lot like the one issued to you, but this has a high-capacity magazine. Check it out."

Boone had always loved the heft of the M4, a hybrid of the old M16. It was a short assault rifle used by the Marines, noted for its ability to shoot more rounds in less time than most handguns.

"This the automatic?"

"It sure is. Fully. A thousand rounds a minute, and this one has the thirty-shot magazine."

"Sweet."

"Thought you'd like it. Bet you wished you'd had it in the garage the other night."

Boone chuckled. "We were trying to be inconspicuous. You think an assault rifle might have given me away? Anyway, you're stalling, Pete. You didn't bring me in here to show me your M4."

Pete hesitated, then took back the rifle, wiping it down and carefully placing it back into the safe. He pointed to the visitor's chair and returned to behind his desk.

"Do you trust me, Boone?"

"Always have."

"But I mean now."

"I'm not sure."

"I appreciate that honesty. It's no secret that I have brought charges against someone you care about."

"I'm in love with her, sir."

"All right, then. And my wife has long advised me to never bad-mouth a spouse or a loved one."

"Say what you need to say, Commander."

"Oh, I plan to. But I know this will not be easy for you."

"I need to hear it."

"Yes. You do. Detective, Haeley Lamonica is not the woman you think she is."

"I'm listening."

"Are you? Or are you just tolerating me?"

"I didn't say I was agreeing. But I am listening."

"It should not be a surprise that she is a single mother."

Boone fought to keep his cool. "She made a mistake a long time ago. That is no indication of the woman I know."

Pete Wade looked away and licked his lips. "This is not easy for me, Boone. But I need to tell you that it *is* an indication of the woman I know."

Boone flinched. "I was unaware you knew her that well."

"I know her well enough. You know she had a relationship with Garrett Fox, not only while he was on the staff here, but even after he was reassigned."

"I have heard that charge."

"It's true. In fact, it's the reason I sent him back to the 11th."

"You're telling me that while he and I were on patrol together, he was in a relationship with Haeley?"

"I'm sorry."

"So am I. Or I would be if I believed it."

"You may believe it."

"Because you say so?"

"Don't make me show you the evidence. Take my word for it."

"Why would I do that?"

Pete sighed and ran a hand through his short hair. "I need to ask you to keep my confidence. Can you do that?"

"Of course."

"For the sake of my wife, I hope I never have to testify to this, but for the sake of our friendship and—I hope—our continued professional relationship, I am going out on a limb."

Wade paused as if waiting for permission, but Boone wasn't biting.

"To my shame, I have not always been a model of marital fidelity. Does that surprise you?"

"It's none of my business, sir."

"But does it surprise you?"

Boone shrugged. "As a matter of fact, it does."

"I'm not proud of it. But this will surprise you too. On more than one occasion, I and a woman other than my wife double-dated—for lack of a better term—with Garrett and Haeley."

Boone realized he had been sitting without moving for several minutes. He was overheated, sweating, and wishing he were anywhere but right there right then. His voice broke and he had to clear his throat midsentence. "And where exactly, uh, would this have taken place?"

"Well, we were not honorable men," Pete said, "but we're not stupid. It was out of state. Indiana. At a little-known club where people didn't know us and didn't ask questions."

Why would Pete be saying this if it weren't true?

"So you and Fox were buddies off the job?"

Pete cocked his head. "*Buddies* may be overstating it. Partners in unsavory activities, let's say. But it all went down the toilet."

"Yeah, I'm curious about that," Boone said. "How far down could it have gone for Fox to later be in line for the job I got?"

"Sadly, that was my fault. I knew better, but I felt pressured by Garrett. He had gotten sloppy and noisy. You know confidentiality and humility were never his strong points."

"Do I."

"The sad fact is, I demoted him back to the street, and at first he seemed to take it all right. Undercover is a stressful deal. But then he applied for the job you got, and when I at first said no way, he threatened to go to my wife or to Fletch with the news that I had condoned his dalliances with a coworker. I couldn't have that."

Boone stood and paced.

"I'm not done," Wade said.

"Neither am I. I just can't sit still."

"I understand."

"I'll bet you do."

Wade held up a hand. "I know. I know, okay? Believe me, I am trying to protect you. And you need to know exactly who you're dealing with."

Here was the second man in just a few days to warn him to tread lightly with Haeley Lamonica.

"So," Boone said, "you're telling me that Garrett getting caught trying to lie for me and winding up prosecuted by Internal Affairs himself is the only thing that saved you from having to give him my job?"

Pete nodded. "Happiest day of my life. And relief? I don't mind telling you I recommitted myself to my marriage and have never looked back."

Good for you, Boone thought, but he couldn't say it aloud and mask his sarcasm.

What a mess.

Boone was suddenly weak-kneed and had to sit again. Pete seemed to take that as his cue to stand. "You can see that Garrett had all kinds of motives to do what he did. Not only did he have significant issues with me, but you seemed to have taken his girlfriend from him too."

"So what's her motive, Pete?"

"Maybe she was intimidated. Maybe she needed the money. Five grand can sound like an awful lot to a clerical worker. But she also didn't want you to know about her and Fox."

"Do you realize what kind of a hypocrite she would have to be?"

"I don't follow," Pete said.

"An awful lot of our time together is spent in church."

"Oh, well, come on!"

"What?"

"You think I'm not a churchgoer too, Boone? I'm a deacon! That's why nobody suspected me."

Boone lowered his head. "So she's hiding her real self behind some phony piety."

"I can speak only for myself. That's what I was doing."

Boone rubbed his eyes with his good hand. "What am I supposed to do with all this, Pete?"

"Just don't jeopardize your career by backing the wrong horse. I know what's on the horizon for you, and I'd hate to see this get in the way of that."

Again it occurred to Boone that if Haeley proved to be other than he believed, even the Major Case Squad assignment would lose all appeal.

Pete came around the desk, extending his hand. The last thing Boone wanted was to shake it, but he offered a weak hand. He staggered into the hallway, fearing with everything that was in him that it was true. Pete brushed past him to join his wife, and Jack motioned to Boone that it was time he should say something to Fletcher Galloway.

Boone found Fletch looking for him. "You got a minute?" the former chief said. Boone followed the man into his empty office, wishing he could be done with all this.

It was strange to see Galloway in his cavernous space with nothing on the desk or credenza, pictures down from the wall leaving faded squares of color. "Sorry for the way I look," Boone said.

"Don't give it a second thought. I don't know how you get dressed at all."

"I have to be a contortionist. Listen, Chief, let me talk first, okay? I don't want to neglect to say what I need to."

Galloway's face appeared to fall, as if he had heard enough accolades for one day.

"I promise to keep it short. I just want to say it's been a privilege, an experience I won't forget. And if I wind up at Major Case, I'll owe a lot of it to you."

"Nonsense," Galloway said. "You owe your whole career to Jack Keller, not to mention that you lived up to everything he said about you. Get healthy and get back in the game, hear?"

"That's my goal."

"Now let me tell you something, Drake. I don't like what's going on here, and you need to know I don't believe a word of it."

"You don't?"

"'Course I don't. You learn something with as many years as I've spent on the job, and I think I know people. Garrett Fox is poison; I saw that from the beginning. If I couldn't have gotten in the way of his taking the job you got, I would have quit then. And Haeley? Everything in me tells me she's good people."

Boone had to suppress a laugh. That phrase was not one he had ever expected to hear from Fletcher Galloway.

"Now I know you've got a thing for Haeley, and you know that because she's a coworker, you have to be very careful. And if anything comes of your relationship, you also know you have to check with downtown on whether it's okay. I tend to think it will be, if you're in separate divisions."

"You sound like you think she's going to be exonerated."

"I do."

"That's a huge relief, sir."

"It won't be easy, but I don't believe this Fox thing for a second. I can't tell you the number of times she complained about him being inappropriate with her. And I warned him. I thought all that was over when he was reassigned. Now I don't know what he's got on Pete, but you didn't hear me say that."

"That's why you're leaving? Because you don't want to see Pete fall?"

Fletcher shrugged. "That's part of it. But my time is past anyway. I'm never going to see better than what you accomplished, so, you know. . . . But I thought I knew Pete. Jack tells me there's some evidence that may justify all this, and you know Pete has been tops for years. But I just don't know."

"Chief, you have no idea how this encourages me. I was about to throw in the towel."

"Don't do that."

"Don't worry."

"Just do me a favor, Drake. Leave me out of it. I'm old, I'm tired, and I'm through."

"You know I hired Fritz—"

"I know, and I like it."

"He wants me to look into some of this stuff for him. You think that's a good idea?"

"If I was still your boss, I'd tell you to run as far from that as you can."

"But now?"

"Like I said, just leave me out of it."

Leaving, Boone was not as confident as he felt he should have been. It wasn't like the old man to go on feelings. It wasn't like Boone either, but right then his feeling was that he would be investigating Haeley as much to know the truth for himself as for any other reason.

15

★★★★

BACK IN THE GAME

MONDAY, FEBRUARY 8, 12:30 P.M.

Boone's plan upon leaving the party was to nose around at Haeley's bank. Apparently the same employee had processed both deposits to her account, and he wanted to see what the teller remembered.

But on his way out, Boone found himself having to work through a phalanx of partygoers who all seemed to be looking for their coats and saying their good-byes. He overheard Jack Keller confirm with Pete Wade that they had a one o'clock meeting.

It was innocuous and should have been inconsequential, but if Boone Drake was anything, he was a trained observer who followed his hunches. Something gave him pause. Hurrying out, tugging his parka over his slinged shoulder, he began rehearsing what wasn't adding up.

Pete Wade was punctual to a fault. Boone had never known him to be late for anything—a meeting, a ride, a stakeout, a dinner, anything. So what?

Well, Pete was helping his wife put on her coat, and he was wearing his. Was he just walking her to her car? They lived in Naperville, farther away than CPD regulations allowed, but apparently winked at by the brass due to Wade's years on the job and pristine record. But there was no way he could run her home and get back in time for a one o'clock meeting, nearly sixty miles round trip.

Was Boone overly suspicious? He wasn't about to dismiss anything. He hurried to his car and pulled around the corner to where he could see the exit of the CPD parking garage. The effort nearly spent him. He sat panting, shoulder aching, lung stabbing, breath fogging his window as Mrs. Lamonica's car fought to heat up.

He was watching for Commander Wade's black, late-model, top-of-the-line Toyota Avalon sedan. And here it came. Boone was suddenly overcome with self-doubt. What was the matter with him? Wade could easily be dropping his wife anywhere. A store? Her own lunch date? But why hadn't they driven separately if he had a post-party meeting? Surely Thelma Wade had her own car.

Boone hung back a block, grateful for a fogged-up windshield and, of course, the out-of-state plates. Pete Wade was a trained observer too, but the last thing he would suspect was to be followed now.

A little more than ten minutes later Boone followed Pete Wade off the Kennedy Expressway to Ohio Street, where he exited and drove into the River North area. Boone nearly lost him at a light on LaSalle but saw the Avalon turn onto a tree-lined street. He pulled around the corner just in time to see Wade head down an alley leading to a motorized gate that opened as he neared it.

Hanging back in the shadows, Boone had an unobstructed view of the Wades' car. It didn't appear the couple were looking at each other, let alone talking. Pete stopped before a row of garage doors that served a block-long complex of high-end, three-story brownstones. He reached to his sun visor and one of the doors opened, revealing a white matching version of his car. Boone memorized the license number.

Mrs. Wade left the car, seemingly without a word, and appeared to stride wearily into the garage. Pete pulled away out the other end of the alley long before the garage door closed, so Boone assumed his wife had hit a switch from inside. Boone was only guessing, but because Pete had clearly triggered the automatic gate and door, it appeared this was no visit. These people lived here.

He pulled out his cell phone and dialed.

"This is Keller."

"Jack, where does Pete Wade live?"

"Naperville. It's no secret. And don't make anything of it. CPD is aware and unwilling to make an issue of it."

"You ever been to his place?"

"No. They aren't really that social."

"You know the address?"

"I could get it, but what're you gonna do with it? I mean, he's in the phone book."

"Okay, great."

"Boones, don't go there."

"What do you think I'm going to do, ring the bell?"

"Then what?"

"Just curious. Does he also have a place in Chicago?"

"Not to my knowledge. Where are you going with this?"

"What kind of money would Pete make? . . . You there, Jack?"

Keller swore. "C'mon, Boones. What're you up to?"

"Just tell me."

"Over a hundred and fifty thou. Maybe close to two hundred. Now leave him alone. I know you don't like what he's got on Haeley—"

That was the understatement of the year. "Thanks for the info."

"I told you nothing; remember that."

"Remember what?"

"That's my boy. You know you should be as far from this investigation as you can get."

"And you know that's not going to happen."

"Yeah, I guess I do."

Before pulling out, Boone called Fritz Zappolo.

"Sorry, sir, he's with a client."

"I have just one question."

Sigh. "Hold please."

When Zappolo came on, he was agitated. "You've got to let me handle my other cases since I'm doing yours basically free."

"I know. Sorry. Let me give you an address. All I want to know is the property value."

"Like I've got time for that."

"Fritz. You've got hot and cold running secretaries. Put

one of 'em on it and have her call me. Should take all of five minutes. You've got my number."

Boone left his phone open and set it on the passenger seat, then headed for Haeley's bank. If a call came, all he would have to do was hit Answer and Speaker. By the time he reached the bank parking lot more than half an hour later, however, only two calls had come. One had been from Haeley and the other from Francisco Sosa. Bad as it made him feel, Boone had immediately hung up on both calls.

As he sat in the parking lot, Boone called the bank, identified himself as a CPD detective, and asked to talk to the manager. He was informed she was not in and was redirected to the assistant manager.

When the man came on, he eschewed pleasantries and demanded to know "what this is about."

"I'll be there in ten minutes and would like to talk with the teller who processed the two deposits into Haeley Lamonica's account on January—"

"I know when it was, Detective. We have already been through this, answered all the department's questions and—as you probably know—the questions of the US Attorney's office, too."

"Just routine follow-up, sir. Sorry."

"That's what it always is. We're not a big branch. Our margins are slim. Our people are stretched and overworked. I can't afford to have them away from their stations all the time—"

"I'll handle this with the utmost dispatch."

"How long?"

"No promises, but it should be just a few minutes."

"No promises?"

"Only to be as brief as I can."

"She's about to go on break. I'll have Mrs. Archibald in my office, and I'll be prepared to give you some privacy."

"I appreciate it."

"Like I've got a choice. It's this or a warrant, right?"

"Probably so. Thanks for cooperating."

"Whatever."

Boone called Pastor Sosa and apologized for having been unavailable. "Not a problem, Boone. Just checking in. You okay?"

"Matter of fact, I'm not and could use a little of your time."

"You say when. I have meetings this evening but I'm available late."

"I hate to ask that. You've got a family, and—"

"They'll be asleep, and I'm taking tomorrow off to spend with them. Where do you want to meet?"

Boone hesitated. Talk about hating to ask . . . "Well, I've been doing a lot of running today, and I'm pretty wiped out."

"Your place, then. Ten okay?"

"You'll forgive me if I doze off?"

"No."

That got Boone's attention. "Really?"

"I'm kidding, but I'm coming at your request, bro. Take a nap before I get there."

"You got it."

He called Haeley. "I was driving; sorry."

"Boone, has Zappolo told you that I may have to go back in? This time to the MCC."

"Why?"

"It's what the US Attorney wants is all I know. I told Mr. Zappolo that if he didn't want his client to disappear he'd better guarantee my mother can take custody of Max."

"And . . . ?"

"He told me not to worry about incarceration yet. He just wanted me to plan ahead. I said, 'And how am I supposed to do that?' Golden-tongued hotshot didn't know what to say."

"I'm on it, Haeley; that's all I can tell you. Can I ask you something, though?"

"Always. Boone, if you don't know I have no secrets from you, you don't know me at all. You know me, don't you?"

"I hope so."

"That wasn't what I wanted to hear. What do you want to know?"

"You told me you never even socialized with Garrett Fox."

"Yes?"

"How about Pete Wade? . . . Haeley?"

"I'm here."

"I'm asking about Pete Wade."

Her voice suddenly sounded flat. "And what are you asking?"

"Did you ever socialize with Pete Wade, ever have a meal with him?"

"Only with you."

"Pardon?"

"When you came on board, we all went to the Chop House for lunch. You, me, Chief Galloway, Jack, and Pete."

"Never another time anywhere? During the workday or otherwise?"

"What, you want me to take a polygraph?"

"I hope it doesn't come to that."

"Well, I hope not too. But listen to me, Boone. I'll submit to anything anytime anywhere, but I won't take a polygraph to convince you. If you don't believe me, our future doesn't exist. You got that?"

He hesitated in spite of himself.

"Boone, tell me you believe me."

"You're saying zero socializing with either Fox or Wade."

"Ask me again and I'll hang up on you."

"I'll take that as a no."

And she hung up on him anyway.

Boone was about to get out of the car when his phone chirped and he recognized the number.

"Drake."

"Sir, this is Stephanie from Zappolo and Associates. I have the information you requested. The real estate values in question are as follows: there are eight virtually identical brownstones connected on that block. They are all the same age and basic layout, though some have been upgraded, some not. Three have been sold within the last two years. Three others have sold twice in ten years. That is the only reason for the disparity in the values. Anyway, the units are valued at a low of 1.3 million and a high of 1.6. One is currently for sale at 1.75 but is not expected to sell for more than a million and a half."

"Very helpful." Boone gave Stephanie the address he had seen above the garage Mrs. Wade entered.

"Recently remodeled. Valued at just over 1.5."

"Is there a name associated with that unit?"

He heard her leafing through papers. "The owner is listed as Thelma Johnson."

"No kidding. Can you do me one more favor, Stephanie?"

"If I'm able."

"Check the property value on an address in Naperville."

"If it's in the public record, I'll do what I can."

"Problem is, I don't know the address. I just have a name. Peter Wade."

"I'll call you back."

1:45 P.M.

When Boone entered the bank, the assistant manager emerged from his glassed-in office and said, "Drake?"

Boone nodded and showed his ID.

"Mrs. Archibald is right there. I'll make myself scarce."

The woman proved to be a massive Texan who spilled out of her chair. As she accepted Boone's handshake and introduced herself with a thick accent, his phone rang again. "Excuse me just a moment."

It was Stephanie. "You know, Detective," she said, "there are several Wades in Naperville, but no Peters."

"Hmm."

"Something jumped out at me, though. A house purchased nearly nine years ago for $890,000 is in the name of Thelma Johnson. Seemed an interesting coincidence."

"Sure does. What would that place be worth today?"

"Thought you might ask. Similar homes in the neighborhood increased a hundred percent in nine years, then lost value during the recession. Looks like most of them are valued at about a million and a half now."

She gave him the address.

"I owe you, Stephanie."

"Anytime, sir."

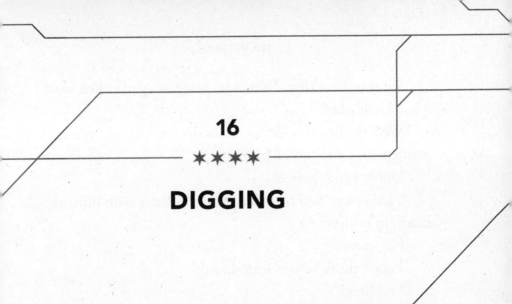

16

★ ★ ★ ★

DIGGING

"This is so excitin'," Mrs. Archibald said, her perfume overwhelming Boone. She had huge rosy cheeks she apparently felt should not go unadorned, and her rouge was clownish. "I've never been interviewed by so many legal officials. And you're also with the police department?"

"Yes, ma'am," Boone said, draping his parka over the back of a chair. He was aware Mrs. Archibald was staring at his shoulder-holstered Beretta, normally hidden by a suit coat. He sat and balanced his notepad on his knee, trying to manage it all with one hand.

"My goodness, what happened to you?"

"Wasn't watching where I was going. I'm a klutz."

She trilled a laugh. "That makes two of us. I fell gettin' out of the shower the other day. Bruised my hip something awful."

"Sorry to hear that. Now, who else have you talked with, Mrs. Archibald?"

"Well, the first was also a policeman. An African American gentleman. I don't recall his name."

"Older, white-haired?"

"That's him! And he had a younger officer with him, also black, in uniform."

"His name?"

"I don't think he was introduced."

"And then?"

"A couple of younger people from maybe the State's Attorney's office?"

"Could it have been the US Attorney's office?"

"Yes, sir, it surely could have been, not that I would know the difference. It was a man and a woman, certainly still in their twenties. I think they told me they were legal assistants."

"Well, I apologize if this is redundant. I know it can be frustrating to have to rehearse the same thing over and over."

"Oh, I don't mind! Makes me feel special."

"Let me make this quick, ma'am. I understand you processed both Ms. Lamonica's deposits on the day in question."

"I did. I've waited on her before. Nice young lady."

"And what do you remember? Did she make both deposits at the same time?"

"Oh no. She only made the one. Her paycheck."

"Is that right? And what about the other? Who made that transaction?"

"Her uncle. He's so sweet. She wasn't gone five minutes when he got in my line, even though there were shorter ones. I was puzzled till he told me what was going on. So precious."

"And what was going on, ma'am?"

"Well, he wanted me because he knew I'd waited on her. I think he'd actually been waiting out of sight."

"Is that so?" Boone was scribbling, hoping he'd be able to read his own writing.

"He was the cutest little thing. Well, not little, but short, know what I mean?"

"Not little?"

"Stocky, I'd say. He was wearing a hat, but he had really dark hair, maybe black."

"How old would you guess?"

"Oh, I don't know. Thirties? Maybe five years older than you."

"And he made a deposit to Ms. Lamonica's account?"

"He did. He didn't quite know how to go about it. He said he was her uncle and that he wanted to surprise her. He didn't have her account number or anything, and he wanted to do it in cash."

Boone looked up. "Cash?"

"He pulled out a little envelope from another bank, like the ones we use when we give people more than ten bills."

"What bank?"

"I couldn't tell you. Sorry. I just noticed it wasn't one of ours. Anyway, he had fifty hundred-dollar bills, and he was kinda shy about it. He kept it right in front of him, you know, like he didn't want anybody else knowing his business. He asked me if there was any way he could just have it deposited into his niece's account. He even said something like, 'I know you can't be giving out any of her information, but if I could just get a receipt that proves I did this . . .'

"I told him he surely could. I took the money, counted it out for the cameras, filled out a receipt with just the last few digits of her account number on it, then turned my monitor around—covering the confidential information with my hand, of course—and showed him her name and the deposit. I was careful not to even show him her balance. I mean, I didn't doubt he was her uncle. Who else would give somebody an anonymous gift like that? But I'm not to give out any information on any of our customers without their permission, unless, you know, it's to law-enforcement officials."

"I really appreciate this. Anything else?"

"Well, yes, there was something. I know he didn't like being touched."

"Ma'am?"

"Oh, it's just something silly I've got in trouble with before, and I'm working on it. I'm a toucher. Sometimes, like with an elderly person or a child, if they seem lonely or scared or something, when I'm thanking them for their business, sometimes I'll just squeeze their hand. One old man reported me." Here she whispered. "Frankly, I think he's one of those germophobes, you know? My boss told me to be careful of people's personal space. Like I say, I'm working on it."

"And you touched Ms. Lamonica's, uh, uncle?"

"I couldn't help myself. He was just so sweet. I wish I could see her face when she checks her balance. You just know she's gonna call, all worried about the mistake. But I put a note in her file so whoever checks it will be able to tell her it was an anonymous gift and totally hers."

"He didn't like being touched?"

"Well, he jerked his hand away, so I guess."

Boone turned at the assistant manager's knock, and the man pointed at his watch and mouthed, "Two o'clock."

"Oh, my," Mrs. Archibald said. "My break's over."

Boone rose. "We're done, unless you can think of anything else." He put his pen and notebook away and maneuvered a card from his wallet. Mrs. Archibald took it and accepted his help extracting her from the chair.

"I hope nobody's in trouble," she said.

"Well, you're certainly not."

"I was pretty sure I did everything right. And I don't think Ms. Lamonica's uncle did anything wrong."

"To my knowledge, none of Ms. Lamonica's relatives have anything to worry about. You know we just look into out-of-the-ordinary transactions."

"Oh yes. I always thought ten thousand was the cutoff, but that's your business."

As Mrs. Archibald hurried back to work, Boone told the assistant manager he needed something else.

"Why doesn't that surprise me?" the man said.

"Do I need a warrant? I don't think either of us wants that, do we?"

"Hardly. If it's in my power to get what you need, I'll do my best."

"I need to see the videos of the day in question."

"The others already looked at all of those and downloaded shots of Ms. Lamonica making her transactions."

"Transactions, plural?"

"I thought it was plural."

"And did they download pictures of the subsequent deposit?"

"Not to my knowledge."

"But they were informed of it?"

"My understanding is that Mrs. Archibald told everyone the same story."

"May I see the recordings?"

The assistant manager returned in a few minutes with a DVD he popped into his computer. He advanced to the time of Haeley's deposit, turning the monitor so Boone could see. "You can advance with the mouse or the arrows."

The camera angle was from above and behind Mrs. Archibald and showed each customer full-on as they approached and transacted their business. Haeley looked sober and in a hurry, though she seemed to force a smile at Mrs. Archibald's greeting. Her deposit took just a few seconds, and she hurried off, probably to pick up Max.

The camera soon showed the man in question fourth in line, though there was no clear view of his face. He wore a long overcoat and a brimmed hat. Boone was sure it was Garrett Fox. He could hardly wait for the straight-on look.

But when he finally came into view, the DVD went haywire. Blocks of color and streaks of white blocked any clear view. "Is this in the recording or is something wrong with your computer?"

The assistant manager leaned close. He pulled the DVD out and polished it on his shirt. Before reinserting it he clicked on YouTube and found a random video. "No problems here," he said.

He put the DVD back in and returned to the spot. Same problem. And it lasted until Mrs. Archibald reached for the man's hand and he quickly pulled away. The assistant manager shook his head. "We've talked to her about that."

"Who had access to this DVD?"

"Well, me, the manager, and the other law-enforcement personnel who've been here."

"Anyone have it alone?"

"Yes, I think both the police department and the US Attorney's office."

"How easy is it to mess up one of these?"

"Not hard if you know what you're doing. You click on Record, go to an editing program, and just fiddle with the mouse."

"Brilliant."

"Well, we don't expect people to do that."

"And yet someone did, didn't they? Seems you'd protect these kinds of things."

"Protect them from law enforcement? Who'd have thought of that?"

The early-afternoon sun was still prominent, but the temperature had dropped. Boone sat in Mrs. Lamonica's car in the parking lot of the bank, shivering and rubbing his palm on his thigh. What a disaster this was turning into. Everything he dug into left him with more questions, but his energy level was so low and his pain so intense that he found it hard to concentrate.

Boone was long overdue for his meds, but he didn't dare drive under the influence. There was just too much to do. He talked himself out of driving all the way to Naperville just to see Pete Wade's house. He knew enough about it, if indeed

Pete's wife's maiden name was Johnson and it was where they lived, to tell him more than he wanted to know.

Boone wanted to talk with Haeley, knowing how agitated she had to be about possibly being incarcerated again. But more important, he couldn't have her taking his questions personally. He knew how it all sounded, but she would face much tougher scrutiny in court. These were professionals he was dealing with, and they would be given the benefit of the doubt. If Pete Wade went so far as to say in court what he had said to Boone, who would doubt him? How could Boone even doubt him? A man of that caliber falsely admitting to a personal failure? Boone couldn't imagine Wade stooping that low.

As the car heated up, Boone took a call from Dr. Bob Valdez, the surgeon who was scheduled to work on his shoulder in exactly one week. "Been looking forward to meeting you," the doctor said.

"And I didn't expect to talk with you until the pre-op, sir," Boone said, a smile in his voice. "Don't you have people who can make these calls?"

"Ah, I had a minute, and I have some questions. I'm looking at your X-rays and your MRI, and of course I see all the bullet fragments. Can you tell me what kind of metal that is? If I find I have to leave any of it in, I'll need to know that."

"You're worried it might be lead?"

"Exactly."

"I guess that's the advantage of being shot with a Glock."

"Sir?"

"It's an Austrian make. More than half the law-enforcement agencies in the US use them. The Chicago PD is pretty much mostly using Berettas, but a Glock is optional. Anyway, Glock discourages using lead bullets because they have a different kind of rifling. I don't know how much of this you want to know."

"I think I know what rifling is," the doctor said. "Isn't that the grooves cut in the barrel that give the bullet its rotation?"

"Exactly. And Glock uses what they call polygonal rifling rather than the usual squared-off grooves. Apparently lead could build up on the rifling and damage the weapon."

"So unless the guy who shot you was using some ill-advised ammunition, you shouldn't have any lead in you."

"That's my guess. But let me check with the evidence guys and be sure, if it's important."

"Believe me, it's important."

They reconfirmed Boone's pre-op interview appointment a few days hence, and when he hung up, Boone dialed another number.

"Chicago Crime Lab."

"Detective Boone Drake calling for Dr. Ragnar Waldemarr."

When Waldemarr came on he said, "It's been a while, Detective. You've been a busy boy."

"Busier than I bargained for. How long are you in the lab today?"

"I have a meeting at four. What do you need?"

"I want a look at the evidence gathered at the shooting site."

"Yours, I assume."

"Right. It was a Glock, right? And the spent shell?"

"And blood—yours and the shooter's. You want to see that?"

"I've seen enough of that. Just the shooting stuff."

"GSR?"

"Gunshot residue would be good."

"Come soon as you can then. I have to leave by quarter to."

Boone made one more call before he left. "Jack, I need another favor."

"You're pushing the envelope, Boones."

"I know, but you love me, so you can't help yourself."

"Yeah, yeah. What now?"

"I need you to run a plate for me."

"What are we, back on the street? Why can't you do this?"

"You said yourself I shouldn't be related to this case. By the way, how'd your one o'clock meeting go with Pete?"

"How'd you know about that?"

"I'm a detective, Jack. I know everything. You taught me well."

"It was no big deal."

"I didn't say it was."

"It went fine."

"Good. Run this number for me, will you?" He recited it.

"Okay, but then can we be done with this?"

"I'm seeing it through to the end."

"I never thought I'd say this, Boones, but I'm going to be glad when you go under the knife again so you'll be off the streets for a while."

"That's cold. I was kinda hoping you'd take over in my absence."

"Don't start."

"C'mon, Jack. I know you're a justice freak, and what's happening here is not just."

"So all the evidence against Haeley—?"

"Is turning out to be bull."

"No bias on your part."

"You know better than that."

Jack was silent awhile. Then, "I like Haeley. You know that. But Pete and I go back to the academy, before you were born. It's awful hard to question his judgment."

Now it was Boone's turn to fall silent. How he wanted to tell Jack even a little of what Pete had told him. And about the property and cars Pete seemed to own. A hundred fifty to two hundred grand a year was nothing to sneeze at, but was it enough to buy those things? Besides, Pete hadn't always made that, and he had put kids through college. But Boone knew with all that was in him that these houses were going to prove to have been paid off. "I know, Jack," he said finally. "Can we just mutually agree to keep open minds and let the evidence tell the story?"

"That's all I ask, Boones."

Again Boone laid his cell phone open on the passenger seat, ready to punch Answer and Speaker if necessary. Then he headed to a parking garage near the US Customs building on Canal Street. Among other things, the structure housed the Chicago division of the Federal Bureau of Investigation's gang crime unit and crime lab.

Boone was woozy and weary as he made his way through the frigid garage to the elevators, trying to tell himself he already had enough to take suspicion off Haeley. But he wasn't completely sure himself. Just before emerging near the crime lab, he took a call from Jack.

"New Toyota Avalon registered to Thelma Johnson, West Oak Street, Chicago. Significant?"

"Might be. Thanks. You don't happen to be sitting in front of your computer—"

"Yes, what?" Jack said, sighing.

"Just by chance, does she own other vehicles?"

Boone heard keystrokes, then a whistle through Jack's teeth. "Hmph. Two others. Good call. Couple of brand-new Bimmers, both 760Li's, one black, one white. Has 'em listed at a different address, though. Naperville."

"What would those go for, Jack? It should be there in the stats."

More keystrokes. "Hmm. She got a deal. They retail in the high 130s. She got the two for a quarter million even, tax included. Whoever this is is well heeled, Boones. She paid without financing."

"Wow." He tried to sound nonchalant with his thanks but apparently failed.

"What's all this about?" Jack said.

"I don't know yet. If it starts to make sense, I'll get back to you."

"Can I stop playing secretary now?"

"Only for now. It's kind of fun having you at my beck and call."

"Ooh, if you were here right now . . ."

"What, Jack? What would you do to your favorite protégé?"

"How does a nice playful smack on the shoulder sound?"

3:00 P.M.

Dr. Ragnar Waldemarr met Boone in the foyer outside the crime lab, and it was obvious he was troubled. "You're not going to be happy, Detective."

Boone followed the doctor to an anteroom of one of the largest evidence caches in the city. Two cardboard boxes lay on the table, each with its lid set off to the side. A short stack of paper sat in front of the boxes.

"We have evidence missing, Drake."

"Don't tell me . . . the Glock?"

"And the shell casing."

"But they're both still listed on the sheet, right?"

"Naturally."

"And you have a record of who has been in here?"

"Sure."

"Cameras?"

"You know we do."

"Then it should be easy to—"

"If someone hadn't gotten to the recordings, yes."

"You have got to be kidding me."

"I wish. The problem is that the DVDs for the last two weeks are blank. As you can imagine, we've had dozens of personnel in here to study evidence, and each is logged in and out with a record of what they are looking at. We rarely, if ever, have occasion to check our tapes. But clearly the equipment has been malfunctioning for a long time. I only just now turned it to Record, so you and I can smile for the camera."

"What was it set on when you got to it?"

"Play."

"That makes no sense."

"Well, at the very least it's going to be hard to prove it was malfeasance. It could have easily been an accident. But it makes for quite a coincidence that we also have evidence missing. I mean, I checked the discs only because of that. As soon as I got the boxes down, I knew. A box with a gun has a certain heft to it. But see for yourself."

In the box marked *Weapon, shell casings, crime scene photos, garage diagram* lay a full velveteen sack.

"I just checked that," Waldemarr said. "It contains all twenty shell casings from the two Beretta M9 service pistols the officers emptied into the shooter. The single shell casing from the Glock is gone."

Boone pulled from the box a thin manila envelope. Inside was a folder containing photos of the garage where the shooting had taken place—from the stairwell door to his blood on the floor—and a dozen pictures of the riddled body of the bad guy. There was also a rough, hand-drawn sketch of the area indicating where the shots had originated—both from the assailant and from the responding officers.

The other box, marked *Blood, DNA, clothing*, was intact.

Among the stack of documents was a long list of those who had signed in and out for the privilege of studying the evidence. It included Jack, Pete, Friedrich Zappolo, various evidence technicians, members of the court, and personnel from the US Attorney's office.

"You'll want to add your John Henry, Drake."

Boone studied the list as he signed. "Who's this?"

Waldemarr leaned in. "Antoine Johnson. Works out of the 18th, lists himself as an evidence tech. May be called to testify, I guess. But wasn't the shooter killed?"

"Yeah, but we're looking at conspiracy here. The gun could help with that."

"Oh, there is the GSR I mentioned."

Waldemarr retrieved a small envelope that contained a

clear pouch with what appeared to be tissue scrapings. "From the shooter's trigger hand. The residue is consistent with the makeup of the bullet from a Glock .45."

"No lead?"

"No lead."

"Let me see the specs on the gun."

Waldemarr pulled out a card. "This means nothing without the hardware."

"It didn't happen to be a 30, did it? The subcompact?"

The doctor shook his head. "Full-size. I want to say a 39 with the .45 GAP caliber."

"Good memory," Boone said, studying the notes. "But like you say, we're in trouble trying to connect this to a conspiracy without the hardware."

"Not totally," Waldemarr said. "You're forgetting they'll call me to the stand. I bring a modicum of credibility."

"But you would be biased toward the Chicago PD."

"My notes are based on my personal examination of the weapon the evidence techs delivered. It proved to have fired one round. And we had the shell casing for that."

"Had."

"And now all we have is you, Boone."

Boone laughed. He *was* the case.

"Just make sure your surgeon delivers to me what he pulls from your shoulder. If it doesn't match up with a Glock 39 with .45 GAP bullets, I'll throw in the towel."

17

****

THE DILEMMA

By the time Boone had parked Mrs. Lamonica's car a few blocks away, so no one would connect him with the vehicle, and finally reached his apartment, he was so weak he could barely put one foot in front of the other. And he realized that he had not eaten anything at Fletcher Galloway's party. A piece of cake might have tided him over. But also nothing since? And no meds? What was he thinking?

Boone knew better than to medicate himself on an empty stomach, so he staggered to the kitchen and pawed through the refrigerator. All he found were sandwich fixings, and having to prepare something seemed the worst idea he could imagine.

Above the fridge was a half bag of corn puffs, which strangely appealed. He'd been working out regularly and eating well before the shooting, but now he just wanted sustenance. And had that been a bottle of chocolate milk in the refrigerator? With a shudder he sat on the couch and found both weirdly satisfying.

Boone turned on the news, then took his meds. Before he knew it, the news anchors' heads were swimming, their patter making no sense, and he had collapsed to his right side.

About twenty minutes later he was awakened by his phone. It was Haeley.

"Oh, I'm so glad you called," he slurred. "I didn't want to leave it the way it was."

She sounded flat. "I don't want to feel like I have to convince you, Boone. You're more than my lawyer's investigator. At least I hope you are."

"I am. Believe me, I am."

"What's the matter with you, anyway? You sound drunk."

"You know better'n 'at."

"Just now taking your meds?"

"Uh-huh."

"Get some rest. You need me to come over there? Because you know I will. Mom's here, and—"

"I'd love that, but Franch—Franz—Fr—Fff—Pastor Sosa's coming later."

"Take a nap, love, will you?"

"Jus' for you."

"Yeah, okay."

"I do want to see you, Hael."

"Tomorrow."

"Promise?"

"If I'm not in jail," she said.

"Anything new on that? I wasn't able to get back to Fritz today."

Haeley hesitated. "He's sounding pessimistic, frankly. You up to hearing this?"

Boone sat up, trying to focus. "Yeah." He wanted to tell her that what he was finding would keep her out of jail. But he wasn't so sure.

"I can't leave Max again, not even with my mom. And if I wind up heading back to a place like County, I might run first, and I'm not kidding."

"Don't say that."

"Boone, I'm dead serious. I will not go through that again. I have never been more scared in my life."

"But, Haeley, I know better than anyone that no one can run anymore. There's too much technology. People can run only so long, and when they're caught, they're guilty."

"Even if they're innocent. Or Zappolo would say not guilty."

"They're guilty of running."

After a pause, Haeley said, "You know I'm not really going to run. But I swear if I had to go back to jail, I don't know what I might do."

"I hear you."

"I want to be heard."

Boone felt himself about to collapse again. "I want to be careful to underpromise and overdeliver. But if what I've been uncovering starts coming together, we're going to get through this."

"Oh, my. I know you're trying to be encouraging, but you

know what I'm hearing? That if the evidence doesn't come together, we're *not* going to get through this."

"Haeley, you need to hear me. The meds are really kicking in. The only thing that could get between you and me is if I found out you were not who I thought you were."

"Boone."

"Sue me. What am I supposed to think? The people out to get you make a living at building cases, being thorough, being convincing. We've got our work cut out for us."

"I'm ready. For Max. For us. Are you, Boone?"

10:05 P.M.

Boone awoke to the doorbell, wondering if he had answered Haeley or even hung up. His phone was open and on the floor.

"Just as I feared," Francisco said as he breezed in. "I woke you, didn't I?"

Boone nodded.

"You want to just go to bed?"

"No."

"I'm looking at an empty bag of corn puffs and an empty bottle of chocolate milk. You ought to be glad I'm not your dad."

"Trust me, I'm glad."

"We're going out."

"Oh, Pastor, no."

"Unless you can show me something nutritional around here that I can whip together, I'm not taking no for an answer."

"Busted. I've got nothing."

Sosa pointed to Boone's coat and waggled a follow-me finger. In truth, Boone liked the idea. *I can sleep when I'm dead. Which may be soon.* He retrieved his shoulder holster and apologized for refusing Sosa's offer to help him with his coat. "Gotta do this myself. Unless you're moving in."

"Fair enough. You carry the weapon everywhere?"

"We all do. Goes with the job."

As they headed out the door, Francisco said, "You want me to turn off some lights?"

"No. I don't like to advertise I'm gone. Let people think I'm here."

A few minutes and four blocks later, Boone and Francisco slid into a booth at a diner, and the pastor did the ordering. Boone couldn't imagine a healthy meal there, but Francisco mixed and matched and found him protein and vegetables. "I think you covered the carbs and dairy earlier."

The good food cleared Boone's mind, but he knew he still needed sleep. He spilled everything to Sosa, admitting that he had his doubts about Haeley.

"Still?"

Boone shrugged. "Now at least I know what we're up against."

"Don't be so hard on yourself, Boone. I've been disappointed by people I would have vouched for."

"What am I going to do if the evidence is irrefutable?"

"God is just. Remember that. Maybe it's time you quit trying to teach Pascual and let him teach you. Just look what's becoming of that man. Spiritually he's growing like a weed. Are you?"

"I feel stalled. I was doing okay until the shooting."

"Rehab ought to help you focus."

"The meds kind of get in the way."

"I'm not buying it, Boone. Don't hide behind your pills and your pain. Don't hide behind what's happening with Haeley or Pascual or your parents or your boss or even your surgery. There is such a thing as the survival of the spiritual—"

"You keep telling me that."

"So start hearing me. Your relationship with God is on you. You know he's doing his part. He's not going anywhere. You stay in the Word. Maintain your prayer life. Stay in church. You don't have to feel your best; you don't even have to feel sane. Just do your part. Stay at it. Everybody who depends on you deserves that. You deserve it."

"I don't deserve anything."

Pastor Sosa sat back and seemed to study Boone. "I stand corrected. You're right. You don't deserve anything. None of us does. But the unsearchable riches of Christ are available to you. What kind of fool would you be to not partake?"

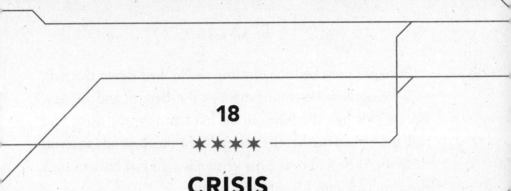

18

★★★★

CRISIS

As Francisco pulled up in front of his apartment building, Boone stopped midsentence and stared at the front of the complex. The glass front door was ajar and the foyer light off.

"What?" Sosa said.

Boone held up a hand. "Stay right here. If I'm not back in five minutes, call 911."

Boone opened the door and drew his Beretta as he slid out of the car.

"Shouldn't you call for backup or something? You're in no shape to—"

Boone kicked the door shut and stayed in the shadows as he moved toward the front door, peering at his place, second on the right upstairs. He crept up the stairs, knowing where to step to stay on the carpet and avoid the creaks.

When he reached the landing, he looked down the hall, wondering how he would manage the Beretta and his key. Boone switched the 9mm to his left hand, in the sling, and realized he had neither the strength nor the fortitude to stand the pain. If he had to use his key, he would just have to tuck the gun back into his shoulder holster.

Two steps down the hall showed him his door had been forced open. Who could have done that without bothering the neighbors? Boone tiptoed to it, saw that it could have been quietly pried and not kicked in, and listened for any movement. He gently pushed the door with the barrel of his gun. It opened onto a ransacked scene.

This was either a simple breaking and entering burglary—unlikely—or someone looking for him. Had he been there, sleeping and out of reach of the Beretta, he'd be a dead man.

Nothing appeared stolen. Expensive electronics still in place. No, this was what Boone had feared. The question now was whether it was more than one guy—and were they gone? He crouched before the bedroom door, light-headed, then kicked it open, weapon ready.

Cold air assaulted him from the window. Clearly, the intruder had not left the way he had come. The fire escape had been activated, the mobile ladder extended. Sosa would have to help him put that back.

Boone closed everything and locked the damaged door, then made his way back down. Sosa left the car as soon as Boone came into view. "You all right?"

Boone nodded and beckoned him to follow him around the building, into the alley, and up to the fire escape. "It's weighted and counterbalanced, so just grab the bottom rung and swing it up with a little oomph."

The ladder clanging back into place caused lights to come on in a couple of other units. An elderly man opened his third-floor window and called out, "Who goes there?" That hit Boone as quaint, but he quickly informed the man who he was and that everything was under control.

But was it? If he reported this, Jack would insist on reinstituting his twenty-four-hour-a-day cover. And if he didn't report it, could he stay here? He didn't like being a sitting duck. But who was behind this? The DiLoKi? The Outfit? Those trying to frame Haeley? Or Haeley herself?

Regardless, Boone knew he had to move, if only temporarily.

"How much time have you got, Pastor?"

Sosa looked at his watch. "Till midnight. What do you need?"

"I need to grab some essentials, have you run me to Haeley's and then back to her mother's car. I could do this myself, but I don't know who's watching."

Sosa helped him haul clothes and toiletries from his apartment and pile them into the back of the car. Boone told the pastor where Mrs. Lamonica's car was parked and had him circle that block twice to be sure no suspicious vehicles were about. They quickly moved the stuff from Sosa's car to the other, then returned to Sosa's car and headed toward Haeley's.

On the way Boone called and woke her.

"If I fall asleep talking to you," she said, "we'll be even."

"I was afraid of that," he said. "What were we talking about?"

"Nothing that made sense. You went loopy on me.

I thought about calling you back or even running over there to be sure you were all right, but I knew you needed your rest. You okay now?"

"I am, but I'm on my way to see you. Is that all right?"

"Oh, Boone! I was in bed. Hair up, no makeup, the whole bit. I don't think we're ready for you seeing me like this just yet, do you?"

"What if I bring a pastor along?"

"Sosa's still with you? Are you seriously on your way?"

"Twenty minutes out."

"Give me twenty-five."

MIDNIGHT

As they sat in the car in front of Haeley's place, waiting until the twenty-five minutes had passed, Boone dialed Jack Keller's cell. It immediately went to voice mail. He hated to call the landline, knowing Jack and Margaret had to be down for the night, but he didn't have a choice.

Jack answered, voice thick. "This had better be good. Got another plate you want me to run?"

"I really am sorry, Jack. I need a place to stay."

Suddenly Keller sounded wide awake, as if he had sat up and cleared his head. "Sure, come on over. What's up?"

"No, no, not with you. Still room at the safe house?"

"Yeah. You want me to run you out there?"

"I just need you to clear it and let them know I'm coming."

"So what happened, Boones?"

"Nothing. I just think you're right that I'd be safer there."

Silence.

"Still there, Jack?"

"Oh, I'm still here, but since I was born yesterday, I don't know how to talk yet. What do you take me for, Boones? I'm supposed to think, what, that you just woke up realizing I make more sense than you do? What happened? Somebody take a shot at you, threaten you, what?"

Boone sighed.

"Don't make this multiple choice, Boones. Just tell me."

"Someone broke into my apartment."

Keller swore.

"They went out down the fire escape. Glad I wasn't there."

"How soon can you be, you know? I don't want to say where over the phone."

"Hopefully within an hour. I appreciate this, Jack."

"Hey, what time do you plan to get up tomorrow morning? How about I come see you at about ten thirty?"

"If I'm not up by then, fire me."

"You're doing enough to get yourself fired without my help."

Boone looked at his watch as he got off the phone and apologized to Francisco.

"I don't have to go inside," the pastor said. "It's late—"

"I'm sure she'd love to see you again," Boone said. "And she's gone to some trouble."

"I'll wait here until you call me up."

Boone kept an eye on the second-floor window, and when he saw Haeley wave, he left the car. On the way up he rehearsed what he wanted to tell her—simply that he was going to be away for a while but that he would still be on the case.

He found Haeley in her doorway smiling. Her hair was in rollers, but she had clearly made herself up a bit. And for some reason, Boone was overcome. He was glad she spoke first, because he felt struck dumb.

"You look awful," she said, chuckling. "Long day?"

"Longest I can remember," he managed, and all he wanted was to hold her. He put his arm around her waist as she led him into the apartment and to the couch, a finger to her lips.

"Mom and Max are asleep," she whispered.

"I'd rather kiss you than talk anyway," he said.

"You would, huh?"

"May I?"

"Well, aren't we polite? If the right is mine to give, you have it."

"Hey, that's a line from *How Green Was My Valley*."

"Yes! Boone! We love the same movie!"

Boone leaned forward awkwardly. She helped him remove his parka; then, avoiding the Beretta, she cupped his face in her hands and they fell into a long kiss.

When they separated, Boone said, "Sure glad Francisco offered to wait in the car."

"I should invite him in."

"In time."

"What's going on, Boone?"

"I love you, that's all."

"I know. I love you too. And you're working yourself to death."

"I promise to sleep tonight until I wake up. No alarm clock. No schedule tomorrow. At least not till midmorning."

"That makes me feel better. And I want to know what you turned up today. But curious as I am, you need to get home to bed. Really, you look out on your feet. You're not even going to remember kissing me."

Boone snorted. "If I forget this, dump me quick. Anyway, I wanted to tell you that I need your mother's car for another few days."

"Mom loves your car. She's hoping you'll offer a permanent trade."

Boone agonized over whether to tell her where he was sleeping that night and why. He opted for transparency and regretted it as soon as he saw her look.

"I don't want this to be so real, Boone. What is going on that your life should be in danger?"

"Surely that's not news. I mean, look at me."

"But they're still after you? Why?"

"Haeley, you work at the CPD. You know how big this thing was. A lot of really dangerous people are not happy with what we accomplished."

"I want you off the case, off my case. Let Jack or someone else run with it."

"Jack's too close to Pete. Anyway, I don't want off your case. Why would I?"

Haeley sighed and shook her head. "Truth is, I want you off the job."

"Off the force?"

"Yes! Take the disability! There's a lot of other things you can do."

"Like what?"

"Teach. You know your job better than anybody your age. Young people could learn a lot from you, and you're still young enough to relate to them."

Boone stood and turned his back to her, fearing he would say something he regretted.

"Talk to me, Boone."

He turned to face her. "All right, listen. I'm going to say this once, and I don't want to have to say it again. I'm a cop. It's all I've ever wanted to be and all I ever want to be. My plan is to rehab myself to where I can be fully functioning again, and I don't plan to ever look back. Clear?"

Haeley looked stricken. "Are you angry with me?"

"I just want to be understood. I'll be angry with you only if you continue to fight me on this. We've declared ourselves. We love each other. I hope we have a future together. If we do, I don't want you to ever say you didn't know what you were getting into. We're both going to have to deal with my life being on the line every day. If you can't handle that, I need to know now."

"Wow."

"I'm not trying to be mean, Haeley. Just honest."

"I got it."

"And can you deal with it?"

"Truthfully? I don't know."

He sat again. "Not what I wanted to hear."

"I can be as honest as you, Boone, and I owe that to you."

He nodded. Waiting.

"You've got to understand, love," she said. "You were nearly shot dead, and then, how many nights later, you could easily have been shot again."

"Two words, Hael: Chicago cop."

"I know."

"You wouldn't want me to be other than what I was meant to be, would you?"

"I love you, Boone. I want you safe."

"I love you. But my life is not safe."

"At least it will be tonight," she said.

"That's a promise. And I have to get going. Francisco is going way above and beyond."

"Let me say hi to him."

Boone texted him to meet them in the foyer. When they got to the bottom of the stairs, Francisco was coming in. "Haeley, it's been too long."

She embraced him. "Take care of this guy, will you?"

"I think he can take care of himself," Sosa said.

"That's what I'm banking on."

"I'll be right out," Boone said, and as soon as Francisco said good-bye, Boone kissed Haeley again. "Work it through," he added.

"I'll try."

Boone left feeling cheap. His love and his lingering suspicion were at war.

TUESDAY, FEBRUARY 9, 1:00 A.M.

"Can you ever forgive me, Pastor?" Boone said. "You said you were good till midnight."

"I can sleep later," Sosa said. "Chalk it up to extenuating circumstances."

He turned onto the street where Boone had left Mrs. Lamonica's car. "Oh, no," Boone said.

The windows were shattered, his stuff gone.

"Haeley's mother likes my car. Looks like it's going to be hers."

"Now what?" Sosa said.

"I've got to call it in. I hope the techies can determine whether it's just a random smash and grab or if it was the same people who were at my place."

"If it was them and they saw you storing stuff in there, wouldn't they just stake it out and then follow you? I mean, they want to do more than scare you, don't they? Don't they want you?"

"Very good. You could be a cop. You're leaning toward a random break-in."

"Hoping, I guess."

"Me too."

"You need a ride to the safe house, right? I mean, you can't exactly ride out there in a squad car, can you?"

"Good thinking, but I hate to ask. By the time somebody checks this mess out—and I'd have to be here at least till they get started—it'll be really late."

"I'll work around it."

"But your family, Francisco . . ."

"I'll do what I've got to do, for you and for them."

1:30 A.M.

Boone explained to the crime scene technicians why he had been driving a car registered to a woman in South Carolina. They carefully processed the scene and had the car towed to a city holding lot. Boone decided breaking this news to Haeley's mother could wait.

Forty minutes later, Francisco, with Boone confirming they had not been followed, rolled up to the dilapidated pickup standing guard on the road to the safe house. The undercover cop behind the wheel looked surprised.

"Didn't expect to see you tonight, *padre*," Quincy said. "I knew Righty was coming."

"Good one," Boone said.

"I'm not staying," Sosa said. "Just dropping my little boy off at school."

"Gotcha. See you on your way out."

When they got to the main yard and the chain-link fence, Sosa asked Boone to greet Pascual Candelario for him and tell PC he would visit in a few days. "Will you still be here?"

"Probably, but this is just a base of operations for me. Lots of work to do before surgery."

"What're you going to do for wheels?"

"Jack will find me something."

2:15 A.M.

At the gate, Unger hurried out in his shirtsleeves to let Boone in, waving to Sosa. "Where's your stuff?" Unger said as they moved inside.

Boone told him what had happened.

"Geez, Drake, if it wasn't for bad luck . . ."

Boone texted Jack about his need for clothes, toiletries, and a car. *& I hate 2 ask, but if u could find a plastic surgical shower shield & fresh bandages . . .* He smirked at the thought of Jack's look when he awoke to those requests.

"Third door on the right," Unger said. "Should be comfy."

Through the fake wall and the hanging plastic and down the hall, Boone found himself so eager to collapse into bed, he could hardly move. Fortunately, he had his meds on him. He would be thoroughly anesthetized by the time his head hit the pillow.

The room was large and the furnishings new. He especially appreciated the private bath. But as he began to slowly peel off his clothes, he started at a knock.

"Yeah!"

"It's PC, bro! What you doing here?"

Boone opened the door. "Why are you still up?"

"I'm a night owl," Pascual said. "What can I say? Whoa. Look at you. We'll talk tomorrow!"

"I look that bad?"

PC laughed. "Your eyes ain't even focusing, man. Go to bed."

"Don't mind if I do."

Boone stripped down, took his meds, and carefully stretched out on the bed. He was unconscious within sixty seconds.

19

★ ★ ★ ★

RAMPING UP

Boone awoke in the same position he had fallen asleep in, unaware of having even dreamed. His room was still pitch black, and he realized it was an inner chamber with no windows.

He had roused only because of a nature call and had no idea how long he'd slept. He peered in the darkness for a clock, finally resorting to feeling for his watch. He hit a tiny button on the side that illuminated the dial: 12:04. What time had he gotten here? Had he slept that long?

Boone returned from the bathroom, still logy, and sat on the edge of the bed. He turned on his cell phone and soon a dozen messages invaded. The only ones that interested him were from Jack. The oldest, which had come in at 10:20 that morning, said, *Here. No rush. Stuff outside door.*

An hour later: *Still here, Sleeping Beauty. PC & I r hungry. Let me know when ur up.*

And at noon: *Have 2 b back in city by 3. Tasty lunch awaits u.*

That sounded like heaven. Boone found the bag of stuff outside the door, including a change of wound dressings and a supply of plastic sheeting he could put over his shoulder in the shower.

He texted, ***Thanks 4 everything. Don't eat w/out me. C u soon.***

It took twice as long for Boone to shower and shave and dress than it would have before the shooting. He savored every minute. Keller had found him several sets of oversize sweat suits, and he chose one with the CPD pistol range logo on it.

Pascual and Jack sat waiting at the table in the kitchen. "You look better than you did last night, *amigo*," PC said. "Feel better too, eh?"

"Not till I take my pills. Nothing feels better than that."

"The Frito Bandito is cooking for us today," Jack said.

"I like Mexican."

"How'd you guess?" Pascual said.

"Where's the family?" Boone said.

"Already ate. Probably watching TV."

PC turned to a counter full of ingredients and started mixing.

Keller said, "We going to be able to work if you're on meds?"

"I just have to concentrate. So what's in the envelope?"

"Stuff we need to talk about in private."

"I heard that," PC said. "Can't believe you guys are keepin' secrets."

After lunch, Boone popped his pills and had to admit that Pascual could run his own taco stand. The big Mexican said, "Well, you two have stuff to talk about."

"Yeah," Jack said. "I wouldn't rush you, but I *am* on a schedule."

As Pascual left, Boone passed along Pastor Sosa's greetings.

"He's the best, man," PC said. "Thanks for making that happen."

"You're learning a lot?"

"Oh yeah. I might want to go into ministry myself someday."

Jack wrenched around in his chair. "What're you, nuts? There's nowhere on God's green earth you could go and not be recognized. Don't you know we're working around the clock trying to think of where to stash you when this is all over?"

"I'm trustin' the Lord, man."

"That's all well and good, but unless he can make you look like a little girl, I can't imagine where you can hide, let alone—what did you call it? 'Go into ministry'?"

Pascual's body filled the doorframe. "I was just watching something on TV the other night about a New York Mob guy—"

"I heard about that too," Jack said. "Michael Franzese, right?"

"That's him," PC said. "Sonny's kid. The old Mob boss who's in prison. Michael became a Christian and preaches all over the country."

"You know how unique that is, though," Jack said. "Right?"

Pascual shrugged.

"C'mon, PC. He may be the only guy who ever left the Mob, especially that kind of an outfit—part of the Colombo family—without winding up dead, in prison, or in the witness protection program. Is that what you want?"

"Well, if he can do it—"

"The jury is still out on how long he can stay in the public eye. Maybe it's the religious aspect of it; I don't know. Maybe his enemies are afraid of that. But I can tell you this: you have a hundred times the enemies he ever had. You think the bullet Drake took wasn't intended for you?"

"Don't say that, man. I know. And Boone knows I know."

Keller glanced at his watch. "I mean, I'm glad you're getting good religious counseling or whatever you call it, but don't go dreaming about starting a church. Now Drake and I have really got to get to our business."

Pascual looked crestfallen. He waved as he turned to go, and Keller called after him. "Hey, PC! I'm not mad at you, you know. You're still a hero. I'm just looking out for you."

When PC was gone, Jack stretched. "Go get your notes, Boones. Show me what you've got."

"It'll wait, boss. I need to see what you've got."

"I'm not sure you do."

"Of course I do. The only way I can attack this is to know everything I'm dealing with. Fritz is holding out on me because he's not ready for Haeley to know everything he knows yet."

"Well, if you insist on seeing this, you'll know why. But what do you mean, the only way you can 'attack this'? Be careful not to be giving ammunition to people who say there's no way you can be unbiased."

Boone sighed. "I didn't go into it only on the attack.

I went in scared to death after what I'd heard from Fritz, and frankly, from Pete."

"So Pete told you what he told me?"

"I have no idea what he told you, Jack, but my guess is he told me more. He even swore me to secrecy for part of it."

That seemed to get Jack's attention. "Am I going to have to beat it out of you?"

"'Fraid so. My word is still my bond."

Jack sat staring. "So, what did he tell you that you *can* tell me?"

Boone shook his head. "No you don't. You first."

"Well, did he mention the graphic e-mails that went back and forth between Fox and Haeley?"

"Fritz Zappolo told me. Haven't seen them, but the very idea that she would be stupid enough to put incriminating stuff on her CPD-issue computer is almost enough for me to discount them before I see them."

"That doesn't sound unbiased, Boones."

"Granted, but does she strike you as that stupid?"

Jack stood and paced. "I learned a long time ago that I can't trust my first instincts about people. I have to rely on hard evidence."

"I can't wait to see what you have."

"Boones, did Pete tell you she came on to him?"

"What?"

"No, eh? Maybe he thought he'd said enough."

Boone shook his head. "Talk about royally brainless. Complain about sexual harassment—which you know she did on more than one occasion—and then do something like that? And to a man his age?"

"You never know, Boones. I was a Clinton fan. I even believed his denials. And Eliot Spitzer was a hero of mine. I'm the wrong guy to ask."

"If she came on to Pete, why not you?"

"Maybe she prefers black guys."

"What does that say about Fox? And I'm about as white as they come. Anyway, if that were true, why are there no stories from Fletcher?"

"She would have known better."

"And she would have known better than to engage in anything with Pete or Garrett, and she sure wouldn't have documented it on a department computer. Let me ask you something, Jack. You and Pete go way back, right? Did you ever have reason to wonder about him?"

"In what way are we talking about?"

"His morals."

"Not on the job. He's clean, or we wouldn't be working together."

"I'm talking personal morals. Anything. Any reason to wonder."

Jack, usually quick to answer, seemed to hesitate. His eyes lost focus as if he were somewhere else. "You can't use this, you know. I have no proof."

"I'm just asking for a reason to suspect him."

"This was more'n thirty years ago. 'Fact, I think Pete and Thelma had been married only a few years, had maybe one kid. I remember because me and my first wife were newlyweds then too. Anyway, Pete and I had been sent to the FBI National Academy at Quantico, Virginia, for training. Bunked together."

"What happened?"

"Pete had relatives in the area that he visited the first night after dinner. Got in after midnight. And then, three or four nights in a row, he left just after I hit the sack and came tiptoeing back in at three or four in the morning. He was dragging when we did the physical stuff every day—it was a lot like boot camp.

"Once I asked him where he was every night and he got testy. He stared me down and said, 'I told you I have relatives in the area.' End of story."

"You weren't buying it."

"Oh, he might have seen family that first night; I don't know. But he wasn't seeing them that late every day after that. I've never been a prude, Boones, and I didn't figure it was my place to push him on it. But I admit I did wonder. Why do you ask?"

"Just trying to make this all add up. Before this I never had one question about Pete Wade. He always hit me as the kind of veteran I wanted to be."

"Thanks."

"C'mon. You know what I think of you, Jack. Anyway, most of what I believed about Pete I heard from you."

"He's always been a by-the-book kind of a cop."

Boone nodded. "That's what I saw."

"Seems that would make you lean his way, even when he's saying stuff about your girlfriend."

"It scares me to death."

"Me too," Jack said, "but I had reason to wonder about Haeley."

"You did? Was she ever inappropriate with you?"

"Never."

"Then why?"

"Well, when Garrett Fox was here, he used to brag about his relationship with her."

"He told me he tried and struck out," Boone said.

"I remember doubting him, because he was quite a story-teller. And I also remember thinking that if there was any truth to it, she sure hid it well. It was obvious, at least to me, that she could barely stand to be in his presence. She never looked at him, hardly responded to him, and I even saw her turn up her nose or roll her eyes when he was around. And she complained both to me and to Fletch about things he said.

"I called him on the carpet about it, and I know Fletcher did too. I don't know what he told Fletch, but he told me, 'Aw, she secretly loves it. You know we're seeing each other.'

"I said, 'So you say.'

"But anyway, when Pete told me about the leak that almost got you killed and dredged up the relationship thing again, I didn't know what to think. I admit I assumed maybe I had been wrong and that there had been something going on."

Boone shook his head and sighed. "Like you always say, let's stick with the evidence."

"There *is* evidence, Boones, so be prepared."

Jack sat back down, pulled from his envelope a stack of sheets, and slid them across the table.

Boone held his breath. Did he really want to see these? The fingers of his good hand fluttered as he spread the sheets before him. Within seconds he was giggling.

"What?" Jack said.

"C'mon, boss! You can't possibly take this seriously!"

"Educate me."

"Did whoever retrieved these do their due diligence and establish a base of comparison—a significant sampling of her normal e-mails? That will show her style, idiosyncrasies, all that."

Jack dug through the envelope. "Yes, as a matter of fact I think they did. Here."

It took Boone a few minutes to arrange the pages with one hand, but when he finished, he was certain Jack would see the obvious. "Now this is what I call evidence."

Boone moved away so Jack could lean over for an unobstructed view. "Uh-huh. Mm-hm. Yeah. Wow."

"See it?"

"'Course."

"You'd been getting e-mails from Haeley every day. Had you ever noticed a misspelling, a grammatical error, even a typo or a punctuation goof?"

"Well, I'm not the best at this stuff myself."

"But you can see it, can't you?"

Jack nodded, then shook his head. "I should have seen that both Garrett's and Haeley's e-mails look like they were written by the same person. I mean, the type styles are different, but I've never seen an e-mail from Haeley with that font either. All these sentences that start without a capital letter . . ."

"From both so-called correspondents. And, Jack, all that stuff about how she craves him and what she wants to do with and to him? Come on. Does that sound like her at all?"

"You'd know that better than me."

"Trust me. It's silly, and frankly it reminds me of something I saw on *City Confidential*. In fact, if I can find it, I'll bet it's almost identical. I gotta tell ya, Jack, I'm really glad I saw these. I'd bet the farm these are phonies. But even if we humored the other side for a second, I return to my argument: how dense do they think Haeley is?"

"What about this one?" Jack said, picking through the sheets.

Boone read: *garrett, boon and I have been inimate and he has proposed to me. I'll do anything you say to make sure he doesn't know about us.*

Boone sat back. "How convenient is that? She sets herself up for being charged with doing 'anything you say' to keep the truth from me? And in the process she forgets how to capitalize names, misspells my name and the word *intimate*? Please. Anyway, if she wrote all that other stuff about what she and Garrett were supposed to have done with each other, in colorful language, why does she use refined language for our supposed relationship? The fact is, neither of us believes it would be right for us to be intimate outside marriage, and we aren't even close to that yet. Fact is, we've only kissed a few times. And I have *not* proposed to her."

Jack clasped his hands behind his head and looked at the ceiling. "I've worked with you a long time, Boones. Never knew you to do anything but tell the truth." He stacked the papers and returned them to the envelope. "All right, your turn. What've you got?"

"Do we want to do this here? Place gives me the willies. I know I'm working out of here for a while, but I'm ready to get away for now."

Jack nodded. "I need you to go back downtown with me anyway. I just drove your new wheels here myself."

"What'd you find me?"

"Twelve-year-old Chevy Impala."

"Perfect."

"I thought so. You can lay out your case on the way."

Boone went to his room to get his notes. When he returned, Jack said, "I do have a confession."

"I'm listening."

As they headed out, Jack said, "I sent crime scene investigators to your apartment."

"You didn't."

"It was the right thing to do."

"But I didn't want that. That's why I didn't even call it in."

"Of course you did. I'm a sworn officer of the CPD. You tell me your place was ransacked, that's a report."

"You're splitting hairs. So, what'd they find?"

"Nothing."

"Terrific."

"In a way it is, Boones. What does that tell you?"

"That it wasn't druggies looking for something to fence."

They climbed into the old Chevy, Boone first standing in the cold to remove his parka and sling it into the backseat.

When he was finally in the car Jack fiddled with the heat. "You knew it wasn't druggies when you saw nothing had been stolen. Zero fingerprints, except on the bottom section of the fire-escape ladder—which will turn out to be Pastor Sosa's, right?"

"Right."

"So the clean apartment except for your prints tells you these were pros, probably wearing rubber gloves. They left nothing to chance."

"So they *were* coming to whack me."

Jack nodded. "And I think the same guys trashed Mrs.

Lamonica's car. But that one I don't get. Just trying to scare you? What does that get 'em? Maybe they were frustrated because you'd eluded them again. But it was obvious you had loaded the car so you could go somewhere else. Why wouldn't they follow you to find out where? Anyway, no prints, and the only damage was the back window and the left-rear side window. Already fixed and covered by insurance."

"How do you know it's covered?"

"Insurance docs were in the glove box."

"Tell me Mrs. Lamonica doesn't know yet."

"I saw the car before I came down here," Jack said. "If she can tell anything happened to it, I'd be surprised."

"I owe you."

"Do you ever. All that shopping I did for you? I feel like your nursemaid. Now make it worth my while. Give me both barrels."

"You're not going to like it, Jack. It doesn't look good for your friend."

"Well, you ought to know something about that, speaking of charges that don't look good for a friend."

Boone nodded. "I need you to keep me in line and make sure I'm not jumping to conclusions."

"I trained you better than that."

"But this seems so cut and dried to me, and it just can't be, can it?"

"You tell me."

Boone pulled out his notebook.

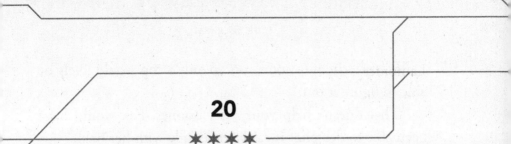

20

★★★★

THE DEAL

As Jack pulled out of the former junkyard complex, he said, "I saw the cell-phone photo I know you've seen. What do you make of that? You going to be able to counter it?"

"The one Garrett supposedly shot of Haeley's meeting notes about where we originally hid Pascual? Think that through, Jack. First, you were at the meeting where she made those notes. You heard Fletch remind her that she was a sworn member of the CPD, even if she wasn't a police officer."

"I did."

"He told her it was her responsibility and that he was making it an oral directive that she immediately lock that document away as soon as the meeting was over."

"And she assured him she would," Jack said.

"It was written in code, too, so only a cop would likely be able to figure it out."

"That doesn't help your case, Boones. Fox would have been able to decipher it easily, especially with her help."

"But here's my question. Why did he need a picture of it? If I even for a second stipulate that he and Haeley were in on this together, does that make sense? She shows him the document, he clarifies with her what it means, and then he tells whoever he needs to in order to get Candelario offed. The cell-phone photo serves only two purposes: to implicate Haeley or to implicate him. He doesn't need it. What was he going to do, forget? That picture was for one purpose only: to frame Haeley."

Jack shrugged. "Can't argue with that."

"Who all have you talked to, by the way?" Boone said.

"Pete, of course, the US Attorney, Garrett, and your guy, Zappolo."

"You talk to Garrett since all this broke?"

Jack nodded. "He made a big point of Haeley having told him about all her lovers."

Boone gritted his teeth. "I keep thinking I want my chance to interrogate him, but I'd better go into it unarmed or I'm likely to put one between his eyes."

"You'll scotch everything by talking to him. You can clearly see his motive in this, can't you?"

"Sure."

"I mean, I don't think he ever forgave you for not standing up for him when he was willing to lie for you."

"You taught me better, Jack. You always said we were all brothers under the blue and that we had each other's back unless someone was unethical, immoral, or criminal."

"I also said when in doubt, you give your partner the benefit. Fox would say that was what he was doing for you. He said under oath he could corroborate your account of having injured the arrestee by accident."

"Even though he didn't believe it."

"Yeah, but he was saying he trusted you, Boones."

"In private he told me he knew I had snapped and crossed the line. Then he goes on the stand and supports my version, only to have a video prove he had his back to the whole incident. That's what nailed him."

"He says you could have saved him."

"Sure. By being unethical myself. My career means more to me than that."

"Anyway, he feels like he was willing to stick his neck out for you and you weren't willing to do the same for him."

"Guess that's true. He was willing to lie. I wasn't."

As they passed into Addison, Jack asked if Boone had seen the transcript of the US Attorney's interview with Haeley's former boyfriend.

"I didn't even know they'd talked to him. Would you believe I don't even know his name?"

"It's in my envelope. The folder is labeled Mannock. DeWayne Mannock. And the US Attorney said he made a big mistake when he referred to him as Mr. Mannock. Apparently the guy insisted he use his first name, then scolded him when he pronounced it as one syllable, like Duane."

"Two syllables?"

"Yep. And the first *e* is long."

"Dee-Wayne?"

"Yeah, like that. DeWayne Mannock."

Boone put his notebook in his pocket and found the folder. "Jack, why do I feel like this is just the start of something between me and him?"

He jiggled the folder with one hand until it slid free of the envelope, but as he was replacing the envelope between the seats so he could manage the rest, his phone rang. Boone tucked the folder under his leg and grabbed his cell, peeking at the readout. "Someone within the department."

"Better take it."

"This is Drake."

"Mr. Drake, this is Brigita Velna. Remember me?"

"Of course! How are you? I didn't expect to hear from you again until after my surgery."

"That was my plan, Officer, but frankly bureaucracy has somehow crept in."

"Sorry?"

"So am I, and to be honest I don't understand it. I'd rather not discuss it by phone, but the fact is that there is a move afoot that makes it important for me to speak to you sooner rather than later. Is there any way you could visit me even this afternoon?"

"Hmm. I am in the middle of something. And I'm underdressed."

"Sir?"

He explained about the sweat suit. "On the other hand, it *is* department issue."

"That's good enough for me. Shall we say this afternoon, as soon as you can get here?"

"This is really that important?"

"I'm afraid so."

"Just a second."

Boone covered the mouthpiece and ran it past Keller.

"Who is she again?"

"The department counselor who works with people who have gone through traumas, fired a shot in the line of duty, been wounded, that kind of thing."

"Lost loved ones."

"Right."

"And what's so important?"

Boone told him what she had said.

"You and I have a lot to cover today, Boones. But tell her yes. I'll be sure I'm out of my three o'clock in time so when you're done with her, I'll be free."

Back on the phone, Boone said, "On my way."

Boone retrieved the Mannock transcript and Jack told him, "The interesting stuff starts on page sixteen."

Boone riffled through the pages. The US Attorney was abbreviated USA.

USA: And what makes you wonder about the paternity of the child in question?

DM: You mean if I'm the dad?

USA: Yes, sir.

DM: 'Cause she was loose. She even liked telling me about all her other lovers.

USA: So you're saying that [name deleted] could not be yours, in your opinion?

DM: Well, he could be, I guess. But I'd say maybe a one-in-ten chance.

Boone tensed, the pain breaking through his medication. The last thing he wanted was to keep reading. "Any more of this relevant?"

"He asks him later if he's ever seen Max."

"Just tell me what DeWayne said."

"Said he had no reason."

Boone looked out the window and shook his head. "Too bad there are metal detectors at the courthouse. Fox and Mannock in the same room? That would be too tempting."

"Don't say that to anyone but me, Boones."

"Don't worry. You know, Haeley was a virgin when she met DeWayne—"

"I don't need to hear that, but I hope you're right."

"Jack, I hope she's going to be my wife someday and that we will all still be friends, maybe even coworkers. You need to know. Haeley and DeWayne lived together for about six weeks before she came to her senses. When she found out she was pregnant, he left and she never saw him again."

"Classy guy."

"See? She went through some deep stuff, came back to her faith, reconciled with her parents, had Max, and pretty much stayed below the radar as she rebuilt her life."

"Until now."

"Exactly."

"You see the photo of him, Boones, there at the end of the transcript."

Boone leafed to an eight-by-ten black-and-white head-shot. "Are you serious? He's a white trash cliché!"

That made Jack laugh. "Gotta love the mullet and the moustache that looks like underarm hair. And what is that? Looks like a tux shirt."

Boone studied it. "It's his work shirt. See the logo of the casino? He wore that to the interview?"

"Perfect."

Boone put everything away, stashed it between the seats, and pulled out his notebook again.

"That looks jammed, Boones. How much information you got for me?"

"Oh, just what I learned from a whole day's work yester-day, that's all."

"We've got only a few more minutes before we hit the city, and traffic is light. Give me the basics."

"No. It's complicated. Hey, after you drop me, you're going to the office, right? There's something I need."

"Oh, goody! I get to play secretary again? Let me stop home for a skirt first."

"That I don't even want to think about."

"Well, I don't have gams like Margaret, but I'd stack 'em up against any other guy my age."

"Spare me."

"So what do you need now, Boones?"

"Thelma Wade's maiden name."

Jack pressed his lips together and shook his head. "Why do you have to be nosing around Pete? It doesn't look good, turning the spotlight on him."

"Jack, the evidence leads me where it leads me. Now if her

maiden name isn't what I think it is, a lot of this goes away. If it *is*, there are things you need to be aware of."

"Well, I knew her maiden name at one time. It's on the tip of my tongue. It should be easy enough to get."

"Without his knowing you're asking?"

"No, I think it makes more sense to let him know that while he's investigating Haeley, we're investigating him! What do you take me for, Boones?"

"Sorry."

"So, do you know the maiden name and just need it confirmed, or . . . ?"

"Maybe," Boone said.

"I remember it's just a normal name, nothing exotic. Miller. Jones. Something plain like that. Hit me with it; see if it rings a bell."

"I can't, Jack. I don't want to suggest anything. I've got to have it confirmed for sure."

"Fair enough. Hey, you going into an office building in a sweat suit and parka with your Beretta peeking out?"

Boone shrugged. "Yes."

"Speaking of classy. All you need now is a mullet and a moustache."

3:10 P.M.

To Boone's surprise, when he got off the elevator, the fifty-ish, matronly, Latvian Brigita Velna was waiting for him. He followed her to her crowded, plain office and was directed to the side table, where she joined him.

"You know me as honest and straightforward, do you not, Officer Drake?"

"If nothing else, ma'am."

"I felt we made a bit of connection while you were working through your trauma."

"I agree," Boone said, wondering if she was overstating it. "I appreciated your help."

"I don't generally get to where conversing with a troubled officer becomes as easy as it did with you. So often they are here against their wills, and they don't want to hear what I have to say."

"You also made it clear that your priority was the CPD and not the employee."

"Like I say, I want to be honest."

"But if you stipulate that with everybody, it might explain some of the distance you feel."

"That and the fact that my looking out for the department means I often recommend keeping affected officers off the job longer than they'd like. You took it well. I appreciated that."

"I was faking it."

She smiled. "I knew that. But you didn't get your back up or file a report on me or lodge an appeal."

"Didn't have the energy."

"Detective, I want to tell you what's going on, but I must first ask for your complete confidence. Because of our history, I am prepared to say more than I ever have to an employee under review. If you'd rather I not—"

"Oh, I'd rather you would."

"As long as we understand each other."

She stood and grabbed a file off her desk, then returned to the table, seeming to study just the first two pages. "As I hinted on the phone, someone downtown is bum-rushing the process with you. Frankly, I think I am being pressured by the brass because the brass is being pressured by someone else."

"Who?"

"I don't know. It's just a hunch."

"Welcome to my world. So what's the thrust?"

"They want you off the job, and they want me to be the one who gets that done."

"I can save you a lot of time and effort, because that's not going to happen."

She held up a hand. "Don't dismiss anything out of hand. You haven't heard this yet. Anyway, if I do what I'm supposed to, follow the directives of my superiors, I have to see this through. For you to counter it, you would have to appeal, and that could hurt me."

"I don't want to do that, ma'am, but that will not keep me from fighting for my job."

"I was afraid of that."

"But you're not surprised."

"No, but I will be if you hear the offer they're making and still refuse."

"They've sweetened the pot that much just to get rid of me? Who am I such a threat to?"

"I don't want to know, but you want to hear this."

"Fire away. Maybe the wrong choice of words."

That made Brigita Velna smile again, and Boone knew that was rare.

"I have to say, Officer, that their suggestion of how to frame this is hard to take issue with. I might have gone this route myself, even without input. I'm sure you're aware of what in my profession we call stress indicators."

"Sure."

"These are measured by major life experiences, good and bad. For instance, being promoted can be nearly as stressful as being fired. Having a child can be nearly as stressful as losing a child. Numbers are associated with the stress levels for such events, and if a person's totals are above a certain figure, they become a candidate for a breakdown—or at least for being at risk as an employee."

"I'm with you."

"All right then, follow this. Some of the most stressful crises in an adult's life are these: the loss of a spouse, the loss of a child, a change of residence, being charged with a crime or malfeasance, a promotion, a life-threatening injury, and major surgery. Any one of those rates so high on the stress list that it raises a red flag. Add another from the same list, even if both were positives—say a promotion and a move—and professionals should take notice. Do you see where I'm going with all this?"

"I'd have to be deaf and blind not to. Would falling in love be on that list?"

"It would. Is that true of you too, Detective?"

"Yes, ma'am."

"Well, congratulations, but that makes you eight for eight. I'm surprised you're sitting up and taking nourishment. If you were me, could you recommend a victim like you for one of the most stressful jobs in the world?"

Boone couldn't suppress a chuckle.

"What?" she said.

"If you only knew."

"Knew what?"

"First, the last thing in the world I would ever call myself is a victim, despite that I have suffered everything you listed above. But how about also adding to the list having your home and car broken into on the same day?"

"Surely you have set some global record."

"I can't be forced to resign, can I?"

Ms. Velna closed her file. "It would be very difficult for the CPD to build a case against someone who has such a high profile right now. You're a hero and you're in the news—which means more stress, by the way. So no, I don't see anyone trying to trump up any charges against you. But if they can encourage you to make this decision on your own, the public knows enough about your ordeals that everyone would understand."

"Except people who really know me. I'm no quitter. I'm going to rehabilitate myself to where I am back to full strength and bring no handicaps to the job. And if the job in the Major Case Squad is still on the table, that's what I want."

"Hold that thought. That offer comes into play here."

Boone sat back. "I'll never really get over the loss of my family, and anyone who claims they could is lying. But time has helped. So has my new relationship. So has getting back on the job."

"Until you were nearly shot to death."

"There was that, yes. But moving was no big deal for me. Being investigated and charged by Internal Affairs was stressful, granted, but being exonerated and then promoted made that a wash. Being shot and looking at surgery, I can't deny the stress there. But I'm channeling that into resolve, just like I did after the tragedy. I'll be obsessive about therapy, my goal being to get as healthy as I can as fast as I can. I would never want a fellow officer to have even one doubt about whether I brought my A game to the street."

"Admirable."

"I'm absolutely committed, ma'am. Need anything more from me?"

"I am obligated to tell you what is being offered."

"I don't care, but I'll listen."

"It's more than full disability."

"How can it be more?"

"I've never seen anything like it. Normally a person disabled in the line of duty would get his full pension and benefits for the rest of his natural life. You are being offered that, including your full salary, including all cost-of-living raises, a multiplier that assumes merit increases, and another that assumes what your salary would have been had you been promoted to chief of the Major Case Squad.

"While you would be permitted to take another full-time job without jeopardizing any of this, clearly you would never have to work another day in your life."

"Wow."

"See?"

"I'd be pretty miserable to live with."

"But financially comfortable."

"That's never been a priority."

"In this day and age? Are you serious, sir?"

"I've never been motivated by great amounts of money, Ms. Velna. Sorry."

The woman rose and put the file back on her desk. "Well, I can say I presented the details to you. You see, the argument from the Chicago Police Department is that you have been not only physically disabled—"

"Which they can't say before we see how successful shoulder surgery is."

She cocked her head. "But you have clearly been psychologically disabled."

"Is that your professional opinion?"

She snorted. "*My* opinion? I find you one of the most remarkable people I have run into on this job. If I were you, I think I'd have surrendered by now. You do seem to have turned all this stress into fuel."

"I like that metaphor."

"Unfortunately, as I explained, you are going to have to fight me and the department and the city on this. Someone wants you gone and has convinced the brass. They couldn't be more generous."

"You have forms or something for filing an appeal? I'll take whatever you've got."

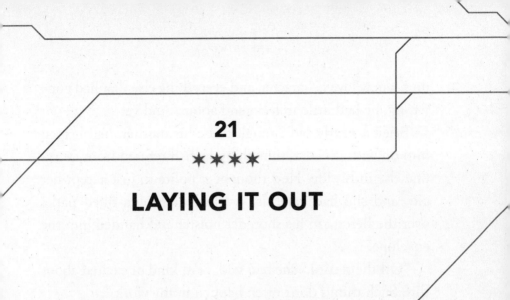

21

★★★★

LAYING IT OUT

Boone Drake stood at the corner waiting for Jack Keller to pick him up. Despite the piercing February wind and that his parka was merely draped over his bad shoulder while he tried to manage the envelope full of forms Brigita Velna had given him, Boone was strangely warmed. The sweat suit that had seemed so toasty indoors was no match for the temperature outside, but even with everything Boone was going through, the encounter with Ms. Velna had left him undeniably encouraged.

He knew that was ridiculous. He had just learned that someone was desperate enough to have him out of the way to have gotten the Chicago Police Department to make him an offer hardly anyone would refuse. And with his wound, the attack on his new love's character, and everything else that had gone wrong, he had little to feel good about. And yet . . .

Brigita, nearly old enough to be his mother, had helped him on with his coat, something he had refused from everyone else in his life. He'd thought it polite to just accept her aid, and she had carefully worked the down-filled parka over the Beretta in his shoulder holster and handed him the envelope.

"Off the record," she had said, "I'm kind of excited about this. Such things don't often happen in my work."

"Ma'am?"

"Fighting city hall. You realize that perfectly defines what you plan to do? They want you out. You want to stay. You're going to put them to the test."

"I'll do everything in my power not to make you look bad, Ms. Velna. I know you're just their mouthpiece—"

"I hope you win. As for my superiors, I don't know what else I could have done. You can't say I wasn't clear about the offer."

Maybe Boone shouldn't have been optimistic about his chances against the powers that be. But her confidential support alone was invigorating.

When Jack pulled up, Boone tucked the envelope under his arm and opened the door. As he slid in, Jack said, "Johnson. Pete's wife's maiden name. It hit me after I dropped you off that I've had a copy of his personnel file in my office since I became his superior. Her name's in there, and I don't know why. You can't even ask applicants that stuff anymore. Is that the name you had for her, Boones?"

"It was what I feared."

"Can't wait to hear why. So, my office? We shut the door and you lay it all out for me?"

"Not your office. Not now."

"Too close to Pete?"

Boone nodded.

"The little conference room down the hall?"

Boone shook his head.

"The one on the second floor?"

"I don't even want us seen together in the building, Jack."

Keller shrugged. "How clandestine do we need to be?"

"Your-eyes-only level."

"Hmm. Crime lab?"

"That'll work," Boone said. "Want me to call Dr. Waldemarr to—?"

"You kiddin'? You can hardly sit there and think with one hand, let alone make a call."

Jack pulled out his own phone and made the arrangements. When he flipped his phone shut, he said, "Gotta love that guy. No questions asked. Said guys are processing some evidence right now, but they should be done by the time we get there."

Though the temperature was lower than the day before, when Boone compared his energy level during the walk into the crime lab with how he had felt yesterday, he realized the benefit of a full night's rest. He was still sore and tired, but he didn't have that on-your-last-legs feeling. And with Jack doing the driving, maybe he could stay on schedule with his meds.

When Dr. Waldemarr emerged, Boone saw over the doctor's shoulder three detectives coming out of the evidence room. He quickly moved away so as not to be seen with Jack. Everybody on the force seemed to know Keller, and because of what Boone himself had accomplished, he had become one of the most recognizable cops on the job too.

When the coast was clear, Jack said, "You think people don't know we were partners and that you work for me now?"

"When we get in there you'll know why I don't want to give rise to any suspicion about what we're up to."

"Gentlemen," the doctor said, "the room is yours for the next ninety minutes."

"Shouldn't need it that long," Jack said. "Unless my cohort here knows better."

One thing Boone liked about the evidence room was that while most of it was filled with metal shelving and seemingly endless rows of boxes that created a maze of dark, narrow corridors, when you pulled something out to examine it, the overhead lights were like the sun. As Jack followed, Boone passed the table where he had examined the evidence from his own shooting the day before. He led his boss around a corner and down a couple of rows to another gray metal table that sat under a wash of track floodlighting.

Boone added his thick, dog-eared notebook to the top of the pile and slid off his coat. He draped it over the back of the chair and sat.

For a blue-collar, seat-of-his-pants street cop, Keller had always been buttoned down when it came to framing a case. Boone had long been impressed by how Jack took careful notes, asked every question imaginable, and set about fashioning a plan of attack.

Keller opened his own worn, black leather notebook,

flipped past several pages full of his small, meticulous hand-writing, and found a fresh page. He tapped his pen on the table, looked up, and said, "I'm all ears and scribbles, Boones. And you know I like to start from the beginning."

"And with my basic premise, my take on how the whole scenario is playing out."

Jack nodded as if pleased with how he had taught Boone. "The basics in a nutshell, please. Just like in court. I'm the jury. Tell me what you're going to tell me, what it's going to mean, then tell me, and then tell me what you told me."

Boone had one chance to get this right. Jack was not a patient guy. If Boone had been distracted by some rabbit trail, or if he had jumped to some conclusion, Jack would ferret it out and not let up. And if Boone lost his best ally, the case against Haeley would prevail, and all would be lost. If that happened, Boone wondered how long the city's retirement offer might stay on the table.

Nah.

Boone studied his notes and took a breath. "All right. Even the limited evidence I have collected so far should show that Haeley is innocent—"

He stopped at Jack's raised hand. "Innocent?" Jack said. "Or do you mean not guilty?"

"My bad. In this case she is both innocent *and* not guilty, but I realize I have to be more precise in the presence of opposing counsel."

"Proceed."

"I confess my thrust here has been to not only exonerate Haeley but to also determine why she was charged in the first place and what that says about the person or persons who have leveled the charges."

"And further," Jack said, "given that you're going to show me why Haeley is not guilty, what conclusion did you draw about her accusers?"

"That they were playing a misdirection game. To turn the spotlight on someone else—in this case, a not-guilty party—and to delay seriously investigating anyone else."

"Like Pete himself."

"Pete and Garrett Fox."

"Well, we know Fox is a scoundrel. Getting something to stick on Wade is going to be a chore. First you're going to have to convince me."

Boone paused and leafed through the first several pages of his notebook. "You told me Pete makes around two hundred thousand."

"I was a little high on that. Looking in his file for his wife's maiden name, I noticed his last raise took him into the middle one eighties."

"About how long would you say he's been earning six figures?"

"Not long. Maybe four years."

"Jack, did he or his wife come from money?"

Keller chuckled. "No, I know that for sure. Until a few years ago, she had to work. Some kind of sales, I think. Commission. Pete said she never really made much at it and he was glad when he got promoted so she could quit."

"No rich relatives? An inheritance? Anything like that?"

"Don't think so. You've got to tell me what you're driving at."

"You tell me, should a civil servant with a salary like Pete's be able to afford two homes—one in Chicago and one in the suburbs—together worth more than three million dollars? And should he also be able to afford four new cars worth three hundred and twenty thousand dollars?"

Jack looked dubious. "Naturally, you're going to tell me where you came up with this, but lots of cops spend beyond their means and are deep in debt. And with that kind of a salary, lots of banks will extend—"

"The cars and the houses are paid for."

"C'mon! I've been in Pete's Toyota. You have too. Remember how thrilled he was when he got that car? I mean, it's nice, but I guarantee it didn't even cost forty grand."

"Would you believe he has a matching white one for his wife?"

"I didn't know, but okay, about seventy grand in cars. Certain people like certain things."

"Like mansions?"

"I doubt they live in a—"

"Not *a*. Two."

"And you're trying to tell me one of them is right here in the city?"

Boone told how he had trailed Pete and saw it, then checked out the details. He described it. "And here's the best part. Cars and houses—all this stuff—is in Thelma Johnson's name."

"You're not serious."

"So does that give you any idea how long Pete's been on the take?"

Keller sat shaking his head. "I don't see what this has to do with the case. Just because a guy has some admittedly suspicious holdings doesn't make him a dirty cop. And even if it does, it doesn't make him one that would leak information that puts a fellow officer in harm's way."

"Harm's way, Jack? Harm's way? You're talking to the 'fellow officer.' Can I get you to go as far as mortal danger?"

"Fair enough."

The whole discussion reminded Boone of his obliterated shoulder, and the pain stabbed anew. Amazing, after having medicated himself at lunch, but the drugs were good for only so long.

Jack pulled out his cell phone and punched numbers. "Doc? Is there a vending machine or something close by? Need a coupla cups of coffee. . . . No, no, really, we need a little walk anyway."

Down the hall they found a coffee machine that dropped a flimsy cup under a stream of boiling water and splashed a clump of powdered coffee into the mix. A tiny wood stirrer slipped in when the cup was full.

Boone studied his. "Something tells me Starbucks is safe."

The cups were so hot Jack had to dig out the perforated flaps that created a makeshift handle. "These will be cool enough in an hour or so," he said as he grabbed a handful of sugars and powdered cream packets.

Back in the evidence room they tried making something drinkable out of their concoctions. Jack sipped his gingerly and laughed. "I been a cop a long time, Boones, and I've endured a lot of sorry excuses for coffee. But this . . ."

"As long as I can wash down my pills with it . . ."

"Shouldn't you have something to eat with those?"

"I still feel stuffed from lunch."

"Yeah, but just to be safe. What do you like?"

"Bread."

"Let me check."

While Jack was gone, Boone glanced over his notes again, realizing he had finally gotten his boss's attention. Keller had a way of delaying his true response, especially when the evidence was overwhelming.

"This is all I found," Jack said, bearing a glazed donut.

"Better not thank me till you determine how stale it is."

Pretty stale. But a bite did the trick. "Am I on the right track with any of this, Jack?"

Keller sniffed. "Hate to admit it. But I'm also thinking like a defense attorney. One plus one doesn't always equal two, you know. Things are not always as they appear."

"Any other clichés we can work into the report?"

"Just sayin'. To take down a man with a record like Pete Wade's, you're going to have to have both barrels loaded. What else you got?"

Boone walked him through his visit to the bank. Jack looked genuinely confused.

"I told you I've talked to the principals, right?" Keller said. "And no one said a thing about any uncle. But that should be easy enough to document with evidence. Surely the bank's security cameras would—"

"Sabotaged." Boone explained what he had discovered.

"Couldn't have been a glitch? Had to be sabotage?"

"Pretty coincidental, wouldn't you say? Everything in the tape corroborates the testimony of the teller, and she says she told everyone the same story. Yet the face is not recognizable, and no one but me seems to have heard her account."

"And you have no doubt that the man in question was Fox?"

"If you saw the tape, you'd know. And she said short, stocky, black hair, and about five years older than me. How close is that?"

Boone mentioned her memory of the man's apparently being touchy, pulling away from her hand.

"Actually, that seals it for me," Jack said.

Boone shot him a double take. "Really?"

"Oh yeah! You didn't know that about Fox? Very territorial. Big protector of his personal space."

"Why didn't I know that? He was my partner for a while."

"You're not an encroacher, I guess. We all told stories of Garrett's idiosyncrasies. No less than Fletcher himself would casually put a hand on Fox's shoulder when he chatted with him, just to watch him squirm."

"You know what I want to know, Jack? Who went with Pete to question the teller? I can't see Pete doctoring the tape, but it appears he brought someone who knew what he was doing, and it was done before the US Attorney's legal assistants got to it. And why didn't anyone repeat the story of the uncle, even without visual evidence? It's eyewitness testimony."

"Probably coached, Boones. I can see someone telling them that without the tape, there's no evidence. Wonder how hard it would be to find out where Fox banks. We're looking for a five-K cash withdrawal."

Boone rubbed his forehead. "They've been sloppy. I mean, Pete himself showing up at the bank? But would they be stupid enough to have Pete withdraw cash from his own account? That would be as bright as they expected Haeley to be, incriminating herself on a CPD computer."

"I doubt you're going to find the withdrawal from *Pete's* account."

"How about Thelma's?" Boone said. "That would be consistent with everything else it appears Pete is trying to hide."

"Good thinking. She wouldn't have paid cash for those Bimmers. If you dig a little, you should be able to find the bank that handled that deal."

Boone called Zappolo's office and asked for Stephanie. "You like this kind of work," he said. "Don't you?"

"I'd rather do what you do than what I do most every day."

"You're aware I was shot recently."

"Yeah, well, I did say *most* every day."

"Today you're doing it," he said. He told her what he needed and asked her to call him back as soon as she could.

While he waited, Boone carefully walked Keller through the rest of what he had discovered, including right there in the crime lab evidence room the day before.

Jack looked stricken. "You're not saying . . . ?"

Boone nodded.

"A second surveillance tape affected?" Keller said. "Two related to the same case? What are the odds?"

Boone said, "I'm going to ask Dr. Waldemarr to show you the list he showed me of the people with access to the evidence," but as he reached for his phone, it rang and the readout showed Friedrich Zappolo's office.

"This is going to be Stephanie. Ask Doc for the sheet."

Jack left and Boone took the call. "Talk to me, Nancy Drew."

Stephanie laughed. "The cars in question were paid for by a direct transfer to the BMW dealership from the Greater Chicago Savings Bank of Naperville."

"Stephanie, you're the best."

Jack returned, studying a photocopy of the access document. "Antoine Johnson," he muttered. "Antoine Johnson. Why does that name . . ." He slammed a fist on the table, making Boone jump. Jack swore. "You know what you're going to find, Boones? This Antoine Johnson is going to turn out to be the cop that was with Pete at the bank. Works out of the 18th. He's a crime scene investigator. Does a lot of testifying."

"How do you know him?"

"You're gonna love this."

"Don't play with me, Jack."

"I don't think Pete knows I know, or if he does, he won't expect me to remember. Antoine Johnson is Thelma's nephew."

"Cue the violins."

"So what'd your amateur detective have for you?"

Boone told him.

"Just a sec." Jack placed another call on his cell. "Deputy Chief Jack Keller, Chicago PD, calling for Chief Lyons." He covered the phone. "We go way back. If anybody can get something done in Naperville—Hey, Chief!" They traded pleasantries; then Keller got to the point. "Nobody can know where this request came from, but I've got to know if there was a five-thousand-dollar cash withdrawal from the account of Thelma Johnson." He gave Lyons her address and the date parameters. "Doable? . . . You do? Well, why doesn't that surprise me? I'll owe you big-time, Chief."

He hung up and Boone gave him an expectant look.

"Naperville chief knows the president of the bank. He'll call me back."

"Is there anybody you don't know, Jack?"

"Yeah, there is."

"Do tell."

"Margaret. I keep thinking I've got her figured out, but she surprises me every day."

"In good ways, I hope."

"No other."

"You ought to make an honest woman of her."

"I know. But neither of us has too good a track record on that score."

"Still . . ."

"I know. Maybe. Someday. She's my best so far, I can tell you that. Not that she had much competition."

"Margaret's accent reminds me of Haeley's mother," Boone said. "Which reminds me I need to call her about her car."

"You kiddin'? I told you, you say nothing and she'll be none the wiser. That car doesn't look like a thing happened to it. Anyway, what're you gonna tell her, that the guys who wanted you dead broke her windows and stole your stuff? That's gonna give her a good feeling about her daughter's future with you."

"Hopefully she'll appreciate the honesty."

Jack shook his head. "That's your curse, you know. You're honest to a fault."

"Interesting way to put it. By the time I'm your age I'll have learned to lie; is that it?"

"It's called diplomacy, the better part of wisdom. Learning to keep your mouth shut. Hey, I'd better get back to my car. And you need to get back to Addison."

"Uh, yeah, that's a problem. I'm pretty doped up."

"You should have thought of that."

"I didn't know how long we'd be, Jack. Sorry."

"Margaret and I had plans."

"Really sorry. Maybe someone else can run me out to the safe house."

Jack's phone rang. "Chief! That didn't take long. . . . No kidding. Unreal. Like I said, I owe you."

22

★ ★ ★ ★

THE EPIPHANY

JACK SLAPPED HIS PHONE shut with a flourish and gave Boone a look. "You know, I admit I took all the rest of this with a grain of salt."

"You don't think I compiled enough evidence to prove Haeley—"

"I'm talking hard evidence that ties Pete Wade himself to Garrett Fox and the leak to the DiLoKi Brotherhood that almost got you killed."

"And?"

"And Chief Lyons found a five-thousand-dollar cash withdrawal from Thelma Johnson's checking account the day before the deposit to Haeley's account."

"Do they document that somehow? I mean—"

"Way ahead of you, and Chief Lyons was ahead of me. The Greater Chicago Savings Bank of Naperville scans the cash and has the serial numbers. Assuming Haeley's bank does the same, Haeley is as good as cleared, and Pete's life—as he knows it—is over."

"Does that really clear her," Boone said, "or just implicate Pete?"

"Pete's been the one bringing the charges, on his high horse trying to clean up subversion within the department. If we tie him to the money that went to Fox and establish that Fox was the so-called uncle who put the money in Haeley's account, it shouldn't take much for Zappolo to get all charges against her dropped."

Boone struggled to stand.

"You all right, Boones?"

"Woozy."

"Then sit down, man!"

"It's not that, Jack. Are you processing this?"

"I'm not liking it, if that's what you mean."

"No, I mean are you playing it out to its logical conclusion? The ramifications to our case are apocalyptic."

"Tell me."

"You tell me, Jack. Is there a scintilla of doubt that Haeley's bank will have the serial numbers of those hundreds from the deposit, and that they will prove to have come from Thelma's withdrawal?"

"No."

"And regardless whether Thelma knows a thing about the details, this is Pete's doing?"

"Yes."

Boone ran his free hand through his hair. "What are we gonna do?"

"Head back to Haeley's bank. Tie up this loose end."

"We can get anybody to do that. We know what they'll find."

"Agreed."

"Then how do we save Pascual's life, and his mother's, and his son's?"

Jack sat staring. Then he let out a string of expletives without his usual apology. When he stood, his chair hit the floor. He grabbed his coat. "Doc!"

Waldemarr came running. "You guys look awful. Who died?"

"We've got a problem," Jack said, picking up his chair and starting to tidy the table.

"I'll handle all that," the doctor said. "What's up?"

"Rags, you and I go back more'n thirty years. Can I trust you?"

"You know you can."

"I've got a situation here. I've got a rat inside, on the job, and he and I go back too. If I can't trust *him*, who can I trust?"

"Well, unless you're talking about Fletcher Galloway, you know you can trust him."

"Yeah," Boone said. "Too bad he's retired."

"Not yet he's not," Dr. Waldemarr said. "Technically he's on leave. Usually when brass at his level retire, they take their unused vacation, personal days, sick days, comp days, all that. He could be up to six weeks away from actually being officially off the job. I mean, he's probably sipping tropical cocktails with his feet up a long way from here, but if you had to have a trusted ear at high levels, you could do worse."

"Doc, you're a genius."

"So, care to fill me in?"

"Tell you what," Jack said, "you have my word you'll be the first one I debrief on this, but for now I'd just better not. You don't want to be responsible for knowing something this explosive, and I have to somehow keep a lid on this."

"Go do what you have to do. I'll put the room back together."

Boone had been through a lot in his brief career, but as he and Jack Keller hurried through the frigid parking garage and the short day faded to darkness, he felt for the first time like a true brother under the blue. He and Jack didn't have to say it aloud. They were on each other's wavelength and understanding all the ramifications.

And it wasn't pretty. Connecting Pete Wade to the attempt on Pascual Candelario's life by the DiLoKi Brotherhood that had resulted in Boone's nearly lethal injury told them both an ugly truth that needed not even be uttered.

Pete Wade had some kind of connection with Jazzy Villalobos, whether through Garrett Fox or just on his own. He didn't need all the machinations of the cell phone photo of Haeley's notes, her apparent payoff, any of that. That had all been for show, to take the focus off anyone else and aim it at Fox and Haeley.

The explosive part of the equation was that not only had Pete naturally been privy to where Pascual would be and when he would be transferred, but he also now knew every detail about the safe house. If Candelario had been vulnerable in a penthouse apartment in a Chicago high-rise, he and his family were sitting ducks at the refurbished junkyard in Addison.

How many of the people involved in that operation might be in Pete Wade's hip pocket? And even if none were, all of them would have every reason to answer any question from him, follow any directive he gave, and allow him full access to everything and everyone at the compound. Somehow Boone and Jack had to engineer an escape for Pascual Candelario while also exposing Pete.

"We're following up at the bank ourselves," Jack said, making sure Boone was buckled in and his door shut. Boone felt like an albatross, everything taking twice the time.

He told Jack his contact at the bank was the assistant manager, but that he also believed he had the trust of the teller in question. "But I'd rather not have to involve her. I don't want her to know too much because she has no concept of keeping confidences. If Pete called and asked her what was going on, she'd likely tell him everything."

"Get the assistant manager on the phone. Tell him what you need."

Boone dialed and switched to speaker mode.

The assistant manager said, "You again? Will this investigation never end?"

"I apologize, sir, but if it wasn't important, I wouldn't ask."

"And if I'm busy and not eager to start another project on your behalf this close to the end of my day, you just get a warrant and I have to do it anyway, am I right?"

"I don't want to have to resort to that, sir. And I think you'll find this a fairly minor task."

"Then there's no rush?"

Boone hesitated. The guy had him. "I'm afraid it's something I need as soon as possible. In fact, I'm on my way there right now."

"Of course you are."

"I'll be in your debt, sir."

"Nice. A little bank humor for me, Detective Drake?"

"Not intentionally, but if it makes you smile . . ."

"Want to make me smile? Convince me you really are in my debt."

"What do you mean?"

"Well," the man said, "tell me what you want, and I'll tell you how you can make us even for all you've put me through."

Boone told him.

"Well, that isn't a big deal, actually. Yes, we photocopy cash transactions. Our computer then scans the serial numbers of the bills and arranges them in alphanumeric order."

"And the reason for that?"

"So the transaction can be compared with another without doing it all manually."

"I don't follow."

The banker sighed, but Boone had the impression he liked knowing something that Boone didn't. Boone had never worked in fraud or bad checks.

"Well," the assistant manager said, "let's say you're trying to tie the deposit in question to a withdrawal from another bank to see if it's the same currency. Am I warm?"

"I'm listening."

"We have both the photocopies of the actual bills, and we also have the printout of the numbers. Generally one bank sends another bank that printout and they compare it to their own record. If the first serial number on the list and the last serial number on the list match—in this case, the first and last of fifty one-hundred-dollar bills—it stands to reason the others would match too, and those who need to know can assume the transactions correspond with each other."

"Clever. Was that your idea?"

That made the man laugh. "Much as I love your patronizing me, Detective, someone much brighter than I devised that protocol long before my time."

"Well, sir, as I say, I will be in your debt. If you can have a copy of the serial numbers for me when I arrive, I will be happy to try to help you in any way that's appropriate and doable."

The man fell silent, and Boone got the impression he was finding this hard to believe. "Okay," he said finally, "here's the deal. My son is in middle school, and they have a zero-tolerance policy on weapons."

"Not a bad idea. Don't tell me your son took a weapon to school, because that is not something I would be able to help w—"

"Hear me out, please. He's a Boy Scout and he has a pocketknife he carries everywhere he goes, except to school, of course."

"Of course."

"So there's some incident at school. A kid brings a butter knife from home, because he uses it to smooth out the dirt in some model of a turn-of-the-century farm, and he gets in trouble for it. The teacher goes on and on about how she's going to wrap it in newspaper and put it in a paper bag and keep it in her desk and that his parents can come in and retrieve it. Fact is, with the policy, I thought it was a pretty reasonable solution."

"I agree."

"But then she asks if anyone else has anything at all like that in their possession, warning them of the no-tolerance policy. My son, more forthcoming than necessary, tells her he keeps a two-inch pocketknife in a locked saddlebag of his locked bike in the bike rack. The teacher says she assumes that's not an issue as long as the saddlebag stays locked when the bike is on school grounds."

"Again, wise."

"Agreed. But kids talk and it gets around about my son's pocketknife, only when it reaches the principal's office, it sounds like a machete. Some enforcer from the office makes my son go out and get the knife and show it to him. He looks disappointed it's not more menacing, but still he decides it violates the no-tolerance policy and—"

"But he told your son to dig into his locked bike to get it?"

"See what I mean?"

"So what was the upshot?"

"Four-day suspension."

"You've got to be kidding."

Jack spoke up. "Sir?"

"Yes? Who's this?"

"I work with Detective Drake. Tell me the name of your son, the school, the principal, and the phone number."

The man told him.

"By the time we get to the bank, I will have a report for you."

"Please, just don't get my son in more trouble."

"Trust me."

4:30 P.M.

Jack was dialing as he pulled into the bank parking lot; he eventually got through to the principal and put the phone on speaker. He identified himself fully, urging the man to write down his name, his badge number, and to feel free to "call the city and determine that I am who I say I am."

"I'm convinced," the principal said.

Jack rehearsed the story he had heard from the assistant manager of the bank. "Can you confirm this account?"

"That's close enough. I'm afraid we have a no-toler—"

"Has it already gone to the board, and have they voted on it?"

"No, to preclude that I made an executive decision."

"When does the suspension begin?"

"Next Tuesday. The boy is allowed to come Monday, because we're having tests. Then he will be suspended for the rest of the week."

"Yeah, rescind that, okay?"

"I beg your pardon?"

"You heard me, sir. The boy will be in school on Monday and the rest of next week too, and nothing more need be said about it."

"I can't have you telling me how to run my—"

"Oh no," Jack said, "this won't do at all. I'm not hearing what I need to hear. I need to hear you say that we're on the same page."

"But we're not."

"I think we are. You know the no-tolerance policy led to this ridiculous end. You have the power to see to it that it is not carried out."

"I will do no such—"

"Oh, but you will. Because the Chicago PD has a no-tolerance policy regarding many things related to your school in particular."

"Our school in par—"

"Like your bus drivers. We need to check every one of them to be sure the bus company did its job in screening and bonding them. No druggies, no alkies, no ex-cons, no sex offenders, no—"

"That's not on us, sir. That's on the bus company, as you say."

"And yet would it not affect your schedule if each driver were interrogated as he pulled up to the facility?"

Silence.

Jack said, "And we also have a no-tolerance policy on teachers parking on the street past the allowed hours."

"But our parking lot is full, and the ones who do park on the street are gone within a half hour of the time limit."

"Does that sound like zero-tolerance to you?"

Silence.

"Sir, can we get on the same page?"

"I'd like to," the principal said.

"It's easy. I can leave the scrutiny of the bus drivers to the company. I can even look the other way when teachers park on the street a half hour later than the signs allow. And you can just pretend the suspension of the Eagle Scout never happened. No announcement, no apology, no explanation. He just shows up Tuesday, and if anyone squawks, you tell them that you have it under control. Because you do, don't you, sir?"

"Yes. Yes, I do."

"Great talking with you."

"And you, Deputy Chief Keller."

The bank assistant manager looked wary when he welcomed

Boone and Jack into his office. "Yet another officer I have not met," he said, shaking Jack's hand. "This must be a much bigger caper than any of us imagined."

"This should be the end of it," Boone said as the man slid the copies of the currency serial numbers across the desk.

He handed them to Jack, who excused himself and stepped into the corner. Boone heard him on the phone with the Naperville chief of police.

"Think you guys can help with my son?" the executive said. "Your partner said he might have news for me."

"Ask him."

But the man didn't have to. Jack slipped his phone back into his pocket, flashed Boone a thumbs-up, and approached the man's desk. "Glad we could scratch each other's backs," he said.

"Sir?"

"And I'm grateful you didn't ask me to fix a ticket or hassle a pesky neighbor. I don't do that kind of thing. But you hit a hot button with me on that zero-tolerance rule stuff. I mean, Lord knows they have their hands full and have to do something, but Eagle Scouts with pocketknives locked away ought to get some kind of consideration."

"My feeling exactly."

"It's over."

"How so?"

"Tell your son not to talk about it or brag about it. But the suspension has been suspended."

"Seriously?"

"Didn't I tell you I'd have a report for you? That's the report. He goes to school, doesn't miss a day, and when people ask what happened, he can say he doesn't really know. Because he doesn't. And he won't, will he?"

"If you say so."

"I say so."

"Thank you, Officers."

"Now I know this likely disappoints you, sir," Boone said. "But this is almost certainly the last time we'll be in here."

The man smiled. "I'll miss you, but I'll get over it."

23

✦✦✦✦

INVOLVING FLETCH

TUESDAY, FEBRUARY 9, 5:15 P.M.

"You're a pro, Boones," Jack said as they returned to the car. "What you did yesterday—I got to tell you, that was just good, old-fashioned, shoe-leather police work."

"Hardly satisfying."

"It will be, when we get Pete before he gets to PC."

"That's it in a nutshell, isn't it, Jack? But what's Pete waiting for? If he has people at the safe house, why not take out Pascual immediately?"

"He's got to make it look either justified or like an accident."

"That doesn't have to take long. We've got to move."

Keller nodded. "Doc Waldemarr was right, you know. I don't know who to trust but Fletcher Galloway."

"Fletch made it pretty clear to me he wanted out," Boone said. "Why would he want back in?"

"'Cause he's all cop, that's why. You know he was skeptical of Pete's crusade against Haeley."

"He told me he wasn't buying it. He wouldn't say anything bad about Pete, and I don't think he suspected his motives, but it didn't feel right to him. He wanted to put it behind him."

Jack pulled into traffic. "Can't let him do that. He may think he's gone, but if he has a rat in his old division, he'll want to help trap it and kill it."

"Where we going, Jack? Or are you just driving so you can think?"

"To Fletch's, on the West Side. Don't know why. It's not like I'm gonna just show up at his door." He handed Boone his cell phone. "I'd better call first. I got him on speed dial there. Hit it for me, will you, and put it on speaker. He won't mind."

Fletch's home phone went to voice mail. "Hey, Fletch!" Jack said. "Boones and me are gonna be in your neighborhood tonight and were wondering if we could drop in and visit you. We'd love to see you."

Within minutes, Galloway called. "You 'member I retired, right?"

"Hello to you too, boss."

"Not boss anymore. Holy moley, Keller, didn't we just have cake the other day? That was my last supper."

"So you don't even ever want to see us again?"

"'Course. But tonight I'm taking the wife to the Old Man and the Sea."

"That fifty-year-old movie?"

"It's a restaurant! You know what kind of seafood I like, don't you?"

"You only told me this one a hundred and forty times."

"Seafood."

"That's as funny as it's ever been."

"I know when you're mocking me, Keller."

"Chief, we need to see you tonight. What time you getting back?"

"Thought it was a social call."

"It is. And a little more."

"After my bedtime is when I'm getting home. Now I'm just starting to get used to not setting an alarm clock. Can't this wait, Jack, really?"

"It can't, Fletch. I'm sorry."

"Just don't make me come and meet you somewhere. Going out with the wife is my agenda for the evening. If you want to come over after she's in bed, I can give you till midnight. That work for you guys?"

"Yes, sir. You want to just call me when the coast is clear?"

"Good idea. Figure around ten. I like to watch the news, but one of my sons taught me how to tape it."

"You're gonna be dangerous, Chief."

"I'm already dangerous, and you know it."

"We're heading your way; is there a good place for us to eat?"

"What're you looking for? And don't tell me seafood. I don't want to run into you at the Old Man and the Sea."

"Boones looks like he's about to keel over, so I'm guessing heavy, greasy, and American."

Boone had to admit that sounded pretty good just then.

"Rollo's on South Ashland. You know it?"

"Pilsen area?"

"Yeah, but this is steaks, chops, one of those sports bars."

"We'll find it and wait for your call. Have a nice time yourself."

"Oh, I plan to. At least I did. Now I got to put up with you two yahoos in the middle of the night."

Boone checked in with Haeley but was careful not to get into specifics. On the other hand, he wanted to encourage her. "I can't tell you much," he said, "but let me just say, you're going to be *very* happy."

"That sounds good."

She didn't sound convinced. "Better than good," he said. "I've got to try to reach Zappolo tonight. But first I need to talk with your mother."

"About what?"

"Car stuff."

When Mrs. Lamonica came on, Boone filled her in on what had happened and assured her that her car was already as good as new.

"That's too bad," she said. "I meant to tell you that if anything happened to it, I would just have to take yours."

"Maybe we can still work that out," he said.

"You think I'm kidding."

"Actually, you sound serious, ma'am."

"I am. Now this damage wasn't caused by somebody who was after you, was it?"

"No way to tell for sure. Let's just treat it as vandalism, why don't we? Reported, dealt with, covered by insurance."

"So, ready to be traded for yours."

Boone laughed. "When you're ready to look at the Blue Book and work out a deal, we'll talk."

Haeley's mother put her daughter back on.

"I've been thinking more about MCC. With my mother here with Max—"

"Haeley, I told you you'd be happy. Do you think I'd say something like that if I thought there was still a chance that you would wind up back in jail?"

"What're you saying?"

"I'm saying I can't go into details, but you're not going back, all right? That's a guarantee."

"You can't make promises like that."

"I just did."

"I've never wanted to believe you more than I do right this minute, Boone."

"I don't know what I have to do to convince you, Hael."

She sighed. "I've learned there's no such animal as a sure thing."

"Wow," Boone said. "That's depressing."

"I'll tell you what's depressing, love. Jail. Whatever you do, don't get me started."

"Haeley, listen—"

"I really don't want to talk about it, Boone, and I mean it. See you tomorrow?"

"I hope so."

"What does that mean?"

"Things are breaking in the case. I'll update you as I can."

"Mm-hm."

Boone wished she trusted him so she could sleep well. But he knew better.

Traffic was stop and go all the way to the West Side, and by the time Jack pulled into the parking lot of Rollo's Sports Bar, it was the middle of the evening. The place looked jammed to overflowing. The lot showed over a dozen sports cars, hinting at the average age—and income—of the clientele. People waited in the lobby, but more huddled outside.

Jack found one of the few remaining parking spots at the far end of the lot. "I've never been shy about using the badge to get a table."

"We're in no hurry."

"I'm not in a hurry to stand out in the cold either, Boones. Though the polar ice cap might be preferable to this overheated crate."

"I'll go put our name in," Boone said. "Wait here."

Boone made his way through the parking lot, noticing decals reading CWCC in the back windows of many of the hot cars. He hadn't realized how close they must be to Chicago West Community College. The football coach there attended Francisco Sosa's church. Boone had even gotten him to give a few tips to a boys' class there.

As Boone maneuvered through the crowd outside and waiting inside the door, many said, "Long wait, pal. And already pretty raucous in there."

He nodded and kept moving till he reached the hostess podium and put in his name. The young woman looked harried. The noise was deafening, and older patrons didn't appear happy.

"Community college football team," she explained. "Guess they just had their post-season awards ceremony and they came here to get tanked. People are complaining, but there's like forty of 'em, and they're throwing stuff. I don't know what to do."

"Call the cops. How many of these college guys are old enough to drink anyway?"

"We card 'em, but maybe they've got fake IDs. Anyway, it would take the cops forever to get here this time of night. I think we're okay if it doesn't get any worse."

As if on cue, glass shattered. Someone had thrown a beer mug over the bartender's head, and the rest of the footballers laughed hysterically. Other customers were leaving, some without even pretending to pay.

The people outside pressed in to see what was going on, and the people trying to get out had to push their way through. And now the football players appeared to be playing keep-away with beer mugs. Every few seconds one would crash to the floor.

"Who's in charge of those guys?" Boone said. "Any coaches here from CWCC?"

"Nobody," the hostess said. "The players just all came in here after practice, I think. Almost all at the same time."

The people rushing out finally turned the tide, and those waiting began to leave too.

"There goes our business," the girl said.

Boone knew Jack would be in soon after seeing people running out. He pulled out his phone and quickly searched his contacts, finding Coach Newt Joseph's number.

"Hey, Coach, I don't know if you remember me, but I'm Boone Drake and we used to go to the same—"

"Sure, Boone. Worked with your boys. I've seen you a lot in the news lately."

Boone filled him in on what was happening. "Your guys got a reason to be letting their hair down tonight?"

"I just left 'em after celebrating their season. They were all going out to eat together. Sounded innocent enough. I'm on my way. Give me ten minutes."

Soon the place was empty except for the football team, and they seemed to be feeling no pain. Running, throwing, laughing, yelling, breaking things. The manager kept bellowing that he was going to call the police, but they laughed him off.

Jack finally showed. "What . . . ? What do you want to do, Boones?"

"I called the coach. Wait for him unless it gets worse?"

"What're we gonna do, draw down on forty guys?"

"Don't tempt me," Boone said.

A few minutes later the team had organized an impromptu scrimmage and were tackling each other in puddles of booze. The manager was still yelling, but the footballers found pool cues and were winging them at him, making him duck.

Finally Boone advanced, flashing his badge and shouting, "Chicago Police Department!"

"What're you gonna do, gimp? Cuff us all?"

"We might!" Jack said.

"All two of you? Bring it on!"

Just when it looked like the whole team was going to advance on the cops, the team suddenly fell silent. The kids froze. Boone turned to see Coach Joseph behind him. He edged between the cops and stood with his arms folded, surveying the scene.

"Single file," he said quietly, and the team immediately fell into queue. "Out," he said, and they began slowly filing past him, heads down. "My office tomorrow morning, 7:00," he said as the first passed. "My office, 7:10," he said to the next. "My office, 7:20. My office, 7:30 . . ."

When the last kid made his way out, the coach turned to Boone. "Thanks for calling me," he said just above a whisper. He apologized to the hostess and asked to see the manager. "Be sure and send me a bill," he said, pulling his business card from his wallet.

"We're covered by insurance," the man said.

"Don't even file the claim. My guys will pay every last cent, and you'll be getting in-person apologies from them too."

"Okay then, if you insist."

"I do. And if you want to estimate how much business you lost because of this, I'll make sure they cover that too."

"That would be hard to—"

"You know what a normal night brings in. Just be reasonable with me, and we'll get it taken care of."

They shook hands, and the coach approached the cops. "I'd really appreciate it if CWCC was not mentioned in any report."

"Report of what?" Jack said. "What happened?"

The coach nodded. "Thanks."

"You get tired of coaching, I got a job for you," Jack said. "No kiddin'. Wouldn't he make a great cop, Boones?"

"The best. Command the respect of forty kids without raising your voice? You can't teach that."

"What good is it if my influence works only when I'm present?" Newt said.

"Anyway, good job, Coach."

"True test will be Saturday when I try to figure out which of these guys deserves to be on the field."

"Judging by what you just pulled off," Jack said, "I have

a feeling you'll figure it out. Hey, can we buy you dinner? We're about to sit down, and it looks like we'll be their only business for a while."

"I appreciate it, but the family's waiting. And thanks again for, you know, keeping this quiet."

"Impressive guy," Jack said as they sat. "Those kids either fear him or really want to play."

"I'd like to be a fly on the wall of his office tomorrow morning. Wouldn't you?"

Keller smiled. "Reminds me a little of Fletch. Never heard him raise his voice either. He was always the epitome of reason, always seemed open to questions and other ideas. But you danged sure knew when he'd made a decision. He spoke a language called *directive*."

Boone ordered a huge meal, hardly thinking or caring whether he would feel obligated to eat it all. All he knew was that he deserved it.

"Tell me, Jack. Put yourself in Chief Galloway's shoes. If you were him, would you want to have anything at all to do with busting Pete?"

Boone appreciated that Jack didn't respond without thinking. He cocked his head, then seemed to study the ceiling. "He's not going to like it, that's for sure. But once he sees all the evidence, yeah, he'll be in. How can he not? It's going to get messy and noisy. You think the press won't be all over this if Pete goes down? How would that look for Fletch, to have jumped off a sinking ship?"

Boone shrugged. "I never got the feeling Fletch much cared how things looked. But you're right; he won't be able to walk away from this until he's had a hand in cleaning it up."

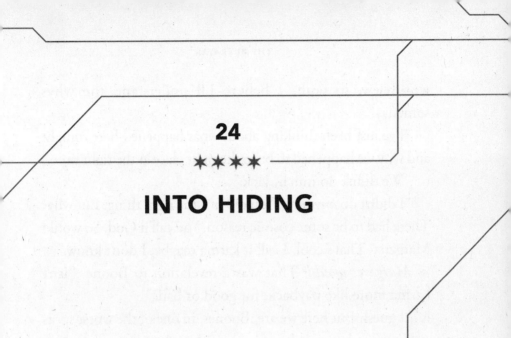

24

★★★★

INTO HIDING

Boone broke protocol and followed Jack Keller's lead in ordering dessert, despite that he was stuffed and already feeling logy.

"I'm gonna regret grazing at this feed trough," he said, though his latest round of meds was kicking in and he felt warm and comfortable in the mostly empty restaurant. "I'll probably fall asleep on Fletch Galloway's couch."

Jack was looking remarkably civilian, attacking a goopy bowl of something covered in whipped cream. "You think things happen for a reason, Boones?"

Boone snorted. "You're asking me? Things have happened to me I'll never figure out this side of heaven. . . ."

"Sorry. Didn't mean to go there."

"It's all right. But you know the afterlife fits in with my

worldview, so yeah, I believe I'll understand the whys someday."

"I've just been thinking about what happened here tonight and why we happened to be in the right place at the right time."

"We didn't do much, Jack."

"I didn't do *anything*. You did just the right thing. But why? There had to be some cosmic reason. You call it God. So would Margaret. That's cool. I call it karma maybe; I don't know."

Margaret would? That was a revelation to Boone. "Isn't karma more like payback, for good or bad?"

"I guess. But here we are, Boones, in one of the worst spots either of us has ever been in—on the job, I mean—and we wander into this strange deal and find kids tearing up the place. I could see a rookie cop firing off a round into the ceiling, facing a thing like this."

"And losing his job."

"For sure. But what are outnumbered, overmatched cops supposed to do—call for backup, and then what? By the time help gets here, the thing's way out of hand."

"Where you going with this, Jack? It made sense to call the coach and I happened to know him."

"Just happened to?"

Boone shrugged. "Yeah."

"Guess I read more into it, that's all."

"What? We've switched roles? You going spiritual on me now, Jack?"

Keller cocked his head. "Maybe. That so bad?"

"You brought it up, so you tell me. What do you make of it?"

"I just think we're supposed to learn from it."

"So teach me."

"You taught me, Boones. That's the point. You see the parallel between this and our case?"

"Hardly."

"You've been teaching me on that, too. I put a lot of stock in Pete's reputation, his years of service, his loyalty, his friendship—or what I thought was friendship. Looks like I've been wrong for a long time."

"I hope Fletch sees it the way you do."

Jack looked away and shook his head.

"What?"

Toying with his spoon, Jack said, "I'd hate to be Fletcher Galloway tonight. I mean, it's one thing, me being wrong about a colleague. But Fletch made Pete Wade who he is. And he credits Wade with a lot of his own success and reputation."

"You think he's going to defend Pete?"

"Fletch is no dummy. He knows evidence when he sees it."

They sat for an hour, chatting idly. Finally Jack said, "Question is, does Haeley's lawyer know evidence when he sees it? You want to call him before too long, right? Better do that while I'm checking with Fletch to be sure he's home."

Boone got the recorded night message at the lawyer's office—no surprise. He hesitated to call the man's cell at that time of night, but if this wasn't a priority, he didn't know what was. Friedrich Zappolo answered on the first ring.

"Drake, I'm glad you called," he said, not even waiting to hear what Boone wanted. "The US Attorney wants Haeley back in custody and is sending—"

"No way! They can't do that. Listen, I've got—"

"You'd better listen to me, Drake. They're sending officers

to her place in the morning to book her at MCC, and I've been advised to urge her to make arrangements for her son."

"I guaranteed her this wouldn't happen, Fritz. You've got to stop this."

"I've exhausted every angle I can think of. Unless you have something compelling, this thing is going down tomorrow."

"Believe me, I have more than enough evidence for you."

Fritz hesitated, which encouraged Boone. "It has to be a lot, and it has to be solid, and I don't want any of it by phone."

"Then where? When? I'm telling you, she's completely in the clear, and there's no way she can survive another night in jail."

"MCC is not County, you know."

"You wouldn't be able to persuade her there's a difference."

Zappolo sighed heavily. "I really don't want to be up late tonight, Drake. But we need to do something about that kid if we can't get in the way of this before tomorrow."

"How much does Haeley know?" Boone said.

"I was about to call her, but I assume she's putting the boy down and will soon be turning in herself."

"And then there'll be no way she can sleep with this staring her in the face. Listen, Fritz, do me a favor. Can you hide her for tonight?"

"You want me disbarred?"

"Just put her up somewhere. I'll pay for it. Trust me, as soon as we get together, you'll have everything you need to keep her out of jail. But for now, we need to get her out of her apartment."

"I'm not harboring her mother and the kid too."

Boone realized Zappolo was considering getting Haeley out of sight so she wouldn't be accessible in the morning. "Okay, tell her I'll call her later but right now she needs to send her mother and Max to my parents' in downstate Illinois. And Mrs. Lamonica should use my car, not her own." Boone gave him the address and directions. "So you'll do this, Fritz? I know it's a lot to ask."

"You have no idea. You're asking an officer of the court to hide an arrestee from federal authorities. When this comes home to roost, and you know it will, I'm going to have to prove overwhelming extenuating circumstances. Otherwise I'm disbarred at best, jailed at worst."

"Should I send Haeley to my parents' place too?"

"No! That's pushing things. They can force me to produce her, you know, and if she's downstate it only makes things worse."

"Got it. I can't tell you how much I appreciate—"

"I don't care about that, Boone. I need to be able to defend my actions as soon as this is traced to me. I can't put it off until she turns up missing tomorrow morning. You think they're not going to come straight to me first, and then to you?"

Jack had paid the bill over the manager's objections and was now signaling Boone it was time to go.

"Here's the best I can do tonight, Fritz. I have to cover all my bases within the CPD; then I can meet you anywhere, anytime, but it'll be late. Sorry. I know you have to be as exhausted as I am."

"I'm due in court in the morning, Boone. I'm going to have to deal with Haeley tonight and see if I can sneak in a catnap before you and I get together."

"Can't you get a continuance or something?"

"You watch too much TV. And there's an advantage to being in court tomorrow—I'll be harder for the feds to reach. Get back to me as soon as you can."

"Calling won't wake your wife or anyone, will it?"

Zappolo laughed. "This job has already cost me two wives and two girlfriends. If I even talk about getting married again, sue me, will you, Boone?"

10:00 P.M.

In the car, Boone said, "So Fletch is ready for us?"

"Sort of."

"What's that mean?"

"Just that I assumed he'd wait till Dorothy went to bed."

"You're not saying . . . ?"

"She wants to see us."

"Thinks it's a social call?"

"That's what I asked him," Jack said. "He said he told her we were coming to say hi, and she didn't buy it. Wife of a cop, ya know."

"But she can't be in on the conversation."

Jack sniffed. "We'll just have to put her mind at ease."

"Easier said than done."

"You know her, Boones?"

"Enough to know she doesn't play the role of the little woman."

Twenty minutes later, Boone's phone chirped. "This is Haeley."

"Keep it short," Jack said. "We're close."

"Hey, Hael."

"Just tell me why I had to hear this from Mr. Zappolo."

"Listen, we're going to have all kinds of time to chat this whole thing through, but right now—"

"Boone," she said, "Mom and Max are gone, and I'm hiding so I don't go to jail. This so goes against my grain. I'd rather defend myself right now."

"I promised I'd get to the bottom of this, and I did."

"You also promised this wouldn't happen, Boone, and here I am cooling my heels when I'm ready to tear somebody's head off."

"Your job is to lie low until I get everything I've found to Fritz. He's taking a huge risk—"

"He's made that quite clear."

"You need to trust me."

"And you need to get Mr. Zappolo what he needs as fast as you can."

"I'll see him yet tonight."

"Good. Remind him what I said. I want Max back, and I'm not going to jail."

Boone fell silent, fatigue washing over him. "You do know," he said at last, "that everything I'm doing is for you."

"I do. But give me the tools and the freedom and, and—"

"A weapon?"

"Yes! And then watch me."

"You'll have lots of time to be anything but a victim if Jack and I do our jobs. Right now you can't do anything without looking worse."

"I hate it."

"I know. Now I'd better call my parents."

Jack pulled to the curb a block from Fletcher Galloway's

house in a modest neighborhood. "Get your call made, Boones. Let's not keep the man waiting."

Boone was glad his dad answered the phone. "Sorry if I woke you."

"Just heading to bed. Everything all right? Your mom's picking up the extension."

"No, Dad—"

"Hello?"

"Oh, hi, Mom. Can I talk just to Dad for a second, then to you?"

"What's wrong?"

"I'll tell you everything in a second, Mom. Now can I just—?"

"We have no secrets, and if I'm going to hear everything anyway, let's cut out the middleman. What's the trouble?"

Boone didn't have time to fight with her. "I need to call on your gift of hospitality for a day or two—I hope not longer."

"You've lost your place?"

"No. Now, Mom, listen. I can't go into details, but I need you to put up Haeley's mother and Max for a couple of days."

"Why? Where's Haeley?"

"I'll be able to tell you when it's all over, Mom. I don't even know where Haeley is right now."

"What does that mean?"

"Nothing suspicious. It's just the way it has to be, and that's all I'm going to say. Mrs. Lamonica is going to show up late tonight, well after midnight, in my car. They just need a place to stay, and no one else can know they're there."

"I don't like this, Boone."

"I know it's not fair to keep you in the dark. I wouldn't if

I had a choice. But I also know you and Dad to be the most hospitable people I've ever known. So can you do this for me?"

His mother was quiet. She whispered, "It's true we consider our home the home of anyone who needs it. Missionaries, the homeless—"

"I know. You're the best. So . . . ?"

"Of course we'll do our part. But as soon as you're able, I want the whole story."

Boone followed Jack up the driveway to the back door of Fletcher Galloway's bungalow, mindful of how unassuming the place appeared compared to what he knew of Pete Wade's two homes. But Fletch had long been known as fiscally conservative. A tightwad, actually. Put a bunch of kids through college and drove modest cars.

"They're both in the kitchen," Jack said.

"Great."

25

★★★★

DOROTHY'S WARNING

Boone had trouble keeping a straight face. Naturally, he had never seen Fletcher Galloway dressed for bed, and he certainly had never seen Dorothy that way either. It seemed strange to see this handsome, late-sixties black woman in a long robe over pajamas, wearing fuzzy slippers, yet still with her hair just so and her makeup in place after the evening out with her husband.

Fletcher himself was dressed the same way, striped pajama pants showing at the bottom of his robe. He greeted the cops warmly, beginning a fancy handclasp with Jack, then seeming to resign himself to a conventional shake. "Forgot," he said. "White boys got no style."

"Guilty," Jack said, winking at Boone while reaching to

shake Dorothy's hand. "An unexpected pleasure to get to see you too, ma'am."

"Mm-hm," she said, seeming to reluctantly extend her hand.

The Galloways sat next to each other on a couch near the fireplace in a small TV room next to the kitchen at the back of the house. It struck Boone as dated but cozy. Dorothy looked locked and loaded; Fletcher, nervous and wary.

"Sorry," Jack said, settling into one of the matching lounge chairs next to Boone, "but we don't have time for small talk."

"You don't say," Dorothy said. "Normally you would at this time of night?"

"No. Doesn't surprise me you're as good an investigator as your husband—"

"Okay, listen, Jack Keller. Don't patronize me. I see what's happening here, so let me say my piece and I'll leave you gentlemen to whatever it is you think is important enough to drive all the way—"

Jack began to speak, but she stopped him by raising a hand.

"Something's up," she said, "and I don't need to know what. This one here, he won't tell me because he knows better. He's never brought his work home, and I didn't expect him to. I'm glad he didn't.

"But let me tell you this. Whatever you think is important enough to bring you here had better be worth the trouble. Fletcher has been retired only a couple of days, and I'm not about to lose him back to the job. If it's advice you're after, he'll give it to you. But if you're here because you think you just can't get along without him, well, too bad. He always said his greatest satisfaction came from seeing his people succeed. Hanging on to the old boss is not succeeding.

"Now, he gave himself to the CPD for a lot of years. It's taken its toll, and I prayed he would get a chance to enjoy life before the years got away from us. Since the end of the party, when we walked out of that office for the last time, I've seen a new man. It's like the weight of the world rolled off his shoulders. Know what I mean?"

Boone nodded and saw Jack do the same. Again Jack appeared to want to say something, but Dorothy cut him off, inhaling loudly and shaking her head.

"Hear me out. This man here is sleeping. He's smiling. He's even walkin' with me every morning, and we're enjoying life like we haven't since before we had kids. You do one thing to jeopardize that, you're gonna answer to me. You got it?"

"Yes, ma'am."

"He's already distracted himself wondering what it's all about. I don't want that. Call me selfish, but I want him all to myself now."

"I understand," Jack said.

"You may think you do, but you don't. What Fletcher's told me about you over the years? You're just like he was. What's the highest compliment you guys give each other?"

Boone said, "He's all cop."

"That's it," she said. "And when I heard people say that about my husband, I knew what it meant, and I was proud. I'm still proud. But I also know what it cost. Because it cost me, too. Well, no more. Don't be trying to take him back."

Jack cleared his throat. "One thing about your husband, Mrs. Galloway: we always knew where he stood. He didn't talk in riddles. I see it runs in the family. Boones and me, we got the message."

"Well, all right, then," she said, standing. This brought all three men to their feet. "I'll say good night. And I'll also say don't make this a habit. Next time you come here it better be because your cholesterol is a quart low. We can talk kids and grandkids and sports and church and anything you want except . . . well, you know."

"Like I say, ma'am, rest assured that Boones and I heard you."

"Then come're and give me a hug, both of you. I'm about to put up my hair and wash my face, so you won't be seeing any more of me tonight."

Dorothy pecked her husband on the cheek and said, "I know where your gun's at, Fletcher."

Fletch widened his eyes in feigned terror and they all laughed. Dorothy wagged a finger at Jack and Boone. "It's got more'n one bullet."

When she was gone, the three men sat quietly staring at the floor.

"Wow, you're a lucky man, Chief," Boone said.

"You don't have to tell me."

"Just saying, I'd give anything to have a wife who'd say something like that at the end of my career."

Galloway nodded. "The end isn't easy. But it's easier when you're happy with your partner. She worried about me, prayed for me, every minute I was on duty. Even the last twenty years when I was behind the desk and not likely to see action."

"Because she knew," Jack said. "I remember at least three times when you went right to the scene, while the action was still going down. No one expected you to. No one would have even questioned your waiting for a briefing. But your men were out there, so—"

"So was I. There's a way to do a job and a way not to do it."

"And you always did it the right way."

"Okay, enough shinin' each other's shoes," Galloway said. "I want both barrels, and I want 'em now. What's happening?"

"Well, Boones here is going to fill you in, but first we've got to get something out of the way. It's about whether you're officially retired yet or are still a sworn offi—"

"We both know the answer to that, Jack, but she doesn't. My official severance date is March 1, but for all practical purposes, I'm out now and nobody—but you and Drake here, apparently—is expecting anything out of me but to act like a retiree. And I've been okay with that up to now."

"You want to keep it that way? Because we don't have to involve you. It's your call."

Fletcher Galloway gave Jack Keller a look that would have put a wart on a gravestone. "Yeah, that's me, Jack. Let you guys show up with some bee in your bonnet that's already stung you clear to the brain, and you think I don't at least want to know what it's about?"

Boone leaned forward. "If I may, Chief . . . As you can imagine, anything big enough to bring us to your door is likely going to be something that will engage you. But it's not going to make you happy. In fact, it's going to turn your stomach. Frankly, I don't think it's something that's going to let you pretend you're carefree, the way Dorothy likes you."

"I'm pretty good at compartmentalizing, Drake. If I have to keep it from her, act like things are okay, I can do that."

"I'm not so sure," Jack said.

Fletcher sat back and sighed. "I'm not going to want to hear this, am I?"

Boone shook his head.

Fletcher stood and moved to the fireplace, turning his back on Jack and Boone. He grabbed a brass tool and poked at a log. "Is it what I feared?"

Jack and Boone looked at each other. "Not sure we know what you feared, boss," Jack said.

Fletcher turned to face them, suddenly looking his age. "Pete Wade." He settled back on the couch, somehow appearing heavier now, sodden, as if it would take the both of them to help him up again. "We go way back, Jack. You know that."

Jack nodded.

"We worked together before there was a policy manual. Before Personnel became Human Resources. Before affirmative action and sexual harassment and anger management and political correctness. Back then every other cop had your back and you had his, and there was never even a question. We would have taken a bullet for each other."

Boone was grateful Jack let the silence hang in the air, lending gravity to Fletcher's memories.

Galloway covered his face with his hands and rubbed his eyes. "I knew this didn't smell right. I as much as flat-out told you that, didn't I, Drake?"

"You did. I thought you were just making me feel good because you knew I had a thing for Haeley."

"You ought to know me better'n that. I don't say things

to make people feel good. I told you I disagreed with Pete, thought he was on the wrong track. But you've got to trust a man you've known as long as I've known Wade and who has that much history with you."

"Forgive me for asking," Jack said, "but is that why you left so soon after the big bust and Boone's shooting? You knew something was fishy in your own office and you wanted to distance yourself from it?"

Galloway seemed to study the ceiling. "I wouldn't do that. I wasn't running from anything. I hoped it would go away and my fears would be proven wrong. But it didn't sit right. One thing that won't surprise me is that young Ms. Lamonica is in the clear. Am I right about that?"

"Yes. Boones has been personally investigating the case for her attorney."

"Fritz." That brought a wry smile to Fletch's face. "The guy we love to hate and hate to love. Perfect choice. Anyway, if I know Haeley Lamonica, there was no way she had any part in this, unless by accident. I mean, that would be serious, but not a crime."

"She's going to be cleared," Boone said. "But Pete is dirty. There's no other way to say it, and I know you don't want anything but the unvarnished truth."

"You got that right. Now when you say dirty . . ."

"You're going to have to hear it all," Boone said. "Then you'll know. The tough part is that it goes well beyond this case."

"Don't tell me that! This case is enough! Something he did almost got a fellow officer killed. Almost got a prime witness killed. There doesn't have to be any more."

"And yet there is, Fletch," Jack said. "I'm so sorry to have to dump this on you. But there is."

Fletcher Galloway slowly rocked until he was in position to rise again. He shuffled into the kitchen. "You guys need anything?"

They didn't respond.

The old man opened the refrigerator and stood staring in. Finally he idly grabbed a bottle of water and slowly returned. He looked as grave as Boone had ever seen him, and the last thing Boone wanted was to lay out such a devastating case.

But there was no way around it.

Galloway removed the cap from his water bottle but made no move to drink from it. He just sat shaking his head and breathing loudly through his nose.

26

★★★★

BOONE'S ASSIGNMENT

Jack led Boone painstakingly, deliberately, as he laid out every scintilla of evidence he had uncovered.

Boone wondered whether Fletcher Galloway would have the energy to stay with him, the stamina even to stay awake. But as he ticked off the litany of revelations, it struck him again that the older man had been much more than a suit, a desk cop, an executive. He had paid his dues, earned his chops, demonstrated street smarts, and embodied all the other clichés fellow cops used about the old-timers.

Galloway's eyelids didn't seem to even flicker as the clock dragged on. Rather, it appeared the man began to smolder like the dying embers in the fireplace. As the room cooled, Fletch seemed to fold in upon himself, his body segueing into heat-conservation mode. His brow was knit, and he squinted as he took in the awful information.

He had begun with his hands in his lap. Soon he slid them under his thighs. Finally he crossed his legs and then his arms. By the end he was swaying slightly as the terrible weight of the allegations seemed to settle over him.

It was midnight when Boone finished, and his temptation to keep rehashing details was thwarted by Jack's look—which wouldn't have been clearer if he had dragged a finger across his throat. Fletcher finally looked away, tucking his lower lip behind his upper teeth and clearing his throat. Finally he took a drag on the water. Boone felt as if he had just told the man one of his children had been murdered.

Fletch suddenly seemed distracted by the fireplace. He unfolded himself and rose slowly, making a ceremony of untying and loosening his robe, then closing it again and retying it. He shuffled to the hearth, where he rebuilt the fire with fresh kindling and logs.

As the flames grew and the moisture in the wood heated and snapped and hissed, Galloway kept his back to Boone and Jack, warmed his hands, then thrust them into the wide pockets of the robe. He stood there, head down.

Boone shifted and inhaled, ready to express his sympathy for what Fletch had just learned about his old friend. Jack held a finger to his lips. Keller knew the boss. If he felt it important to just let him be, let him find his own voice, Boone could do that.

At last Fletch turned to face them. "You boys ready for something to drink now?"

Boone started to decline, but Jack asked for a water, so he

followed suit. With Fletch a few steps away in the kitchen, Jack whispered, "Just let him get used to this."

When he returned, the old chief tossed the bottles to the cops and sat again, finding his own bottle. He tilted his head back, downing the rest. Fletcher screwed the cap back on and fired the bottle into the kitchen trash more than fifteen feet away.

"Probably give me a headache," he said, massaging his forehead with probing fingers. "That'd be a relief."

He let out a low, resigned expletive, then glanced quickly at the ceiling as if fearing his wife could hear him. "Forgive me, boys," he said. "You know I'm a churchgoin' man and I know better. But sometimes no other word works."

Boone had not expected to feel so for a man in such pain.

"You know what this reminds me of?" Galloway said. "Jackie Selebi."

Boone raised his eyebrows at Jack, who nodded.

"That Interpol guy," Jack said.

"Hero of mine," Fletcher said. "Man of color in a place like that . . ."

"Not familiar," Boone said.

Fletcher pressed his lips together. "He went from being a member of South Africa's parliament to president of Interpol. I heard him at an international conference once. Tried to model myself after the man. Then more'n ten years ago he gets named South Africa's police commissioner. His acceptance speech, about how he would attack corruption so they could 'fight crime with clean hands'—something like that— man, that was good, so inspiring. . . ."

"You've made copies of that for all us command officers," Jack said.

Fletcher nodded slowly. "And now he's doing fifteen years."

"For what?" Boone said.

"Taking bribes from a drug-lord murder suspect. I took his picture off my wall, threw away the rest of the copies of his speech. He's appealing the verdict, but I followed the trial. Another one bites the dust. Lot of young cops are gonna have the same reaction when Pete goes down."

Suddenly Fletcher seemed to shake his funk and engage. "How good an actor are you, Drake?"

"Sir?"

"You know what kind of danger this puts Candelario in, right? There's nothing about this case Pete doesn't know. It's obvious he and Fox are in cahoots, and it won't be long before they try again to take out Pascual. We've got to get to Pete before he or whoever he assigns gets to PC, and that could be anybody for all we know. Even somebody already assigned to the safe house."

"But you asked about my—"

"Ability to act. This is going to require a sting. You've got to convince Pete that he got to you, won you over, trashed whatever you thought you knew about Haeley, the whole bit. That's the only thing that will slow him. If he thinks you're closing in on the truth, he'll act quick. And if he knows you've found him out, Pascual Candelario's as good as dead."

Boone glanced at Jack. "That's why we're here. But the sting is a new wrinkle. Leave it to you to come up with that. Problem is, I'm about to keel over and still have to try to get together with Zappolo yet tonight. If I don't get some sleep—"

"Where you gonna sleep, man?" Fletch said. "From what you tell me, not your apartment. You go back to the safe house and Pete and Garrett have you and Candelario together, just where they want you."

"He can stay with Margaret and me," Jack said. "But how do we stall Pete in the meantime?"

"Text him," Fletch said. "Not at this hour. Too suspicious. Just tell him he was right and you need to talk when you get in. Bang it out now and schedule it to go a little after eight in the morning tomorrow."

"How do you know all this techie stuff, Chief?"

"I got grandkids."

"So, we get him slowed down," Boone said. "Then what? We've still got to get PC and his family out of there."

Fletcher sighed. "Don't know. Don't care."

Boone shot him a double take. "You serious?"

"'Course not. That's just my way of saying that you have the best planning man sitting right next to you. When I had a problem like this, I assigned it to Jack and quit worrying about it. This one is trickier, though. While you're trying to sting one of the smartest cops in the history of the CPD, Keller has to figure a way to get an oversize, tattooed Mexican and his mother and child away from a safe house without even his guards knowing it. I wouldn't wish it on anybody else."

"Getting them out of there is one thing," Jack said. "Finding a new place for them is another. Where in the world . . . ?"

"First things first, Jack," Fletch said. "Get Boone to Zappolo and then to bed, will you? He needs to be getting his sorry self ready for surgery, and we've got him in the middle of this mess."

"Don't worry about me," Boone said. "I'm worried about you."

"Me?" Fletch said. "This isn't the first time I've had my heart broke. Maybe you didn't know, but Dorothy and me, we had a prodigal."

"I didn't know."

"That says a lot for Jack. Man knows how to keep a confidence."

"Dang straight," Jack said. "Nobody's business but yours. Anyway, she came back to you, didn't she?"

"To us and to God, thank the Lord. Little ones of her own now. She'll find what a pain parenting can be sometimes."

"That how you feel about Pete?" Boone said. "Like a son?"

Galloway shook his head. "More like a younger brother. But it's not like he can come back from this the way our sweetie did. Tell you one thing: one of you two pulls something like this on me, I'm more likely to put a bullet in you."

Boone forced a smile. "That what happens to cops who have been married a long time? They and their wives decide to settle everything with a weapon?"

"Fortunately," Fletch said, "both of us are all bark and little bite. But one of you failing me like Pete has would be hard to take. Him? I don't know. Shocks me in one way. But there were always parts of him I didn't know—guess that's obvious now. I mean, I thought we were close. But we never were, not really. Not off the job. That's the true test."

"You and I haven't been close off the job either, boss," Jack said.

"Yeah, but you weren't secretive about anything. I knew about every wife and girlfriend. I knew I could drop in on you anytime and you'd welcome me. I didn't ever get that sense from Pete. Now I know why. Sad, man. Just flat sad."

"Sorry," Boone said. "I wish I'd had different news."

"I'm sorry too," Fletcher said. "But I'm going to get some satisfaction out of seeing him busted. Nothing gets to me like one of our own breaching the public trust. That was some job you did. Your emotions could've gotten in the way, but it looks to me like you just logged the hours and stayed after it. Good, solid detective work."

"Thanks, but there wasn't much joy in it. It's nice to know I'm going to clear Haeley, but what she went through . . ."

"It could've been worse. Take satisfaction in that." Fletcher rose and walked them to the back door. "You sting 'im good, Drake, and Keller here will plan the escape. Keep me posted, but otherwise, for the sake of my marriage, I need you to leave me out of it, hear?"

As Jack pulled away from the house, Boone saw the light go out in the family room where they had met and noticed a light still on upstairs.

"So much for Dorothy not caring about the details," Boone said.

Jack shook his head. "Believe me, he'll tell her precious little."

Boone phoned Zappolo and told him Jack would join them. They agreed on the 'Round the Clock restaurant on North Sheridan.

"You sure that's what Jack wants?" Fritz said. "We have history."

"Give me that phone," Jack said, wrenching it from

Boone's hand and laughing. "I heard that, you rascal. You've got history with every self-respecting cop. Every bad guy we bust, you get 'im exonerated."

"So, one of us is doing our job."

"Boones has done his on this case, so you're getting this one handed to you on a silver platter."

"Look forward to seeing you too, Jack."

Boone fought to stay awake and realized he had lost the battle when he awoke as Keller parked at the restaurant.

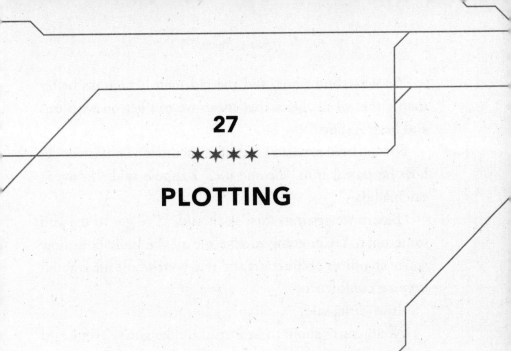

27

PLOTTING

Boone dragged himself into the 'Round the Clock restaurant, still stuffed from dinner. It warmed him to see Fritz Zappolo looking every bit as frazzled as he. The lawyer wore a steel-gray suit with all the trimmings: patent leather shoes, tasteful jewelry, a silver collar stickpin, an iridescent tie, manicured fingernails, and coif slicked back just so. But the bags under his eyes lay in dark circles, and if Boone hadn't known better, he would have said the man's pupils were fixed and dilated.

Usually courtly and deferential, Zappolo made no attempt to stand. He just nodded wearily as Boone and Jack joined him in a secluded booth.

"You look like I feel, Drake," he said.

"You stole my line."

"So we're both shot, and the old man here looks better than either of us. Does that mean we can get on with this and keep it short?"

Fritz ordered a massive breakfast that made Boone wonder how he stayed trim. "So sue me," Zappolo said. "I haven't eaten all day."

"Before we get into this," Jack said, "I've got to tell you something. You're going to give me all the bull about how you're an officer of the court and that your whole life is about keeping confidences—"

"It is," Fritz said.

"Well, you're about to hear stuff unlike you've ever heard before, and it involves a dirty cop. If it gets out before we can stop him, lives are in danger, so—"

"Jack, listen to me," Fritz said. "I know we pull each other's chains all the time, and maybe we do come at the law from fundamentally different perspectives. But you need to know that I take this stuff seriously. You don't have to worry about me breaking confidences, especially if lives are on the line. Okay?"

"I appreciate it," Jack said.

Somehow Zappolo ate every bite of the colossal breakfast, never taking his eyes off Boone as he rehearsed everything he had learned. Jack leaned away from the table, and Boone heard him letting Margaret know they would have a guest and that she shouldn't wait up.

When Boone's recitation ended, Zappolo slid his empty plate to the middle of the table. "I think you just saved my career."

"Were you seriously worried?" Jack said.

"You bet I was. You know what I'm doing for this guy?"

"Harboring a fugitive, the way I hear it."

"Keep your voice down. It appears now that I am merely being a champion of justice. One can't, by definition, harbor an innocent party. I'm merely protecting her from false arrest."

"Did you just use the word *innocent*?" Boone said.

"Guilty. I mean, yes, innocent. I won't lecture you anymore. She's not just 'not guilty.' She's innocent."

"I'd love to hear you say that just one more time."

"In your dreams. I don't grovel."

"Just thank the kid," Jack said. "He saved your bacon."

"Kudos," Zappolo said. "And I mean that, Drake. I seriously thought the best I was going to be able to do was to keep the little boy's name out of the record. Now it appears I'll keep even her out of court."

"I never worried about her being convicted."

"You should have. This was hardly a slam dunk. In fact, I wouldn't have bet against the other side. Now I'm licking my chops over the potential wrongful arrest suit."

Boone rubbed his eyes and yawned, the deep ache in his shoulder telling him it was time for more meds. But he didn't want Jack to have to carry him into his and Margaret's apartment. "So, all that blather about your not caring whether Haeley was guilty—"

"Was just that. You knew it. On one level, it's true. I've defended a lot of guilty people. I have a job to do and I do it the best I know how."

"Tell me about it," Jack said. "I don't know how you sleep."

"Like a baby, and don't go for the old joke, Jack. So what're you going to do about your real problem?"

"Still trying to process Wade," Keller said.

"You may not have much time."

"No! You're a cop now too? Just keep all this privileged, will you?"

"No! You're a lawyer now too? Just let me get to bed, will you?"

WEDNESDAY, FEBRUARY 10, 2:00 A.M.

Boone timed his meds so he was still ambulatory by the time he and Jack reached Jack's apartment. But just barely.

"Margaret's got you in her reading room."

"Concrete floor would work for me."

"Then you'll be thrilled."

Boone was. The tiny room at the other end of the apartment from Jack and Margaret's bedroom was cozy with a firm bed. She had laid out some clothes for him, and a bathroom sat next door. There he found a drape of plastic sheeting and adhesive tape, no doubt Jack's idea.

Boone slowly undressed and collapsed into the bed, but just before he turned off the bedside lamp, he was distracted by Margaret's bookshelves. Images were swimming, but he was certain he saw some Christian books, authors whose names he recognized, even a few Bibles in various translations.

He didn't want to be judgmental, but Margaret was Jack's live-in girlfriend, and he thought she had as many former husbands as Jack had former wives. Could she be interested in spiritual things?

Boone reached for the lamp and found it too far. He would have to wrench himself up and over. But that could wait while he mustered the strength and energy. Several seconds later he forced his eyes open, only to find that the lamp seemed even farther away now. *Give me another minute,* he told himself. But soon he was drifting, drifting.

Boone had to quit living like this. He had gotten a full night's sleep the night before, but now he had ruined it by going a hundred miles an hour all day and half the night. How long could he sleep in? Neither Jack nor Margaret would wake him, but he and Jack had planning to do. Whatever happened, he didn't want to spook Pete Wade. Everything had to look normal.

Boone woke a couple of minutes before 9 a.m., the lamp still on but the shade and curtains pulled tight against the sun. He also smelled breakfast—Margaret seemed to think of everything. Jack had told him more than once that she was the smartest and kindest woman he had ever been involved with. She sure seemed good for Jack.

Boone had become more proficient at managing his showering, shaving, and dressing with one hand. It still took longer than normal, of course, but certainly not twice the time, as it had in the beginning. When he was ready to go, Boone felt surprisingly perky.

Somehow Margaret looked her usual outdoorsy self even first thing in the morning. Jack always looked the same, as if he had already worked out and was ready to go. Which was true.

Jack suggested they eat quickly and get going. "We've got a lot of talking to do on the way, and I don't think it should look like we came together. You go in and I'll find some reason to call in late."

"Oh, Jack, let the boy take his time and eat."

"You know I can't tell you what's going on, Margaret, but trust me, we don't have time to dawdle."

"Well, then, eat."

Boone was intrigued to see Margaret bow her head briefly before she picked up her fork. He squinted at her. "I don't want to embarrass you, ma'am, but—"

"You embarrass me by calling me ma'am."

"Well, you just called me a boy."

"Compared to us, you are a boy, Boone. But I'm sorry. I won't call you boy if you don't call me ma'am. That *really* sounds old."

"Anyway, were you just praying there?"

"That okay with y'all?"

"'Course. I just . . . I mean, I didn't—"

"You didn't know I was raised like you? Church and Sunday school, VBS in the summers, Bible camp, the whole thing."

"No kidding?"

"You're wondering what happened?"

"I didn't say that."

"But you're surprised?"

Boone shrugged and nodded.

"We don't have time for this right now," Jack said.

Margaret raised an eyebrow. "So how is it you told me all about Boone being a born-againer and you didn't tell him about me?"

"That's your business. Let us get past our case and you two can have a prayer meeting or whatever it is you types do."

"Don't you love it, Boone?" she said. "Now we're typed."

Boone didn't want to get in the middle of it, but he was shocked.

"You're wondering how a Christian girl grows up to live in sin."

"Margaret, listen," Boone said, "I know how life can invade. When I lost my family—"

"You had a crisis of faith, Boone. You didn't turn to the dark side. C'mon, you're curious."

"Don't assume I'm going to tell you how you should live."

"Well, I want to talk about it. But I'm gettin' the evil eye from my man here, so another time."

Boone realized he must have looked embarrassed.

"Don't worry about us," Margaret said. "The ol' man adores me."

28

★★★★

THE APPROACH

By the time Jack wheeled into the parking garage downtown at Chicago Police headquarters, Boone had texted Pete Wade. He had first bounced off Jack the idea of just informing Pete that they needed to talk.

"That could spook him, Boones. You have to make him think he's gotten to you, not make him worry about what you've found."

So Boone texted, *Pete, I'm going to be in the office later today. Open for lunch? Crow is on the menu for me.*

"Perfect," Jack said. "I'm going to make myself scarce so he doesn't see us together. Keep me posted."

"I feel as nervous as when we were transferring PC," Boone said. "This shouldn't be dangerous."

"Of course it will. This'll be as important and dicey a conversation as you've ever had. You blow this and he gets the drift that you're onto him, well, you know what that means for Pascual and his family."

"Thanks for nothing."

"It's not my job to make you feel better, Boones. You *should* be nervous. Use that edge. Fletch asked you how good an actor you were."

Boone just sat nodding, wishing he could put this off. Maybe even till after Monday's surgery. Dealing with the pain and the meds and worrying about the operation—not to mention the memory of the gunshot—had left him few resources.

Boone hoped he could somehow soldier through this and do what needed to be done. If he and Jack and anyone else involved could succeed at taking down Wade and Fox and protect PC and his family—and Boone—in the process, there would be plenty of time for sleep later.

He could go into his open-shoulder surgery with a sense of accomplishment, and Haeley would be free and able to be there for him.

As long as he had to have his body repaired, this could be the best of all possible worlds. Put bad cops away. Protect a witness and his family. Preserve his own future. Pursue a life with Haeley and Max. And turn down the Chicago Police Department's lucrative early-retirement offer and take the chief's job in the new Major Case Squad.

As Boone made his way through the frigid, echoing

parking garage toward the elevators to the Organized Crime Division, he forced himself to focus. He had one job: convince Pete Wade that he had pulled the wool over Boone's eyes. That was the only way to buy time.

For the sting to be effective, Boone had to get Pete to drag it out of him. He couldn't appear too eager. If he barged in, pushing Wade to have lunch so he could admit he'd been wrong and Wade right about Haeley, he could look obvious. The key was to make Wade come to him.

Haeley's replacement looked surprised to see Boone. "Thought you were out until after your surgery, sir."

"Technically I am. Just putzing around in my office."

"And if someone calls for you?"

"I have a short list of who I will talk to. And they have my cell number."

"So you're not here?"

"Officially, that's right."

"That our hero?" a voice called from down the hall.

"Hey, Pete," Boone said as flatly as he could manage.

Wade wandered out, smiling. "Got your text. Lunch works for me. The Barrel sound all right?"

Boone worked at looking distracted, somber. "Yeah," he whispered.

Pete followed Boone into his office. "Do we need to talk right now?"

"Nah, it'll wait. Just need a little counsel is all. You know, just wondering where I go from here."

Pete looked concerned. "Sure. I understand. Shall we say twelve thirty?"

As Pete returned to his own office, Boone stepped out and

said to the new woman, just loud enough for Pete to hear, "I won't take any calls from Ms. Lamonica or her lawyer."

"And that is?"

"Friedrich Zappolo."

Boone closed his door, sat in a corner, and called Haeley.

"I was so hoping you'd call," she said, sounding weary.

"Haeley, I need to talk with you sometime about Margaret."

"Jack's Margaret? What about her?"

"It'll keep, but I think she's searching. Spiritually."

"Who'd have guessed?"

"Not me. I've always wondered how to get through to Jack. He'd be such a great believer. Maybe she's the key."

"You have an unusual mind, Boone. All we're going through right now, and you're thinking about Jack's soul."

"Guess that is kinda crazy."

"I'd say it's progress, love. You've been preoccupied for a long time, first about you."

"And now about you."

"And I appreciate it. By the way, I talked with Max and my mother this morning. Your mother got on the line."

"Sorry."

"No, she was great. I'll let her tell you why. I persuaded her to wait for your call. Do call her."

Boone looked at his watch. "Guess I can call her now. You're not going to tell me what it's about?"

"Nope. I'm waiting to hear from Zappolo."

"Yeah, listen, about that—he has more than enough to keep you out of MCC and even get you back on the job, but—"

"He'd better, Boone."

"He even wants to go for the big settlement, but he can't breathe a word of the evidence until we get a few things accomplished on our end. If it gets out, it scotches our whole plan."

"Who's *we*?"

"Jack and me. We've got all the ammunition we need, but we can't fire until the time is right, or it all goes up in smoke. Let me ask you something. I know this is presumptuous, but if you could choose to be a stay-at-home mom, would you?"

Silence.

"Painful subject?"

"Very."

"Sorry. And it's none of my business."

"Well, I hope it's your business, Boone. Or am I totally misreading what's going on between us?"

"I want to be in your future, if that's what you mean."

"So what you just asked is totally your business. Have I not made it clear to you how hard it is for me to leave Max every day? I hate it. I hate myself for it. It's my own fault, and I live with the guilt."

Boone strolled to his door, peeking out to be sure no one was in the area. "I wouldn't blame you if you wanted to be more than—"

"A mom? You and I have a lot of getting acquainted to do. I love my job, and it's where I met you, so I can't complain. Sure, someday I'd like to be in the workforce just by my own choice. But not till Max is in school, and even then only when he's gone from the house."

"Then maybe you ought to start getting your head around the settlement Fritz has been talking about. You were falsely arrested, falsely imprisoned—"

"Would I have to testify about what happened to me at Cook County? Because I wouldn't."

"Not even if it meant enough money so that you would never have to work again unless you wanted to?"

"Who's going to pay that? The department? The city? This wasn't their fault. This is on Pete, and he's not going to pay."

"The CPD, the city—they're insured against suits like this."

"It doesn't feel right."

"You don't have to decide right now."

"Thanks. I do have a few other things on my mind. Meanwhile, call your mom, will you?"

"Too late. She's calling me."

"Call me later, Boone. Bye."

Boone switched calls. "Hi, Mom. I sure appreciate your—"

"Oh, honey, listen. Mrs. Lamonica was so tired by the time they got here that I helped her get Max down and then insisted she sleep all she wanted. She took me up on it and I'm so glad she did. Max is . . . well, what can I say? He loves me! He got up early and came padding out and took to me like I don't know what! He sits on my lap, gives me hugs, and smiles and everything."

"Imagine."

"Yes, imagine. I haven't had this much attention from a child since you and your brothers were little. You're going to have a time pulling this tiny guy away from me. You going to make me his grandma someday?"

"Mom!"

"Well, all right, so he reflects well on his mother. Whatever you think of me, you don't think I'm blind, do you? I can see what's happening between you and Haeley." His mother began whispering. "Her mom is watching Max now, but it's obvious Haeley is a different person now than she was when . . . you know—"

"She made a mistake."

"Exactly. And your father is enamored of this boy too."

"You don't say."

"And his other grandma is delightful."

"*Other* grandma?"

"Okay, I'm ahead of myself. But unless you're asleep at the wheel, you need to see what you have in that girl."

"You don't have to tell me."

"Now how long do we get to keep Max?"

"Not sure. But maybe when things settle down up here, Haeley and I will come down there."

"We'd love that!"

Boone spent the rest of the time before his lunch date riffling through his in-box and checking his computer. Little could keep him occupied, however, as he agonized over the ruse he had to pull on Pete. It would be no small chore, fooling a man who had made a career of reading people.

Boone's fondest wish was to get to the end of this ordeal in time to go into his operation with a clear mind. Maybe Brigita Velna was right. The stress had to catch up to him at some point. Like now. He had to do his best police work ever, when his reservoir of resources was close to an all-time low.

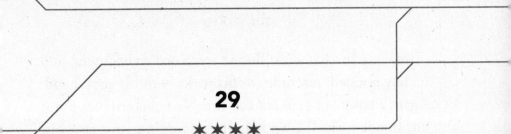

29

★★★★

THE LUNCH

WEDNESDAY, FEBRUARY 10, 12:30 P.M.

"Shall we take my car, buddy?" Pete Wade said, pulling on his long overcoat as he peered into Boone's office.

It was the first time Pete had ever used a familiar moniker for him, but that wasn't all that struck Boone. Pete was normally formal, almost stiff. Unlike most of the personnel in the Organized Crime Division, he generally eschewed suits and ties and wore a uniform at least four days a week, occasionally even his dress blues, as today. What was that about? Maybe he had a meeting with the brass. Boone didn't care to ask. He feared it could mean a meeting with the US Attorney.

Pete rarely offered to drive either, usually using an unmarked squad or allowing a subordinate or at least a newer cop—like Boone—to drive.

Staying in character, Boone remained tight-lipped and merely nodded, reaching for his parka with his good hand. Again wholly out of character, Pete Wade helped him put it on. Boone turned down help from most everyone else, but he didn't want to do anything to interrupt what was going on with Pete. The man was trying to impress him somehow, to endear himself to Boone with a rare air of deference and concern. Maybe Pete was hoping Boone had come to his senses.

As they headed toward the parking garage, Pete actually gently put a hand on Boone's shoulder and guided him out of the elevator. It wasn't that Pete had ever been rude or snooty, but servility had simply never been part of his character.

As they reached the glass door leading to the frigid garage, Pete said, "Why don't you wait here where it's warm, and I'll bring the car around."

Pete seemed to be trying to emasculate him, and every fiber of Boone's being wanted to brush off the offer and show that he wasn't letting an injury hold him back. But he was desperate to communicate to Pete in word and action that he was shell-shocked—not because of his injury but because of what he had learned about Haeley.

So he just nodded and stood inside the glass door, shoulders hunched against the draft. When Pete pulled up a few minutes later in the very car Boone had followed to the Wades' River North condo, Boone headed out into the frosty garage, only to see Pete hurry from the car to open the passenger door.

"Thanks," Boone muttered, gingerly sliding in. Before he could reach for the seat belt, awkward with his right hand but manageable, Pete grabbed it and buckled him in. Boone held his breath at the smell of English Leather cologne, an interesting and archaic choice for Pete.

Boone whispered another weary thank-you, rattled by the usually reserved Wade's having invaded anyone else's personal space, let alone his.

"Sure thing, pal," Pete said. The last time Boone had been spoken to this way was by a salesman. Adjusting the heat while maneuvering out of the garage, Pete said, "So, how's it been going with the shoulder and all?"

Blech. Boone preferred the standoffish Pete to this version. "Slow but sure," Boone said. "I'm going to be obsessive after surgery so I can get back on the job."

"Seriously?" Pete said, waving at the garage attendant as he pulled onto the street. "Impressive. Most guys would jump at the chance for full disability."

"I don't even know if they're going to let me come back."

"*They*? Who's they? It's your call, isn't it, Boone?"

Whose side was Pete on?

"I guess it's my call," Boone said. "Unless it turns out I'm incapacitated."

"The injury that bad?"

Boone shrugged. "We'll know more after Monday. But my goal is to come back to full strength."

"Even if you don't, that doesn't mean you have to retire. It just means you couldn't work the streets."

"They're making retirement pretty lucrative."

"How lucrative?"

As if you don't know. You probably designed the plan. "I'm not at liberty to discuss the details, but like you say, most guys would jump at it. But I don't guess too many people my age have ever been offered full benefits."

"If you were older it might turn your head, hm?"

Pete drove just over a mile and pulled into the tiny parking lot next to a hole-in-the-wall restaurant called the Barrel. "Was that what you wanted to talk to me about, Boone? Your future?"

Pete unbuckled Boone and jogged around to his side of the car to open the door. Between the car and the restaurant their breath came in thick, white clouds.

"I think you know what I wanted to talk about, Pete."

"I suppose I do," he said, holding the door. "Something about eating crow."

Boone nodded and fell silent as the hostess showed them to a table in the back, dark and secluded.

It wasn't like Pete to seem distracted, but soon he was chomping popcorn and pickles as if he'd skipped breakfast. Boone ignored the preliminaries and ordered a chicken sandwich. Pete opted for the Reuben.

"So, what's on your mind, Boone?"

"Like I said, I think you know."

"Disappointed? Feel betrayed?"

"Do I ever. How about you, Pete? Have you ever believed in somebody from your heart and then found out they weren't what you thought they were?"

"You kidding? I've *been* that guy. I told you, my wife sees me as her hero, overachiever, decorated cop, civil servant. And like I said, I'm a deacon. I've felt so bad for so long because Thelma still doesn't know what a scoundrel I was."

"That never came out, all that stuff you told me about?"

"I couldn't have that. It would have killed her. And I have to admit, when I had my chance with, you know, the one who's been deceiving you, well, I almost fell again, man."

She has a name. Can't you even say it? Everything in him wanted to pull his Beretta and put one between this liar's eyes. Boone's phone vibrated. Haeley. Perfect. He hit Ignore, then nodded sadly, as if commiserating.

"Hurts, doesn't it?" Pete said.

"It's the worst."

"I mean, you think you know a person . . ."

Pete had no idea how true his words were.

"Thing is, Pete, where do I go from here? It's not bad enough I lose my family. But time does heal. Not totally, probably not ever completely, but I was making progress."

"I know you were. I saw it. We all did. It's not like you're ever going to get over that, but like you say, you were getting back into the swing of things. It was also obvious you were enamored of, uh, Ms. Lamonica, and for that I owe you an apology."

"You what?"

"I'm telling you, man, I knew from the beginning it was headed for the rocks. People like that, women like her, they don't change. Anyway, hard as it is, be glad you're out of it. She and her cohort are going to do a lot of time, you know."

"Looks that way."

"That scumbag Zappolo got her out of County, but the US Attorney's going to put her in MCC today. Fox is out on bond and eager to sing, but unless he gives up something really good—beyond her, because we've got all we need on her—he's back in the can soon too."

"Doesn't surprise me. That he was dirty, I mean."

"Yeah, but you were in love with the girl, eh?"

"Thought we had a future."

"You still thought so the other day, Boone, when I tried to tell you. I could see you weren't ready to hear it, but you're enough of a cop that you couldn't run from the evidence."

Boone nodded. "Painful."

"I'm sure it was. It was painful for me too."

"You?"

"Of course. Can you imagine? Having to bring charges against a coworker and knowing how that was going to affect a friend like you? One of the hardest things I've ever had to do."

When their meals arrived, Boone had lost his appetite. He needed nourishment, so he took a couple of bites and chewed them till they were mush.

Pete continued, "She wasn't exactly a cop, but we consider even support staff like Haeley brothers and sisters under the blue. I didn't want to have to rat out Fox; he was once one of us too. But the evidence pointed to him, and knowing his history, it wasn't so hard. He was no longer a cop, and we'd all been through so much bull with him."

"But Haeley . . ."

"That was a tough one. But because of our previous encounters, you know, I knew she wasn't what she appeared. And I need you to forgive me for not giving you a heads-up before you got too involved. I'm not saying I knew she would violate the public trust, but I for sure knew you were just going to be one in a long line of men. . . ."

Boone fought with everything in him to keep from

hyperventilating. How he was going to enjoy taking down this scoundrel.

"So can you?" Wade said.

"Sorry?"

"Can you forgive me? As a friend and, I hope, a mentor, I owed it to you to warn you. But I took the easy way out, hoped you'd use your investigative powers, find out on your own, and leave me in the clear. I wasn't a good friend."

Boone's phone vibrated again. Haeley. Of course he couldn't take it.

"That wasn't your responsibility." *Anyway, when were we ever friends, Pete? I always felt like I was supposed to kiss your boots.*

"Yeah," Pete said, "but I should have known that emotions can get in the way of judgment. The keen eye you bring to the street—you wouldn't think you have to bring that to a relationship."

"I forgive you," Boone said, cold inside from the depth of the lie. "Let's put it behind us. I'm suffering right now, but I'll get through it. I just want my head clear for Monday."

"Got a good surgeon?"

"So they tell me. But after the operation, I have no idea what I'm going to do."

Pete wiped his mouth, slid his plate forward, and sat back, his leather squeaking. "Boone, if it was me, I'd take the deal from the department. But it's not me we're talking about."

It will be soon enough.

"But why not, Boone? You've got your whole life ahead of you. You could do just about anything else you wanted. It's none of a new employer's business that you're on full disability. You'd be great teaching at the academy, but you can't double-dip on the city. You want two incomes, don't you? Who wouldn't? You've got yourself a dream situation. And you deserve it."

How quickly Pete had forgotten Boone's pain over Haeley. It was all about setting oneself up for the future.

"I'll think about it," Boone said.

"And you know I'll support you whatever you do, give you stellar references, whatever you need."

"You'd do that for me?"

"Absolutely."

"I'm going to have to think hard for a way to thank you for all this, Pete." *I can hardly wait.*

Wade waved him off. "What are friends for? You can tell me something, though. What made you finally come around and see it?"

"The truth about Haeley?"

Pete nodded.

"Oh, I don't know, maybe finally realizing that I was getting inside information from only the best investigator the Chicago PD has ever had."

Pete dipped his head and seemed to fight a smile. "Oh, I don't know about that."

"I do. That's all I've ever heard. And seen close-up. Frankly, I wish you'd been wrong this time, Pete."

Pete pressed his lips together and looked sad. He peered deep into Boone's eyes. "So do I, friend. So do I."

Back at the office, Pete repeated rushing about to open doors for Boone and pledging his continued support.

On the elevator he said, "And let me just restate. This offer you're talking about? That's a gold mine, the lottery, your ship coming in. I know you still want to be a cop, and take it from one who knows, believe me: you'll always be a good one, one hundred percent physically or not. But take the gift, man. Live the rest of your life on two incomes. What's the downside?"

Boone shook his head. "Hard to see one, Pete; I give you that."

As soon as Boone got to his office he called Haeley.

"I was at lunch with you-know-who," he said. "Talking to you would have completely botched the—"

"I understand, but I can't get hold of Zappolo either, and—"

"You know Fritz is in court. He'll call you as soon as he's free."

"I've had enough of this. I want to see Max."

"Call my parents and talk to him."

"Not good enough. I'm going down there."

"Give it another day, Hael."

"But what if someone already got to Zappolo and they're forcing him to tell them where I'm staying? I could be at Metropolitan before you even know it."

"Zappolo is a pro. He's been down this road before. He'll—"

"He's never harbored a fugitive before."

"You're not a fugitive. There's no such thing as harboring an innocent victim."

"Well, I just wanted to let you know that I'm getting out of here now."

"What?"

"You heard me. I'm renting a car."

"You can't do that without a credit card, which means they could trace you in ten minutes. And how long do you think it would take them to figure out where you might be going? You can't exactly take back roads. Just stay put or you're going to make things worse, not to mention make yourself look guilty. Now hang tight, hear?"

"You're going to make a great husband."

He laughed. "Aren't we getting a bit ahead of ourselves?"

"You love me, Boone. You can't help yourself."

"You got that right." He told her of his phone call from his mother and what she had said about Max and Haeley.

"Max was all it took?" she said. "I could tell she was not thrilled with me. . . ."

"No more. She wants to be Max's other grandma."

"She didn't say that."

"She did."

"You're in trouble, buddy. Both your mom and I want her to be Max's other grandma. Maybe it ought to be you trying to escape."

"Escape from you. That'll be the day."

WEDNESDAY, FEBRUARY 10, 2:00 P.M.

Boone met Jack at a corner three blocks from headquarters and slid into his car, shivering.

"You up on your meds?" Jack said.

"Just took 'em. Ought to be high momentarily."

"Stay with me, Boones. You've got to hear this. Am I brilliant or what? Don't answer yet. I gotta show you something." Jack pulled onto the expressway.

"Where we going?" Boone said.

"Indiana."

"I'll bite."

"I couldn't have this done in Illinois, could I? We don't know who's watching. Now tell me how things went with Wade and I'll tell you about my great idea."

Boone did not get the response from Jack he had hoped for when he rehearsed the whole lunchtime conversation with Pete.

"I don't know," Jack said. "It almost sounds too easy. It's like he knows what you're doing and is trying to convince you it worked. Maybe he's still playing you."

"Don't you think I would have been able to read that?"

"You were pretty nervous."

"True."

"So don't trust your own judgment. Here's the thing: If you did convince him, he might think he's got a lot more time to do whatever he wants to do with Pascual. If he's onto you, the clock is ticking."

"We're not moving slow regardless, right?"

"No. But add into the mix that Pete isn't as convinced as you think he is."

"And you think we've got time for a drive into Indiana?"

"We won't be long. I want you to meet a guy. He's the only friend I got who has two first names, except maybe you. This guy's name is Carl Earl. Worked with me in the 18th in a previous life, took early retirement, and got a job handling security for an RV manufacturer in Elkhart, Indiana. He's doing okay for a lot of years. I see him now and then; he seems happy. Then the whole RV thing goes belly-up with the economy. Only a couple of those firms survived, not including his. So they dive into another business altogether, and surprisingly, a lot of their equipment and technology—with a few modifications—fits the new industry."

"Which is?"

"Tricking out trucks for municipalities. They make garbage trucks, sanitation trucks, snowplows—"

"What's the difference between a garbage truck and a sanitation truck?"

"The kind of sanitation truck I'm talking about are those ones that suck the gunk from septic tanks. So I call Carl Earl and I ask him what kind of truck do they make that has room in it for people. He suggests a garbage truck, only the only way people can get into the back of that is through the scooper—you know, that hydraulic thing that grabs the cans and bags and mashes 'em in there."

"No way for people to get into the back of a truck."

"Right. So he suggests a sanitation truck. Says there's a hole in the top that's like the door of a submarine and allows one person at a time to get down in there. And there's room for plenty."

"Why would anybody ever want to do that?"

"I don't know. In case there's a clog, some problem, something that has to be cleaned out."

"Somehow I love my job even more now."

"I hear you, Boones. Now listen. They're making a half dozen of these trucks right now. Most of 'em are done and ready for painting, putting the city name on the outside, all that. Here's my idea. We have 'em paint 'Addison Streets and San' on the side of one of these new trucks, put some temporary foam padding inside the tank, along with some sturdy handles; then we drive that sucker through some slush and mud so it looks old. Maybe we even spray some stinky stuff on it from another truck."

"And the padding and handles are for . . . ?"

"Pascual and his mom and his kid to have something to hang on to, in case the ride is rough."

"Jack, you're not saying . . ."

"Am I brilliant, or what?"

"How do you come up with this stuff?"

Keller shrugged, looking pleased with himself. "We've got to get them out of there, and every other way I could think of would make it obvious to Pete and whoever's working with him what's happening. We get in there, we clog the toilets. I tell everybody I've called the city to come and check the septic; when that truck shows up, nobody's going to want to get close enough to check it. I'll get Carl to drive it. He'll pull it into the back at just the right place where we can get the family out and into the tank before anybody's the wiser."

"Then where do we take them?"

"I haven't got that far yet. I just want them out of the safe house, which ain't so safe anymore."

"I've got it. Come up with a story about how there's something wrong with the truck and it has to be taken back to the outfitter in Elkhart to check it out. That way, if it gets stopped on the highway because it looks suspicious to a state trooper for an Illinois septic truck to be heading into Indiana, Carl has a story. He can even have paperwork."

"Great, Boones! And no statey is going to want to peek into the back of a septic truck."

"We're some team, Jack. I can't wait to see this truck."

30

✴ ✴ ✴ ✴

PROGRESS

Boone wouldn't have recognized Carl Earl as a cop if he'd been wearing a badge. The fat man in his late sixties who emerged from the security shack at the Elkhart truck plant wore untied construction boots, no socks—or maybe anklets or socks that had slid from view—denim coveralls over a bare chest, and an unzipped sweatshirt that provided little protection from the lake-effect, below-zero gusts.

Carl was freckle faced and hatless, despite that he was bald on top with a rim of gray hair that extended over his ears. And he wore gold reading glasses perched precariously on the end of his nose.

He gave Jack a bear hug and shook hands with Boone. "The hero," he said. "I always had that in me, just never the chance to prove it." And he roared with laughter.

"Aren't you cold?" Boone said.

Carl nodded toward the security shack. "Hot as fire in there. Anyways, I got my own installation—" obviously meaning *insulation*. "Been buildin' it up for years!"

He led the cops to an auxiliary white cement-block building at the back of the complex. "Handlin' this job myself," he said. "Obvious reasons."

"Good idea," Jack said. "But I didn't know you were a handyman."

"Built my own house, man. And believe it or not, from wood I harvested from my own tree farm."

"Are you kidding me?" Jack said.

"God's honest truth, JK. Tuned up my own cars too, back when we had to do that kinda thing. Also made myself one of the weapons I used to carry on the street. You knew that."

"I did. It was a monster that shot .50 caliber bullets, wasn't it?"

"That's the one. Watch commander put the kibosh on it. Stewie Lang—'member him?"

"Sure. He's at the 11th now."

Carl raised his eyebrows. "That right? Said he'd never be able to explain to the brass or the press if one of his guys blew a hole like that in a bad guy. Tell you what, there woulda been no wounding anybody with that sucker. Death was the only option."

"You still got it?"

"Shore do. I've hunted with it."

"You have not!"

"I swear. Kilt myself more'n one deer with it. Gotta be sure, though, to get 'em in the head. Normally you wanna shoot a deer through the heart, you know, to be humane about it. But with that monstrosity I'd get so many bullet and bone fragments in the meat that you had to eat careful like."

"You're incorrigible."

"That's nothin'. You know what Jimmy used to like?"

"Your little guy?"

"He ain't so little anymore, Jack. He's almost as big as me. In his forties now."

"No way!"

"Kids of his own. Anyway, when he was little, we'd be out huntin' deer, him with a Winchester and me with my .50, and he'd goad me into shootin' squirrels. Still feel bad about that. Those tiny varmints didn't stand a chance and never knew what hit 'em. That baby made stew of 'em, one shot. Would you believe I did that twice and actually lost sleep over it? I'm no pacifist, but I couldn't make that justifiable, so I quit doin' it."

"Admirable," Boone said.

"Well, doing it even once was shameful."

Inside the building, they came upon a gleaming new white tanker truck.

"Tricked out nice for a municipal vehicle," Carl said. "It's got a digical clock and peda-stool seats."

Boone bit his lip to keep from bursting. How he wished he could spend more time with this fountain of malapropisms.

"What's the smell?" Jack said.

"Glue."

He led the men around the other side of the truck, where two one-gallon cans of glue sat on a pallet. "I know I ought to shut one of 'em at least, but I'd rather the smell and the fumes distipate a bit out here than in the tank when I'm down in there."

"Makes sense," Jack said.

"I can only spend about twenty minutes down in there at a time as it is. Kids get high on that stuff, so they tell me, but I just get a headache and dizzy. Hard to breathe. Can't be good for you. 'Course, I don't suppose too many people carry glue into a tanker truck anyway."

"What's it for?" Boone said.

"Gluin' foam mats to the walls. Jack tells me you want to put people in there while she's rolling. Gonna be hard to keep your feet, though, even with the handles."

"How'd you manage those?"

"Glued two-by-fours to the sides and screwed 'em into those. Wasn't easy, either, because those walls are round. But I figured it out. It's what I do. Wanna see?"

"Sure," Boone said, not sure how he'd manage the built-in iron ladder with one hand.

"Just watch the wire comin' from the ceiling. Leads to the only light I got in there. I wouldn't climb down in, but you ought to be able to see okay from the top."

Boone shed his parka and started up, feeling it in his shoulder as he kept his left arm pressed to his chest and fought to stay steady. At the top he reached the manhole and peered in. The hanging light illuminated an area about six feet square that Carl Earl had fashioned with the kind of foam panels you see at the end of a gym, where basketball players hit the wall on fast breaks. They were wider than the opening.

"How'd you get these through the hole?" he said.

"Just folded 'em over. Wasn't easy, but I managed. They

popped right back into shape. Trouble was, they wanted to straighten themselves out when I was gluing them to the wall too, but eventually I got 'em to work. One advantage of being a big man, know what I mean?"

"No, what *do* you mean?"

"I just glued the wall and glued the back of the panels, then pressed my big old backside against the panels till they stuck. Guy I arrested once asked me if I carried a red hankie in my back pocket so I could make the wide turns. Even I had to laugh at that one."

Boone saw the two-by-fours adhered to the sides, bearing the steel handles. "So, you're done?"

"Well, that's all Jack asked for, but the engineer side of me says you need more."

"What would you add?" Jack said as Boone made his way back down.

"Seating," Carl said. "Found a couple of old car bench seats with seat belts still on 'em." He pointed to them in the corner.

"The Candelarios aren't going to be in there that long, Carl."

"Yeah, but it could be an hour or more at least, am I right?"

Jack nodded.

"I've seen pictures of the Mexican. He's bigger'n I am. He wouldn't have much trouble. But you say there's a grandma and a little boy? They ought to have places to sit, and even use the seat belts."

"How long would that take?"

Carl Earl shrugged. "Not long. I can do it yet today. Unless you need to take it with you when you go."

"I hope I don't. I'm looking for you to drive it, maybe as soon as tomorrow."

"Count on me gettin' it done."

"Can't thank you enough."

"Yes, you can. I'll bill ya."

For the next half hour the three men sat at a tiny wood table in the corner, and Jack outlined the plan. "As soon as you hear from me, you start heading our way. Depending on the time of day and the traffic, you should reach Addison in a little over two hours. Wear something that looks authentic for a city septic-truck driver."

Jack drew a map for Carl and told him he would pave the way by creating the plumbing problem and letting the guards know to allow the truck in. "And you can dirty up the truck so it doesn't look like it just came off the assembly line?"

"Oh, yeah. My sign painter's coming in 'bout half an hour." He pulled from a pocket a sketch of what he had asked the man to paint on the side. "They do the stencil in their shop, then spray it on here in just a few minutes."

"I hope you didn't give 'em this spelling of *Addison*," Jack said. "It's got two *D*s, you know."

The fat man looked stricken. "What? I had the wife proofread this!"

"Chill, Carl. I'm kidding. It's perfect."

"Why, I oughta . . ."

It was dark, and traffic crawled all the way back to Chicago. Boone had taken his meds and should have been mellow, but he was agitated. Something wasn't sitting right.

"Sit still, Boones," Jack said. "When I hit jams like this,

I just resign myself to it. There's nothing we can do but ride it out. There's nowhere to go."

"I'm not worried about the traffic, Jack. Doesn't it strike you as odd that I haven't heard from Haeley or Zappolo by now? Fritz should have been out of court by lunchtime and have gotten back with her."

Jack shrugged. "Don't make too much of it. Maybe he had good news and she didn't want to bother you."

"I don't know. I don't like it."

"So call her."

Boone was reaching for his phone when it rang. Fletcher Galloway.

"Put me on speaker. There's not anybody else there but you and Keller, is there?"

"No, go ahead."

"I got to talk low, because I told the wife you guys just needed a little advice about a case, I gave it to you, and that was the end of it. But I've been noodling this thing and something jumped out at me. Did I get it right that after the break-in at your apartment, you loaded stuff in Haeley's mother's car, then went to see her, and when you got back, the car had been ransacked?"

"Right," Boone said. "And it made us wonder if it was coincidence. Whoever came to the apartment was after me. But if it was the same guys who messed up the car, why didn't they just stake it out and follow me to the safe house?"

"Exactly. Try this on for size. They were just trying to rattle you, throw you off your game, zig when they should have zagged. But they made a big mistake. They told you something they didn't intend to. They didn't need to follow you to the safe house. They wanted to ensure you would go there, worried about who was trashing your apartment and your car, but they didn't need to follow you."

"Because?"

"Think it through, Drake. Because they know where it is."

Boone looked at Jack and shrugged. "All due respect, Chief, but we figure they're working for, you know, the inside guy, and we know he knows where the safe house is. We're worried he's got guys on the inside there, working for him when we think they're working for us."

"Right, but all these guys having all this inside knowledge has me wondering who else they know. How wired in are they? I don't want to say names over the phone, but think of who this guy knows and has worked with over the years. Besides colleagues throughout the department, he knows your lawyer. He knows our evidence guy. He knows people in the US Attorney's office. You see where I'm going?"

"He knows a lot more than we think he knows."

"'Fraid so. Sorry, boys. I'm just saying, you'd better act fast and get your people to safety."

Though the blower was filling the car with heat, Boone shivered. "I've got to ask you, Chief. Do you think there's any way he could know the other, uh, hiding place? Where my friend is?"

"I wouldn't be surprised. And here's why. Your guy, the lawyer, has a history of stashing people here and there. Witnesses, clients, you name it. He's got his favorite places for that kind of thing. Even I know one or two of them. If I was looking for somebody he was hiding, I'd know where to start at least."

"I haven't heard from my friend for quite a while. And I should have. Thanks, Chief. We'll keep you posted."

"Better not. I'm on thin ice with the wife here. Made some promises I got to keep."

"So maybe we just text you?"

"I don't even speak that language, Drake. We'll have you guys over for a barbecue in the spring and you can tell me all about it."

7:04 P.M.

"Talk about a guy retiring before his time," Jack said.

"Yeah, I'm impressed too, but he just made me sick."

"Channel it, Boones. You can whimper or you can take action. Let's get to work."

Boone called Haeley and got her voice mail. His mind raced. If someone was monitoring her phone, he had to confuse them and reassure her. He affected his breeziest tone, as if he suspected nothing and hadn't a care in the world.

"Hey, Hael, it's me. I'm here with Max. See you soon for pizza. Call when you get a chance."

Boone dialed Zappolo, and all he heard was Fritz's voice. "Secure line." *Click.*

"Now what am I supposed to do, Jack? Zappolo wants me to call his secure line, and I have no idea . . . Wait."

"What?"

"I'll try Stephanie in his office."

"It's after hours," Jack said.

"I've got to try." He dialed.

"You have reached the after-hours recording for Friedrich Zappolo and Associates." It was Stephanie's voice. And despite what she said, it sounded live. He had called after hours before, and the voice had been a professional and the message different. "If this is an emergency, you may call our live answering service at the following number. . . ."

"Write this down, Jack!"

Keller scribbled on a pad on the dash. "Aren't we a pair?" he said. "Me driving and you crippled. What's up?"

Boone put the scrap of paper in his lap and dialed.

"This is Stephanie, Mr. Drake. Thank God for caller ID."

"And that was you on the so-called recording, wasn't it? Live?"

"The plan worked. Mr. Zappolo is pretty good at these things. He knew you'd call asking for the secure number."

"So, what is it?"

"I'm it. You've reached my cell. There is no secure phone. Here's what's happened. Someone somehow has breached our security. All three hotels Mr. Z uses to stash people had their fire alarms triggered just after dark. Hundreds of people filed out into the streets until the all-clear signal was given. At the end of it all, Ms. Lamonica did not return to her room."

"Someone got her?"

"That's our fear. Mr. Zappolo told me to tell you he thinks it's the one you believe is behind all this. He could have had people stationed at the three hotels watching for her. Then they probably identified themselves as working for Mr. Z and said she was to come along and meet him."

"She was desperate to hear from him," Boone said.

"Mr. Zappolo suggests that you—I'm reading his scribbled note here—'trigger whatever plan you have to protect your charges.' I assume you know what that means."

"Got it. Thanks."

"Officer, if there's anything I can do . . ."

"I've got your number. Thanks for staying late and all that."

Jack immediately called Carl Earl. "Got an emergency, Carl. What's the status of the truck?"

"Welded the seats in, belts and all. Sign done, paint almost dry."

"Can you leave right now?"

"I can, Jack, but ain't no way I'll make Addison before about nine thirty."

"No choice. You're the man, Carl."

"Can I bring my .50?"

"Don't you dare. I'll see you there."

Both Boone and Jack slid their phones into their pockets, and Boone slammed his fist into his thigh. "I'm dead in the water here, Jack. Someone's got Haeley, and I've got no leads. Plus, we've got to get to the safe house. I've never felt so helpless."

"That Stephanie's something, isn't she?"

"What? Yes, but—"

"I'd like to get her on board at the CPD. Sounds like she'd rather be doing our kind of work anyway, huh?"

"Jack! You're not helping. Yes, I've been impressed by her, but I'm going to kill somebody before I lose another loved one. Can we focus?"

Jack held up a hand, not taking his eyes off the road. "That's what I'm trying to get you to do, Boones. Have I taught you nothing? Now, where are you with your meds and all?"

"Why are we chatting when we should be—?"

"Stop, Boones! Stop!" Jack put both hands on the wheel. "We are stuck in traffic. We're going nowhere fast. Here's the plan: we're going straight to Addison. I'm hoping to beat whoever or whatever Wade has planned for Pascual and his family. We're going to stop up the toilets or make it look like we have, and then I'll tell everybody that Streets and San is on its way. We'll get the family out of there, and then we'll head to Chicago to find Haeley. If we could do it in the opposite order, we would. But it's not like I've got time to drop you anywhere. You want to hitchhike and see if you can find some help?"

"Don't be ridiculous."

"I'm trying to get you to focus, man. By the time we leave Addison, we need to know where we're going. I'm going to arrange to have the Candelario family taken into protective custody, and in a few minutes—because, unlike you right now, I'm thinking like a cop—I'll come up with the perfect place. Meanwhile, you need to shake off the pain, the meds, the fear, the emotion, and figure this thing out. You're thinking like a lover and not like a detective. Now I mean it, Boones. You need me to smack you in the face, conk you on the head, what? You know how frustrating it is to try to do your job when an emotional citizen is in your ear."

"Yeah, I do."

"Well, that's how I feel right now. Don't be that guy, Boones. Be my partner again."

Jack was right. Boone smacked his forehead with his open palm. Then again. *Think!* "All right, Jack, listen. Pete's the mastermind; we know that. Fox is probably out of the picture, lying low, hoping for some kind of a deal. Jazzy Villalobos is too recognizable, but he might be one of the shooters at the safe house if Pete sends in marauders.

"Some of the cops assigned as guards at the safe house have to be Pete's guys, but we don't know who. And who would he send to grab Haeley who could pretend to be working for Fritz? Someone who would know where to take her for safekeeping."

"Don't assume safekeeping, Boones. She knows the truth. She's a threat to Pete and his whole future."

"But if something happens to her, it has to look like an accident and be blamed on an overzealous lawyer."

"Right," Jack said. "But who would Wade use who could put her mind at ease enough to get her to go along?"

"The nephew!"

Jack nodded. "Antoine Johnson. That's good. Maybe. Young, good-looking. Doubt she knows him. Take him out of uniform, dress him in a suit, give him a nice car. He sees Haeley on the street, trying to keep warm while the fire department checks out the hotel, tells her he's an associate of Fritz, who asked him to come get her."

"She'd buy that," Boone said, feeling like he was finally thinking like a cop again. "It might eventually dawn on her that it was too coincidental that he happened by when she was outside. Why wouldn't Fritz have called? But in the spur of the moment, she'd go along with him. And to a place no one knows about except family."

"I'm listening," Jack said.

"The River North condo."

"My man," Jack said. "See how you can be when your mind is right?"

"Right? I'm about to jump out of my skin. I want to get units into the area right now, surround the place, see if they can determine whether she's there, protect her."

"Exactly. How are we going to do that?"

"Who do you trust, Jack?"

"I can think of three old-timers who'd die before they turned to the dark side."

"Fletch," Boone said.

"Of course. And we worked under two more just like him at the 11th."

"Heathcliff Jones and Stewart Lang."

"You got 'em, Boones."

"You don't think they'd hesitate because, you know . . ."

"Not a chance. They find out he's dirty, his color won't matter. Those guys are cops first, man. You saw Fletch's reaction. Jones and Stewie will be all over this."

"I'm calling Fletch."

When Galloway answered, he said, "Drake, I told you to leave me out of this for now."

"It's life or death, boss."

"I'm not your boss, and I can't be doing anything—"

"Your weapon handy?"

"Of course, but—"

"You told me yourself you're still a sworn cop. We need you to save lives tonight."

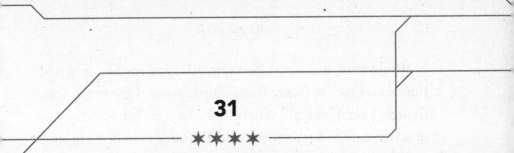

31

★★★★

FIRST MOVE

WEDNESDAY, FEBRUARY 10, 9:40 P.M.

It was one thing, hearing the resolve in Fletcher Galloway's voice and his assurance that "even my wife will understand this." It was another to follow Jack Keller's counsel to keep his emotions—particularly his fear over Haeley's safety—at bay and think like a cop.

That was, Boone knew, crucial to the success of this operation. But even calling this an operation seemed a stretch, because he and Jack were flying by the seats of their pants, using an unmarked squad—stuck in traffic—and a pair of cell phones as their base of operations. The car was outfitted with a police-band radio, but they didn't dare conduct any of their business over a medium so easily monitored.

Fletch agreed with the idea of gathering a small cadre of veterans he would trust, as he said, "with my wife and my life" and told Boone and Jack to "leave River North to me. I got to tell you, though, I get myself killed here in the twilight between the end of active duty and retirement, and Dorothy will kill me again."

The old man also had a great idea. He told Boone, "Zappolo owes us. For the first time he's on our side, so you need to get him to cash in all his chips and find a friendly judge to get us whatever warrants and clearances we need to search residences, even monitor phones. Can you do that?"

"I can ask."

"Finding a judge who can stomach a defense attorney is the chore," Fletch said. "Make sure he knows how bad we need it."

Boone called Stephanie. "Sorry to bother you. Do you have a minute?"

"Officer Drake, I have no life outside the office. I'm in my robe and fuzzy slippers with my hair up, waiting to watch the news, the highlight of my evening."

"Except for helping me out."

"Of course."

"I need Fritz to call my cell from a secure landline. Maybe a pay phone somewhere?"

"A pay phone? Haven't seen one of those in ages."

"Maybe from a friend's house. A phone no one would even think to tap. Problem is, I need to talk to him like yesterday."

"I'm on it."

Boone's phone chirped. A text from Pastor Sosa: *Praying. Check 1 John 4:18a when you get a second. Worth it.*

Boone opened the Bible app on his phone and found the verse: *"There is no fear in love; but perfect love casts out fear."*

Thinking and acting like a pro didn't mean sublimating

his fear, Boone knew. He had been taught well that bravery was anything but an absence of fear. It was the courage to push past fear, to harness it and use it to stay alert.

Boone could not even begin to catalog all that was at stake. A future with Haeley and Max was another form of salvation—not spiritually; he knew better than that. But since the tragedy that had cost him his family and everything he thought he had known about God and life and himself, Boone had been floundering.

Family and friends believed he was on the mend, that his growth had been astounding. He couldn't argue that he had made progress. He had learned that while time was indeed a healer, it was a slow one and not predictable. Waves of emotion still hit him at odd times, woke him in the night, sent him somewhere else while strolling with Haeley or playing with Max. It wasn't fair to them, but what choice did he have? It wasn't fair to him either. It wasn't like Boone chose to be dragged back to a grief so deep and piercing that it was clear he would never be entirely rid of it.

But if there was hope, it was in God, in his faith, in prayer, in Scripture. And the ultimate realization of hope was not forgetting the pain but rather finding a balm for it in the form of a new life, a new love, a new family. To her credit, though Haeley never seemed completely comfortable talking about Nikki and Josh, neither did she seem resentful or indicate any wish that he forget them.

It had to be hard for her, too, in essence competing with the idealized memory of a beautiful woman, her love's first love. Haeley's maturity in this alone was yet another reason Boone so cherished the thought of a future with her.

Was it just his imagination, or did the traffic appear to be abating as Jack skirted the city and set sail for Addison? "We moving a little better?"

"Averaging ten miles an hour faster," Jack said. "It'll open up here in a bit. We should reach the safe house not long after ten."

"This going to look suspicious, our getting a city truck out there in the middle of the night?"

"I'll think of something to make it work," Jack said.

Pray.

It was as if Boone had heard the command aloud. That was a new one for him. He'd been raised a Christian, but not in a tradition where people were spoken to from on high, and he always found himself uncomfortable in the presence of those who were convinced they had been.

And yet here it came again.

Pray.

Boone panicked, worried that God was urging him to pray aloud in front of Jack. He was sure he knew where Jack stood spiritually—respectful, even deferential at times, but nowhere near a man of faith.

Boone decided to pray silently, lowering his head and closing his eyes, knowing he didn't have to do that, either.

As soon as his chin rested on his chest, Boone felt fatigue wash over him. He had skipped his last round of meds and believed that a good idea, given all he had to think about. Being off the narcotics would keep him awake and alert. But there was no arguing that he belonged in bed sound asleep. He fought the drowsiness and told God, *I don't know what to say. I'm listening. I need you; I know that. Keep Haeley safe and help us do whatever we need to do to protect Pascual and his mother and son.*

I will keep him in perfect peace, whose mind is stayed on me. My peace I give to you; not as the world gives do I give to you. Let not your heart be troubled, neither let it be afraid.

Was that God? Had he spoken directly to Boone? Or was Boone just being prompted to remember Scripture? Sosa had always told him that "the Word will not return void."

"Fallin' asleep there, bro?" Jack said.

"Nah. Just praying."

It had slipped out. He'd had no intention of telling Jack, but now it was in the open.

"Well," Jack said, "that can't hurt, I guess."

"Really? Do you pray too?"

"No! Well, yeah, couple of times I have. When I thought I might die. I didn't make any bargains or promises, just called out for help, you know?"

"Sure do."

"One of your kind told me once that God doesn't listen to the prayers of unbelievers, so I can't say whether it got higher than the ceiling."

"Too many of our kind think they know more than they do, Jack. I'm no theologian, but how could a God who created you ignore your cry for help?"

"That's what I kinda hoped. And you know Margaret agrees with you. She's a pray-er, you know. She feels bad because she's living in sin, she says, and she knows God's not happy about that. She told me, 'He's more likely to listen to you than to me right now.'"

Zappolo called.

"You won't believe where I'm calling from," he said.

"Try me."

"I was buying cigars when Stephanie called my cell. My tobacconist let me use his office line. 'Course I've kept him in business for years, so he owes me. What's up?"

Boone told him how desperate they were for warrants and even wiretapping and phone-monitoring privileges.

"That stuff's easier than ever these days," Fritz said, "especially with cell phones. But finding a judge this time of night isn't going to be easy. Not too many look kindly on me, as you can imagine, but I'll do my best."

"But you're on our side this time, Fritz. One of 'em has got to like that. Nobody owes you a favor, anything? Anyone?"

"Hey! You know Peggy Overmeyer?"

"Sounds familiar."

"Name comes with 'the Honorable' before it. Circuit court judge. Known for berating everybody over the smallest stuff—showing up a minute late, misfiling a brief. Loves to show off that way, chastising everybody about the sanctity of the courtroom, specifically *her* courtroom."

"Yeah?"

"Well, *she* owes me. I was in her chambers one day, and she was giving it to me for one thing and another. Then she realizes court's about to be in session, so she jumps up, grabs her robe, and breaks a heel just as she gets to the door. She changes shoes, but she gets to the bench about ninety seconds late. No big deal, but with her reputation, well, she was embarrassed.

"I jogged around the outside of the courtroom and entered from the usual corridor. The other attorneys were eyeing each other and smirking, so I asked permission to address the court. I said, 'Your Honor, I apologize for causing your delay this morning. It won't happen again.'

"She recovered well, said she appreciated that and that, yes, I was forgiven. After the hearing her bailiff said she wanted to see me in chambers. She told me, 'Mr. Zappolo, it was interesting to discover that your heart may not be totally black.'"

Boone enjoyed the story, but time was of the essence. "So, you going to try her?"

"Just hoping she's not an early-to-bed girl."

Boone was relieved to hang up and realize they were already in Addison, less than half a mile from the dirt road that led to the safe house. He had no idea how far behind Carl Earl had to be, but a city worker's being late to an emergency call would only add authenticity.

Boone was dying to know what was happening with Haeley. Guessing she might be at Pete and Thelma Wade's condo was good police thinking, but that didn't mean he was right.

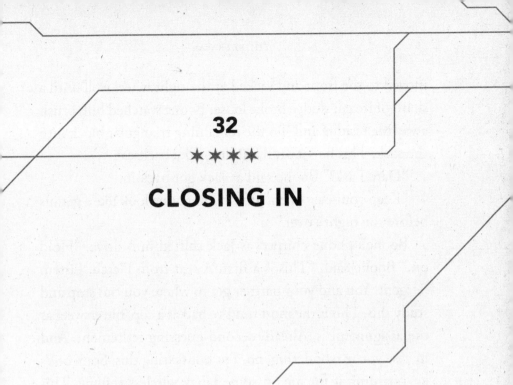

32

★★★★

CLOSING IN

Just outside the area monitored by the Chicago Police Department security unit in charge of the safe house in Addison, Illinois, Jack Keller carefully edged the unmarked Crown Vic squad off the pavement, through a shallow snowdrift, and into a forest preserve parking area.

"What?" Boone said, eager to accomplish whatever needed to be done in Addison so he could make sure Haeley was all right.

"Sit tight," Jack said. "Normally I'd assign you this task, but with you being a cripple . . ."

Jack popped the trunk and slid out of the car. Boone heard him rustling around and then saw that he had apparently removed the jumper cables from their burlap tie sack. Jack moved to the front and kicked at the right wheel well until a shard of frozen sludge broke loose. Boone watched him brush away the residue and slip the remaining triangular block into the sack. This he set on the floor of the backseat.

"Dare I ask?" Boone said as Jack got back in.

"Keep your eyes open, junior. I'm gonna look like a genius before the night's over."

Boone's phone chirped as Jack shifted into drive. "Hold on," Boone said. "This is a first. A text from Fletch. Listen: 'Urgent. You and your partner get to where you can stop and study this. This is the most fun I've had as a cop, bittersweet as the assignment is. Already second-guessing retirement. And in case you're wondering, no, I'm not texting this. Someone's keyboarding it for me on some fancy wireless thingie. This connection is not guaranteed secure, so here's your new numbers, one for each phone. Hang up and don't answer till you get a message from me. It will come in ten or twenty seconds and will be long. Both phones will ring. Hang up now.'"

Jack shoved the Vic back into park, and as they sat there alone in the wintry darkness, illuminated by only their headlights, both cops laid their cell phones on the rubber dashboard pad.

Both phones sounded simultaneously and the men reached to connect. *Write down those new numbers,* Fletch's message read. *I don't know how the techies do it, but both your phones have been reconfigured remotely and are now secure and impenetrable. They may have been secure before, and we have no evidence of anyone breaching their security, but now we know.*

Stewart Lang, Heathcliff Jones, and I have set up shop at the evidence lab with Doc Waldemarr, Judge Peggy Overmeyer, and

Friedrich Zappolo, Esquire. Stewie and Cliff and I have each chosen select beat cops we trust implicitly. They'll work with a SWAT team to handle the operation in River North. We already have visuals that tell us all the lights are on in the residence and that several people are there. We believe both Wades are there, and we can only assume our victim is too.

Boone didn't like Haeley being called a victim, especially, he hoped, prematurely.

Judge Overmeyer approved the warrants, and the tech team is wired in to Pete's, Thelma's, and Antoine's cells, as well as the landline at the condo, Pete's landline in his office, and the landline at their Naperville home.

Best, they have remotely engaged Haeley's phone, muted it, and programmed it to transmit. We don't know for sure where she is, and we assume someone has confiscated her phone, but this could give us our best information.

If we find that the Wades are holding Ms. Lamonica, we will strategize a retrieval. That's polite language for "Somebody's gonna get hurt and it ain't gonna be us." The number at the bottom of this message is the one you should respond to.

"So text back what we're up to," Jack said.

"What *are* we up to? You're gathering stuff for a snowball fight. . . ."

"You get hit with that baby in a snowball fight, and you're dead. What I'm gonna use it for will become obvious soon enough. Just tell 'em we're minutes away."

"How am I going to do that with one hand? Wait, this phone has voice-to-text." As Boone dictated, the words appeared on the screen: *Aim texting this bye voice. Minutes from safe house. Will cause plumbing problem, call in streets and san, and pull*

*our people out in tanker truck. Whole story later, but jacks
using an old friend of yours, Carl earl. For the job.*

Fletch texted back: *Got it. Green light. Muffled sounds from
Lamonica phone. Must be in someone's pocket.*

As Jack stopped for the first security check a few yards up
the dirt road, the cop in the beat-up, idling pickup rolled
down his window. "Deputy Chief Keller," Quincy said,
"didn't expect you this evening."

"Just checking on our man and dropping off my overnight
guest."

Boone leaned over and nodded to Quincy, who nodded
back and jotted on a clipboard.

As Jack drove toward the compound, he slowed and peered
ahead. "You see what I'm seeing, Boones?"

He followed Jack's eyes. "Lots of tracks."

"Pastor Sosa?"

"Probably," Boone said. "But that would have been one
car. There've been a lot more."

Jack stopped and turned around. When he reached the
pickup, the window came down again.

"Who's been here?"

Quincy looked at his clipboard. "Pastor Sosa. That's it for
tonight, till you. Why?"

"Oh, just thought someone else from our office might
have come."

"Nope."

Jack headed back.

"He's lying," Boone said.

"You got that too? What was your first clue?"

"Checking his list."

"Exactly. One visitor and he had to see who it was? Can you handle the Beretta with one hand?"

"I'd love to be tested."

"I'll just bet you would. And I'd wager my pension these tracks are only coming in, not going out, except Sosa's."

"So Quincy is Wade's guy?" Boone said.

"Looks that way. Question is who else, and who joined 'em tonight? We can't believe anything we see here."

When they reached the high fence the dogs barked and snarled, despite their wagging tails giving them away. "Poor things must not get much action, Williams," Boone said as the trainer called them off.

"You're right," Williams said. "You can see in their eyes that they want so bad to work, or play—and it's all the same to them."

But though the dogs seemed to lose interest in Jack and Boone at Williams's command, they didn't retreat to their warm shelter as usual. They sniffed the air and snarled and cavorted. Boone had an idea why. Those extra tire tracks had been no illusion.

Inside the Quonset hut, the shorter of the two disguised guards was dozing, and Unger kicked him when Jack and Boone entered. Both men stood. "Welcome back," Unger said. "Anything we can help with?"

"Nope," Jack said, the heavy burlap bag swinging in his hand. "Feel free to get back to your chores."

Unger chuckled and triggered the opening, while Sleepy cleared his throat and looked confused. Jack and Boone made their way through the hanging plastic curtain.

"Hey, *amigos!*" Pascual Candelario called out, switching

off the TV and laboriously rising from the couch. "What's new?"

"Sosa the only visitor you've seen tonight?"

PC nodded. "Thought I was getting some more when I heard the dogs about an hour ago. False alarm."

"Let's hope," Jack said, then ran down the plan for him.

PC's curious look gave way to a clouded visage. "We're gettin' out of here in a septic truck?"

"You first. Then I'll carry Jose up and hand him down to you. Then I'll help your mama get in."

"Where you takin' us?"

"No idea yet," Jack said. "But it'll be too cold to keep you in that truck for long."

"I know a nice place," Boone said. "Furnished, fancy even. If the first operation gets over in time, it'll be empty and likely well stocked."

"River North?" Jack said. "No way. It'll be a crime scene."

"Not unless somebody's dead. By the time they get Haeley out of there, CPD will have all it needs on Wade and Antoine Johnson, and probably Fox and Villalobos too."

"You're crazy," Jack said. "But it just might work. Nobody will notice an Addison Streets and San truck there in the middle of the night, and if we can get their cars out of the garage, we can pull it in there and unload the family."

"If it'll fit," Boone said. "That's a tall truck. I don't remember the garages being extra tall."

"If we have to pull 'em out in the driveway," Jack said, "so be it. Anybody watching will just be confused."

"I've been called toxic waste," PC said. "But nobody ever

expected to see me come out of one of those trucks. Chief, your bag is leakin'."

"I'm going to stick this in your toilet, Boone. Okay?"

"Mine? Why?"

"Might look suspicious if we show up and all of a sudden Pascual has a plumbing problem. Anyway, we can flood your room without messing up the whole place."

PC and Boone followed Jack into the tiny bathroom connected to the room Boone had stayed in. Jack wrestled the sack over the toilet and slowly lowered the ice chunk into the water. The level immediately rose to the rim. Jack used the bag to cover his hands as he reached to jam the thing into the neck of the bowl. It appeared to want to float, so he kept the pressure on until it was set.

Jack reached for the handle, looking knowingly at Boone and Pascual, and said, "Fire in the hole. Prepare to evacuate."

As soon as he flushed the toilet, it made a racket and water spilled onto the floor. Jack pulled the lid off the tank and disengaged the bobber. That kept the water rushing, and the three men moved back into the TV room.

"Call Carl," Jack said. "I'll go tell the guys up front what the problem is and that we've called the city. We've got to keep everybody out of that bathroom until the ice melts. The slush residue is going to look realistic."

"Gross, man," Pascual said. "You want me to pretend I was asleep? Everybody here knows I'm a night owl."

Jack said, "Just tell 'em you were watching TV when Boone's toilet overflowed. But wake your mother. Let Jose sleep until it's just about time to go. He won't cry or make a fuss, will he?"

"Naw. I'll convince him we're having fun."

"You've all got to dress warm and bring blankets. It's going to be really cold down in there."

Boone slapped his phone shut. "Carl says the roads are opening up, but he's still at least an hour out."

"Hope it's sooner," Jack said. "I still think we've got company."

Boone followed Jack to the front, where Jack told the guards at the counter what happened. Unger made a move like he was going to check it out. "No need to come back there," Jack said. "Got it under control. You can see we're tracking water. I shut off the feed and Streets and San is on its way."

"This time of night?" Unger said.

"Guess they've got an emergency unit for stuff just like this. I'll let everybody know someone's coming."

"Use my walkie-talkie," Unger said, pulling it from under the counter. He depressed the button. "Hut to Front, do you read? Keller wants a word."

"Roger."

"Hey, Quincy. Got a little plumbing problem here and think it's the septic. Streets and San is on its way."

"Everything under control?"

"Yeah, but watch for them. No idea how long they'll be, but they tell me it'll be a white tanker truck."

"Got it. You'll tell Williams?"

"Will do. And can you let me know when the truck gets here? I can lead him right to the tank."

Ten minutes later Boone received a text from Fletcher Galloway. *Just monitored a call to Wade's cell from the guard at the front of the complex there, telling him what's going down.*

Wade doesn't like it but this guy is assuring him he's got it all under control. Wade asked him if everyone else was in place. And he said yes.

So Quincy updates Wade on everything that goes on here, Boone dictated back.

Wade must have more than one insider, though. Ever vigilant.

Lots of tracks in the snow. Jack fears assassins. Our goal is to get our people out of here before anybody gets suspicious. And can we use the river north condo as the new safe house?

Bring them this way. We'll put them somewhere.

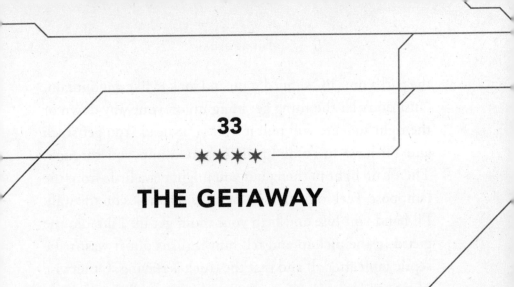

33

★★★★

THE GETAWAY

Pascual Candelario's mother sat holding her sleeping grandson, Jose, whom she had somehow outfitted with a heavy coat and shoes over his footy pajamas. Next to her sat a stack of blankets, two suitcases, and several paper bags. Clearly she had no intention of returning to the safe house.

PC looked pensive and sat with his monstrous parka in his lap.

"Peek out that window next to the door," Jack said, "and if you see only the truck and me, come out immediately. PC, you first. Head up the ladder and down the hatch. My guy says he set it to open easily."

"Am I going to fit in there, man?"

Jack stepped back and studied him. "Let me see you with

335

the parka on." PC slipped it on and looked like a mountain. "Just don't let the thing get hung up on your way down or the tight squeeze will pull it over your head. You get stuck and I'll have to come up there and stomp you through. There's no light in there, but you might get a little from the lamppost. Feel for seats, seat belts, and handles on the wall. I'll hand you Jose and help your mom get in. I'll radio the guard in the pickup and tell him it turns out it wasn't the septic tank after all and that the truck is leaving. Otherwise it's gonna look mighty strange, pulling in and then leaving right away."

Jack and Boone moseyed back up through the maze to the counter, waiting for word. Unger's walkie-talkie buzzed. "Streets and San is here," Quincy said. "Can you put Keller on?"

"Just click it to stay open," Jack said. "This is Keller!"

"Truck's approaching," Quincy said. "After I clear him, you want to tell him where to come to?"

"Sure."

Quincy set his transmitter to stay open as well. "Been expecting you," he said.

"Bet you have," Carl said. "I'm always the most welcome man in town, least till I get down into the muck."

"I'm gonna put someone on who'll tell you how to get to the tank. Hey, you look familiar."

"People tell me that. One of them faces, I guess."

"No, you look like a cop I knew years ago."

"Cop? Ha! Do they let ex-cons be cops these days?"

"Not hardly."

"Then I ain't your man. Been on this job since I got outta the joint thirty years ago. 'Bout to retire."

"Well, you could be his father or his older brother then."

"No cops in my relation," Carl Earl said. "They wouldn't have me."

"I swear you're a dead ringer."

"He was a handsome guy too, eh?"

Quincy laughed. "Keller, you there?"

"I'm here. I'll be waiting by the fence, sir. Follow me to the left and around the back."

As Jack stood at the front door of the Quonset hut watching for the truck, Boone said to the two guards at the counter, "You going to go out and help the driver get his bearings?"

Jack slowly turned, and Boone saw the horror in his eyes. Boone winked at him.

"Not on your life," Unger said. "We're not supposed to move from our posts. Now if he needs to get into the bathroom to look at the plumbing, we can help him."

"Freezing out there," the other said. "And those dogs give me the willies. Why don't *you* help out?"

Boone laughed. "The temperature and the dogs would not be good for my shoulder."

When the truck lights came into sight, Jack headed out. Boone went back through to the living area and past the Candelarios to the back door. Carl slowly backed the truck into place under the light pole as Jack walked alongside, waving for Pascual Candelario to come out.

Boone held the door open, icy wind slicing his face as he scanned for even a shadow of movement. PC pulled on his parka again and lumbered out. "This better work, man," he said. "You guys are *loco*."

Jack helped him get started up the side of the truck, PC yelping at the frozen ladder. "Don't you have any gloves, Pascual? You're going to freeze in there."

"I got good pockets."

Carl Earl opened his door and leaned out. "There's a wheel in the middle of the hatch top. I left it loose. Just spin it to the left."

"What're we gonna do for air in there?" PC said.

"I set the hatch to stay open about an inch," Carl said. "It'll be cold, but at least you'll be able to breathe."

"I'd rather suffocate warm. Never see cold like this in Mexico."

"Keep moving," Jack said. "I'll get Jose."

PC was surprisingly agile getting to the top, but he had to keep stuffing his parka into the hole as he went. Once he dropped out of sight, Jack stepped past Boone, whispering, "See anything?"

Boone shook his head.

Jack approached Mrs. Candelario. "He's still sleeping," she said. "Wrap him in this blanket and cover his face. If he wakes up, he'll be afraid. Just tell him you're taking him to his daddy."

It appeared to Boone that Jack was surprised at the weight of the boy, and it seemed all he could do to manage the ladder with his free hand. As Jack climbed, Jose whimpered and wrenched around, causing Jack to stop and push the little body higher against his shoulder.

"Let's go see Daddy, okay?"

"Daddy!"

"Shh!"

Mrs. Candelario approached Boone, dark eyes peering out at Jack and Jose. "Is he going to be okay?"

"Jack won't let go of him."

But as soon as Jack reached the top he stopped. In the light from the lamppost Boone could see Jack fighting to keep his footing on the curved steel top. He knew he should still be scanning the dark horizon for interlopers, but Boone couldn't look away.

"Hold still, Jose!" Jack hissed. "Pascual! Can you reach Jose?"

Mrs. Candelario set her stuff down and hurried out to the ladder. As she began climbing, Boone heard the telltale sound of the fake wall casing turning on its axis down the hall behind him.

With his good hand, Boone pushed the Candelarios' supplies out the door one by one. He hated to leave paper bags and blankets in the snow, but he couldn't let anyone see those.

Pascual reached through the opening at the top of the truck and gathered in his now-screaming son, shushing him as they descended from sight. Jack lost his footing and began to slide over the side, grabbing the hatch door with one hand and the top of the ladder with the other as PC's mother drew into his view.

"Hang on a second, ma'am! Let me get my bearings."

"Someone's coming!" she said.

Jack let go of the ladder and, attached only to the hatch, grabbed her under one arm. With his feet dangling, he hauled her up to the top rung where she could reach the edge of the opening.

"PC! Get your mom down there!"

Boone heard footsteps. "Jack, get out of sight! Carl, look busy!"

Carl huffed out of the cab while Boone used his foot to slide the supplies away from the door. Jack pulled himself up and over the other side of the truck, and Boone saw only his hands on the wheel atop the hatch door.

There Jack hung on the dark side of the truck as Carl kicked his way through the snow. Boone was just pulling the door shut as Unger arrived from up front.

"So, how's it going, Drake?" he said.

"All right, I guess, but I'm freezing."

Unger peeked through the window. "Driver doesn't look happy."

Even through the closed door, Boone could hear Carl swearing a blue streak. "He doesn't sound happy either. Guess he's decided it's not the septic tank after all."

"Where's Keller?"

"Out there somewhere, trying to help."

"He's a better man than I am."

"We already established that," Boone said, smiling, half expecting to be attacked from every direction in the next second.

Carl came to the door and banged loudly. "Let me in, you lousy—"

Boone quickly opened the door and shushed him. "Sir, we've got a family sleeping in here, including a child. Keep your voice down!"

Red-faced and gasping, Carl almost convinced Boone he was at the end of himself. He whipped off his fogged-up glasses and wiped them with an oily rag. "What do you people take me for?"

Boone put a finger to his lips, and Carl whispered hoarsely. "Call me out in the middle of a night like this. There's nothin' wrong with that septic. Let me see the toilet where this started!"

"It's the bathroom off my room," Boone told Unger. "Can you show him? I'd better find Keller."

Unger took Carl down the hall, and Boone slipped outside. "Jack! We've got him preoccupied. Come get this stuff!"

"I can't get back up!" Jack called, still dangling from the other side of the truck.

"Well, I can't get this stuff into the tanker. What're we gonna do?"

Boone heard a groan and Jack sliding, then a *whomp* as he landed in the snow, feet first and then on his rump. The air seemed to burst from his lungs.

"You all right, Jack?"

"I've been better," he said, slowly rising and coming around the back of the truck. He knocked on the side. "PC! Open the hatch all the way so I can get this stuff in there!"

In three trips up the ladder, Jack dropped the two suitcases and the pile of blankets into the tanker. As he came back down for the last of the supplies, Boone heard Carl and Unger coming. "Get in here, Jack!"

Jack pushed the remaining paper bags aside and tramped in, stamping his feet and rubbing his hands. "So the problem's not in the tank, eh?" he said to Carl.

The older man still looked agitated. "You people didn't need Streets and San! You needed a plumber."

"So we're dumb cops. Our bad."

"Your bad. Gimme a break. Well, I'm not moppin' up that mess in there. That's on you."

He pushed past Boone, giving him a look, and yanked open the door. "Put those sacks on the seat," Boone whispered. "Head toward the city and we'll be in touch. And, Carl, don't stop for anybody."

34

★ ★ ★ ★

ROADBLOCK

Boone watched Carl Earl grunt his way back into the phony Addison Streets and San septic tanker truck cab and slowly roll away from the back of the Quonset hut.

Boone pulled the door shut, freezing to his core, face stinging, shoulder throbbing. It had been too long between meds. He was none too happy to see Officer Unger from the counter out front still hovering.

"Where's the Mexican?" the undercover guard said.

"Probably sleeping," Jack said.

"No way. He usually watches TV till three, and there's no way he'd have slept through all this."

Jack peeled off his coat. "Maybe he's looking after his family.

When we're here, we've got him, so just assume he's safe and sound."

"I'd better check. It's my tail if anything goes wrong."

Jack stepped between Unger and the hallway leading to the Candelarios' bedrooms. "We've got it. Anybody hassles you, you tell 'em you checked with the officer in charge."

"No harm in peeking in to make sure everybody's—"

"Stand down! I said we've got it."

"You're not my superior officer, Keller, at least not on this job."

"I'd advise you not to test that theory, Unger. This witness and his family are under my jurisdiction, and—"

"And so you ought to be happy I'm making sure of their—"

"Back to your post, man. I'm not going to say it again."

Unger set his jaw and appeared to try to stare Jack down. "Okay, but it's not going to be my funeral. You know I got to cover my own backside."

"Do whatever you've got to do," Jack said. "But leave this family to us."

As Unger headed back through the maze toward the front, Boone heard him on his cell. "We've got a problem. I can't get a visual on the family, and Keller isn't allowing me to . . ."

Boone's and Jack's phones rang simultaneously. Fletch.

"Follow that truck!" he said. "Wade just took a call from the perimeter guard saying someone saw people climbing into it."

Boone and Jack caught each other's eyes. The closest route to Jack's car was the way they had come in. Boone could see on Jack's face that he was considering the same thing Boone was: heading out the back and around the side of the building to the car. But there wasn't time.

They rushed through the hanging plastic strips and down the dark corridor to the other set of the same. Just past those, Jack banged on the wall. As it slid open he hurried past the counter with Boone a step behind.

"I shouldn't have opened that," Unger said, his sleepy partner suddenly appearing alert and curious. "Downtown wants you to stay put until somebody calls you."

"Yeah?" Jack said. "Well, be a doll and take a message, will you, sweetie?"

As Jack and Boone reached the front door, Unger yelled into his walkie-talkie, "K-9! Do not let these officers reach their vehicle! Security breach!"

Jack burst through the door, and as the piercing wind hit Boone's face, he saw the trainer, Williams, burst from his shack and heard him cue the dogs. As they came snarling into view, Jack stopped dead. Boone pulled his Beretta and rested his shooting arm across Jack's shoulder.

"Williams!" Boone bellowed. "Control those dogs if you don't want 'em shot dead! Now you know Chief Keller and you trust him."

"I thought I did, yes, sir."

"He's going to go start our car and I'm going to cover him from right here. You make a move for your piece or allow those dogs to take one step toward either of us, you'll wish you hadn't."

"We're all at ease, Drake," Williams said.

Jack slipped away, the dogs following him with their eyes. When the car roared to life, Boone moved slowly toward the gate, gun still leveled at the dogs. "When this all shakes down, Officer, you're going to be glad you were on the right side of it."

As soon as he was through the gate he kicked it shut. Boone was about to holster his weapon when he noticed Williams reaching for the flap snapped over his sidearm. He crouched by the car, aiming directly at the man. "That'll be the worst decision you'll ever make. And the last."

Williams looked frustrated beyond words. He had the bearing of a former special forces veteran, and Boone knew it would haunt him to have been subdued. "When this is all said and done," Boone said, moving to the car door, "we'll talk and you'll thank me."

"You'd better hope that's all I do!"

Boone put his gun away and got into the car, trying to buckle up as Jack punched the accelerator and the squad fishtailed. "Easy," Boone said. "You won't do us any good stuck in the snow."

"No way Carl gets past that pickup. You know Quincy is watching for him. I swear, Boones, somebody's gonna die before they get to that family, and it's not going to be me. Good work back there, by the way. Glad you didn't have to shoot that cannon right next to my ear."

"I didn't want to have to kill a dog, let alone Williams."

"He's a good guy. He has to know that if something's gone bad, it's not because of us."

Boone called Carl. "They're onto us! You within sight of the pickup yet?"

"Terrific. No, this road is so bumpy I'm trying to go easy on my passengers. This yahoo gonna try to stop me, is that what you're tellin' me?"

"No doubt."

"Well, I ain't stoppin'. Fact, I'm gonna slow down and

let you catch up. If you got your man's phone number, tell him and his family to hold on, because I'm blasting through whatever they try to set up."

Boone found the connection to Pascual sketchy—no surprise, with him surrounded by metal. "Can you hear me, PC?"

Jose was crying in the background. "Just barely, man! We're freezing and it's hard to hang on!"

"Well, hold tight, because they're going to try to stop you."

"You should've given me a piece, Drake! How'm I supposed to defend my family?"

"By staying right where you are. You know we won't let anybody even start up the ladder."

"I'm countin' on you!"

The taillights of Carl's truck appeared around the next bend, and Jack flashed his lights. Carl sped up with about a quarter mile to go to the pickup. Boone saw the truck bouncing and swaying and could only imagine what it had to be like for the family, hanging on for their lives in pitch-blackness—and freezing.

Boone called Carl again. "Put your phone on speaker so you can drive with both hands!"

"I'm telling you, Drake, I'm not stopping for this guy."

"Roger. Just know that he knows you're coming. And we have no idea how many others are here and know too."

Sleet hit the squad's windshield, and slush also began to fly up from the truck's back tires. Jack sprayed the window and turned on the wipers. As soon as the blades cut a patch through which they could see, it became clear that Quincy had pulled the pickup across the gravel road.

"I couldn't have hoped for more!" Carl squealed. "I disobeyed, you know!"

"Say again?" Boone said.

"I'm packin'!"

"You hold your fire!" Jack yelled. "Do whatever else you have to do, but no shooting!"

"C'mon, Jack! I know how these things work. I'm automatically a sworn officer for this assignment and covered by CPD insurance. You know I'll take care of business!"

Boone caught sight of the speedometer as Jack punched the gas to keep up. At thirty-five miles an hour on packed snow over pitted gravel, Carl's tanker swerved right as if to go around the back of the pickup. As Quincy threw the pickup into reverse, Carl swung the other way and headed around the front of him, left tires off the road and into the soft drifts, the tanker bouncing and reeling.

Quincy quickly shifted into drive and shot in front of Carl, and the tanker blasted into the front-left tire of the pickup, spinning the smaller truck till it was facing the squad. Jack slammed on the brakes and the car fishtailed, slamming the pickup in the same spot with the back-right quarter panel of the Crown Vic. The impact threw Boone into his own door and then back into Jack, his obliterated shoulder taking the brunt. He howled.

As the pickup spun, having been pushed hard twice by speeding vehicles, its door swung open and Quincy was thrown into the ditch on the other side of the road.

"Gun!" Boone shouted, pulling his own and trying to lower his window with the same hand. A deafening report came from twenty feet past the totaled pickup, which had come to rest with its headlights illuminating Quincy as he dropped in a heap, a hole ripped from one ear through to the other.

"Carl!" Jack shouted.

"He was aimin' to kill you two, Jack!"

"Just get going! We're not alone!"

From the crossroad came three vehicles at top speed, one of them a CPD squad with siren blaring and lights flashing. The other two were late-model luxury cars reminiscent of Pascual Candelario's former colleagues. "A hundred to one Jazzy Villalobos is driving one of those," Boone said.

"He's driving into eternity," Jack said. "Get Fletch to call off any roadblocks between here and the city. And find out where we're supposed to go."

As the marked squad passed the crash site behind them, Boone heard over the police radio on the dash, "Officer down at the safe house!"

35

★★★★

THE CARAVAN

Boone heard rubber on metal behind him to the right and knew the unmarked squad had sustained damage in the crash with the pickup. The blue-and-white immediately caught up to Jack, aiming its spotlight at the rearview mirror.

"He doesn't want to play with me," Jack said, aiming his own spotlight directly back into the driver's eyes.

"Clear out of the way, Officer!" came a voice from the PA speaker in the grille. "In pursuit of that truck!"

Jack grabbed the police radio transmitter. "Back off! We're sentries for that vehicle. Do not interfere!"

When the marked squad car made a move to pass, Jack swerved into its path.

"You are impeding a police department operation!" the officer behind radioed.

"I was about to say the same!" Jack said. "Who am I speaking to?"

"Antoine Johnson of the 18th precinct. I've been given authority to apprehend this truck."

"You're a long way from your jurisdiction, Officer. As your superior, I am ordering you to cease and desist, and we will sort this out later."

"No can do, Keller. Sorry."

"You don't know how sorry. Who are the gangbangers following you?"

There was a pause. Then, "I am alone, sir. But I am arranging for backup, so be prepared to stop."

Boone was on the phone with Fletch. "So Johnson actually identified himself?" Galloway said. "That puts the nails in Wade's coffin. I'll get the superintendent to call off any roadblocks."

Boone told him about the two cars behind Johnson.

"They won't dare get caught in a roadblock anyway. I want them before they peel off. Where are you?"

Boone told him.

"I'll get squads in the area to apprehend them. Have your man in the truck head for the precinct station house on North Sedgwick."

"Roger. Just a few blocks from where the SWAT team is in place, right?"

"Correct. SWAT reports that Wade has left the condo. Somebody's following him. And Haeley's phone is still transmitting. On his way out Wade told his wife that if it rings, Haeley should answer it and say she's back in her hotel, that she was in a shelter for a while and her phone was dead. From what we can tell, it's only Thelma Wade and Haeley there now. We've got the phone transferring speech to text if you want to read it."

"Impossible in the car, Chief. Where can I hear it?"

Fletcher gave him the IP address where he could access the audio.

And as the unlikely caravan made its way from the Eisenhower to the Kennedy, Boone punched in the numbers that gave him access to Haeley's transmitting cell phone. It sounded as if it were within ten feet of the voices.

". . . and you know all this about your husband and me and Officer Fox how?"

"I have my ways."

"He told you?"

"I didn't need him to tell me," Thelma said. "I have eyes. And ears."

"And you're smart."

"Yes, young lady, as a matter of fact, I am."

"Then you know it's all a lie."

"Of course I do."

"You can't be happy about that," Haeley said.

"I wouldn't be happy either way. If it was true, I'd want to strangle him. That he made it up makes it worse. Would you be happy if you were me?"

"Happy about my husband using me?" Haeley said. "No, ma'am, I would not. If you're as smart as you say you are, and as smart as you seem, I'm guessing you haven't been happy for a long time."

There was a lengthy silence. Finally, Haeley spoke again. "So, where did those two go?"

"I believe Peter went to his office. What could look more

innocent than that? That's where he likes to be found when everything has gone down just as he planned it."

"And Fox?"

"Back into his hole. I don't know. He's got some ratty apartment downtown, and he has to lie low. He's angling for some kind of a deal, but he won't get it unless he sings real loud. And I don't guess Peter will let him do that, if you know what I mean."

"Let me ask you something," Haeley said. "How long have you known, and why have you let it go on?"

Another pause. Then, "The truth about Peter? For years. But the kids don't know. They don't even know about this place. For all they know we got a good deal on a house in the suburbs and have two nice cars."

"How do you live with it?"

"I knew he wasn't behaving himself almost from the beginning of our marriage. And when he started putting stuff in my name, I thought he owed it to me. He *did* owe it to me. And I liked it at first. But no amount of stuff can make things all right. Before I knew it, I was as deep into everything as he was."

"You can't leave?"

Boone heard a long sigh and assumed it was Mrs. Wade's. Jack said, "Hey, Boones, check out behind us."

Boone couldn't turn around because of his shoulder, so he lowered the sun visor and adjusted the mirror to where he could see. Several squad cars had seemed to appear out of nowhere and were pulling over the two cars behind Johnson's squad.

"That's not going to end well," Jack said. "Especially if one of 'em really is Villalobos. He's got nothing to lose."

From the other direction a half dozen lit-up squads

screamed through the darkness, exiting and coming across the bridge to enter the expressway from the other side. The gangbangers had waited too long to make their move. There would be no escaping now. Boone hoped there wouldn't be a gunfight, but he could hardly imagine another scenario.

"Antoine Johnson sticks with us and he'll have an awful lot of answering to do," Jack said.

"He'll claim he was just following orders and had no idea."

"Yeah," Jack said. "And the sun might rise in the west tomorrow."

Boone watched the sea of blue flashing lights until they disappeared behind him, as he listened for more between Haeley and Mrs. Wade. He was amazed at Haeley's poise.

"They think I can be bought?"

"Believe it or not," Mrs. Wade said. "You're going to get offered a lot of money. Otherwise, I wouldn't be optimistic about your future."

"Ironic, isn't it, trying to buy me off when I'm accused of taking a bribe?"

"I'll say."

Boone dialed Haeley's cell. He heard someone approach, then Mrs. Wade read off the number.

"That's probably Boone," Haeley said. "I'd better take it."

"You know what to do."

Click.

"Hi, Boone!"

" 'Hi, Boone'? Awful cheery for someone I've been trying to reach since—"

"I'm sorry. There was a fire alarm at my hotel, and since I didn't have my coat on, I was one of many the Salvation

Army took in. And when I got back, my phone went dead. Guess I'd been charging it from an outlet that had a switch, and I didn't know it was off."

"So where are you now?"

"Back at the hotel. Everything's fine."

"Can anybody else hear me?"

"No, I'm fine."

"Tell her you'll take the deal."

"Sorry?"

"Tell her you could use the money. Who couldn't?"

"But, what, how—?"

"We're monitoring it; now play along."

"Okay then, Boone. I'll see you tomorrow. . . . Love you too."

"Very good, missy," Thelma Wade said.

Boone listened carefully but didn't hear the phone being set down. Maybe he could risk texting her.

"I don't need any more trouble," Haeley said. "Anyway, how much money?"

"Depends. I think Peter wants you to testify against Fox. Say Garrett forced you, extorted you, tried to ruin your new relationship."

"In a way, that's true."

"Then take the money," Thelma said. "That's the only thing that will make all this worth it."

"Worth it? All I've been through? How about you? What makes it worth it for you?"

Mrs. Wade snorted. "Nothing. I just don't care anymore. Whatever I ever hoped for, that ship has sailed. But if I don't play this all the way out, I wind up in jail myself."

"But come on, ma'am. Talk about being intimidated, forced."

"I let Peter do it. I'm an accomplice."

"So testify against him to keep yourself free."

"Against my own husband. Against the father of my children."

"How different is that from what you're suggesting I do?"

"It's not going to happen," Mrs. Wade said.

"Where are we, anyway?" Haeley said. "I'm brought here blindfolded with no idea—"

"You're not far from where you started."

"So all those turns . . . I tried to keep track, but I was getting dizzy."

"They just don't want you getting any ideas."

Boone took a chance, believing from the relative clarity of the voices that Haeley still had the phone. He texted her. *Next ring, say it's your mother.*

"Getting a message?" Mrs. Wade said.

"My girlfriend. I can call her later."

Her phone rang. "My mother," she said. "Should I take it?"

"Yes, but remember—"

"Hi, Mom!"

"Order a pizza," Boone said.

"Sorry?"

"Tell her you're hungry."

"Doing fine. Hoping to get back to work soon. I'm kind of busy right now. Can I call you tomorrow?"

"SWAT will bring the pizza."

"Love you too, Mom!"

Fletch texted: *Cops untouched. Three gangbangers in custody. Villalobos to morgue.*

Suicide by cop? Boone tapped in, wondering whether Jazzy had come out shooting, forcing the police to return fire.

No. Suicide by suicide. Must have seen no way out. That made his boys give up easily.

Relieved.

Me too, Drake. How close are you?

Ten minutes.

Call me.

Boone dialed, and when Fletch came on, Boone told him of the pizza idea.

"Perfect. Just tell us when. Wade's taking calls from Johnson; Johnson is telling him where you guys are. We followed Fox home, Wade to the office. Tell Jack we'll have backup at Sedgwick even though we don't think Johnson is dangerous. He's influenced by Wade. We'll intervene there so Jack and Antoine can have it out while PC and his family are being extracted. Then I'll meet you in the garage at our office."

"What's your plan, Chief?"

"Just going to show up in Pete's office. His look will tell me all I need to know, not that there's any mystery left."

"And I can come with you?"

"I may need backup."

"No, you won't."

"But you wouldn't want to miss this, would you, Drake?"

"Not for a million dollars."

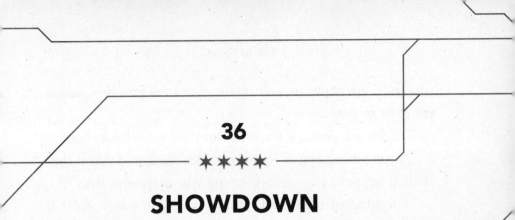

36

✻✻✻✻

SHOWDOWN

When he emerged from the marked squad that pulled in behind Jack and Boone and Carl Earl's phony septic truck at the CPD precinct station house on North Sedgwick, Antoine Johnson proved to be a buff, good-looking man in his late twenties, skin the color of milk chocolate. He looked both agitated and embarrassed.

Half a dozen cops jogged out, guns drawn, and surrounded the truck—something Jack had arranged while Boone was busy monitoring Haeley and talking to Fletcher Galloway.

Boone extricated himself and his excruciating shoulder from the unmarked squad in time to see Jack approach the young Johnson with both palms facing out at chest level. "Officer, you and I are going to have a talk after I tell you how this is going to go down."

"You're protecting a civilian who shot a cop back there!"

"A cop taking aim at fellow officers," Jack said. "And that civilian happens to be a former cop who saved our lives."

"Speaking of fellow officers, do you know how hard it was for me to stay on your tail when other cops were making arrests on the Kennedy?"

"There were plenty of them," Jack said. "They didn't need you. But how do you think your coconspirators felt about your abandoning them?"

"I was told they were with us on this deal," Johnson said.

"And what was this deal, Officer?" Jack said.

"A breach of security at the safe house."

Jack turned to an officer at the precinct. "Take the truck around back and get the family out of the tank. Maximum protective custody until you hear back from me."

The cops directed Carl's truck down a narrow alley between buildings as Antoine Johnson peered after them. "Don't worry," Keller said. "It's all under control now."

"This is one monster snafu," the young cop said.

"Who were you under orders from, son?"

"The Gang Enforcement Section commander of the Organized Crime Division."

"And you don't think I know you two are related?"

Johnson's eyes darted; then he seemed to study the unmarked squad. "What's that smell?"

"That's rubber on steel, Officer," Jack said. "I'm surprised we made it this far."

"What's going on, Chief Keller?"

"You really don't know, do you?"

"I thought I did, and I want to, but I'm freezing."

"Let's get inside," Jack said.

"I'm taking the car," Boone said.

"Take his," Jack said. "Mine's not going to last much longer."

Antoine Johnson shot Jack a double take. "I can't let—"

"Relax. I'll clear it. We'll get you wherever you need to go."

Johnson shrugged. "Keys are in it, Drake. Bring it back in one piece."

As Jack led Johnson inside and Boone was getting into the squad, he heard the young officer saying, "All I know is, Commander Wade—yes, my uncle and a man I have admired all my life—told me . . ."

Was it possible he really didn't know what was happening? Worse than his disappointment in Pete Wade would be his chagrin over being duped.

Fewer than ten minutes later Boone rolled up on the perimeter established by the SWAT team half a block from the Wade condo. Once he had identified himself, he was cleared through to the officer in charge, whom he told about the pizza delivery.

"That'll be perfect, sir. Our assessment at this point is that it is just the two women in there now. We doubt the one is armed, but we want to ensure the safety of the other."

"Let me make the delivery."

"Won't she recognize you?"

"I'll wear the delivery guy's hat and stand close to the peephole. That's all she'll see."

"Okay, but as soon as that door comes open, my guys will overwhelm her with size, noise, and . . . well, you know the drill."

"Just tell 'em to watch the shoulder, eh?"

"You're a hero to these men, sir. Nobody's going to let you get hurt again."

Boone moved through the phalanx of massive bodies outfitted head to toe in black helmets, armored vests, padded gloves, elbow and knee pads, and combat boots. Each carried an M4, a heavy, ugly assault rifle nightmares are made of. The appearance of star troopers alone would give pause to most bad guys. Boone didn't figure Mrs. Wade would offer much resistance.

He waited on the street near a gate that led to the condo complex, shivering in the darkness. Adrenaline fought his ravaged shoulder for attention. Boone would be so glad when this was over.

A few minutes later, a beat-up compact car with a lighted pizza sign on top skidded to the curb. When Boone emerged from the darkness to the light of a nearby streetlamp, the delivery guy opened his door a crack. "I'm not carrying much cash, but I have Mace!"

Boone flashed his badge. "Chicago PD. Just need a second."

The man emerged and approached cautiously, a red thermal bag in one hand, a small canister in the other. "Let me see that ID again."

Boone showed him and introduced himself.

"I know you," the man said. "You've been on the news."

"Good. I'm going to make this delivery for you. I just need

you to give me the pizza and your hat, and there's fifty bucks in it for you."

"Sure! But I gotta get the bag back. Any pie will be cold in sixty seconds in this weather without that."

"Don't need it," Boone said.

Boone pulled the cap down over his eyes, then waited as he slid the box from the bag. "You get yourself clear of the area now, hear?"

"I'd ask what's going on, but I don't suppose—"

"I can tell you? You're right."

Boone moved down the row of condos, and four SWAT team members fell in silently behind him. He approached the door of the fifth one from the street and leaned in so the only thing anyone could see through the peephole from inside was the hat and a bit of his face in the shadows.

He rang the bell. "Pizza!"

When he didn't hear anything, Boone was tempted to peer through the window. But he knew better.

Finally, footsteps.

The inner door opened and Thelma Wade stood there with her purse and only the glass door between them. "How much again?" she said.

"Ticket's in my pocket," Boone muttered. "Can you take the pizza?"

Mrs. Wade set her purse down and opened the door, but as she reached, Boone's four backups slipped past him and stormed in.

"Chicago Police!"

"Down on the ground!"

"Hands behind you!"

"Ms. Lamonica! Are you here? Chicago PD!"

Boone stepped inside just as Haeley appeared.

"You all right, ma'am?" one of the officers said as Haeley held a hand over her mouth and looked down on Thelma Wade, who was being handcuffed. A female SWAT team member suddenly took charge.

"Thelma Wade?"

"Yes."

"You're under arrest for kidnapping, unlawful detainment, and conspiracy to commit extortion. You have the right to remain silent. Anything you say can and will be used against you in a court of law. . . ."

Boone moved past the officers to Haeley, who set her jaw when he wrapped his good arm around her.

"You were great," he whispered. "Like you were made for this."

"All I want is to see Max. How soon can we—?"

"Somebody's going to take you downtown and debrief you. I'll find you later and we can head downstate tonight."

"When did you sleep last, Boone?"

"I don't even remember. But I'll be on adrenaline rush for a while. When this is all over, you can drive, and I'll medicate myself. You can wake me when we get there."

2:15 A.M.

When Boone pulled into the department headquarters parking garage downtown, he found Fletcher Galloway just inside the double glass doors that led to the elevator. Fletch had his hands deep in his pockets, shoulders hunched, and was pacing, his breath visible.

"Get where it's warm, man," Boone said.

"Don't want Pete to know I'm here yet. Anyway, we're waiting on Keller."

"Why?"

"Good job at the condo, but you've been out of the loop. Jack's bringing Officer Johnson with him and one other special guest."

"I'll bite."

"Thelma."

"Seriously?"

"Wants to be here. What can I say? Jack can hardly believe it, but he's become convinced Johnson was duped. And Jack has custody of Thelma. She's ready to come clean. Mostly to get leniency for herself, I guess, but Ms. Lamonica had a big influence on her."

"Haeley has that gift. She's had a big influence on me, too. Where do they have her, by the way?"

"Being interrogated upstairs. Fritz Zappolo is with her. He'll probably bill you for overtime."

Boone wanted to laugh, but Fletch still looked grave. "Tough night for you, boss."

Galloway looked away and nodded. "Some good police work going on, though. Listen, when the rest get here, we're going to meet in the little conference room on three. And if Wade starts to leave before we get to him, the front desk will tip me off. Don't think he's going anywhere, though."

"Why's that?"

"Keller got Johnson to give Pete misleading information. He knows Jazzy is dead, but he thinks Pascual and his family are too. As far as he knows, the only ones who can tie him to the mess are his wife and Garrett Fox. If he'd succeeded and we weren't onto him, he just has to eliminate Fox and control Thelma, and he's home free."

Thelma Wade looked like death and spent most of her time apologizing to her nephew. Antoine had the shell-shocked look of one whose world had caved in before he knew why. The truth seemed to be washing over him in stages. "Uncle Pete's a very persuasive and convincing guy," he said, shaking his head. "Had me go with him to the bank *and* to the evidence lab!"

When they were settled in the meeting room, Fletcher Galloway quickly ran down how he thought the confrontation should go.

"It should start with Drake," Jack Keller said.

"Me?"

"He's dead to rights and we got all we need on him, but you deserve the satisfaction."

"So do I," Thelma said.

"That's for sure," Jack said.

"Don't forget me," Antoine said.

"We'll all get to make our appearances," Fletcher said. "And while this may seem satisfying, seeing a guy get his, it's not a happy day."

Fletch herded everybody to an anteroom down the hall from Pete's office and set Boone's phone to transmit to his own so they could all listen in.

Boone dialed Pete's cell.

"Hey, Boone! What're you doing up?"

"Just heard everything went in the toilet at the safe house."

"Yeah, tough deal. One of the guards was killed too. A guy I assigned there."

"You anywhere we can talk? I'm downtown and I wouldn't be able to sleep anyway."

"I'm in my office, Boone. I don't sleep well after a fellow officer is lost either. Come on over."

37

★ ★ ★ ★

THE PAYOFF

Boone had never seen Pete Wade looking anything but dapper, but here he sat, out of uniform, plaid flannel shirt over jeans. And when he stood to welcome the younger man, Boone noticed his tan construction boots. On his desk lay a stack of papers that looked like busywork, time sheets and the like. Who did that kind of work during the wee hours?

Pete's familiar look of confidence was gone too. He appeared distracted, continually checking his watch. His Glock was strapped into his shoulder holster. He pointed to the chair in front of his desk, and Boone sat.

"Sad day for the CPD, eh?" Boone said.

"Hm? Oh yeah! Press will be all over this. All your great work with Candelario, and most of it goes up in smoke."

"A lot of evidence is already in play."

"Yeah, but—"

"I know," Boone said. "Without the star witness . . ."

"I'm sorrier than ever that you got mixed up in this, Boone."

"Mixed up in it? It was my case, Pete."

"But look what it's cost you. Almost your life. Your shoulder. Your new relationship. Maybe your career."

Do you know, Pete? Do you have any inkling, speaking of relationships and careers? How about your freedom? "I'm pretty disillusioned, I've got to say that," Boone said.

"I can only imagine."

No, you can't.

"But don't let it get you down, Boone. Remember Fletch and Jack and others who walk the talk."

"And you, Pete. Much as I hate that walking the talk cliché, you've been an example to me."

"Oh, well, I don't know about that. To me there's only one way to do this job."

"Mm-hm. Hey, thanks for showing me your Glock the other day. Sweet."

"It is, isn't it?"

"May I see it again?"

Pete unsnapped the flap over the holster, then hesitated, staring at Boone. Had Boone given himself away? He had to get the weapon from Pete so he wasn't dangerous to Boone or to himself.

"You've got me thinking about switching from the Beretta."

"Really?" Pete said, seeming to relax. He handed over the sidearm. "There are a lot of similarities."

Boone hefted the piece. "Still, there's something about a Glock."

"That there is."

"Jazzy always liked the Glocks, didn't he, Pete?"

"Sorry?"

"Villalobos. He was the arms guy for the DiLoKi, and he was a Glock man."

"That so?"

"You tell me, Pete. He was your friend, not mine."

A hardness settled in Wade's eyes. "Give me the gun back, Boone."

"Answer the question. Jazzy get you a good deal on the Glock of your choice?"

"What're you implying?"

"I'm not implying anything. I'm saying it straight out. All the pieces fit, Pete. You and Jazzy, Glocks, Jazzy's nephew taking a shot at me. You and Fox trying to frame Haeley to get to me."

"I want the gun back, now."

"If I give you anything right now, it'll be one between your eyes. You always told me to follow the evidence. In fact, you even told me once to follow the money. Well, I've followed it all, and guess where it all leads?"

"You've got nothing," Pete said, standing now.

Boone rose and cocked the Glock. "Sit. It's over. No more dancing, no more misdirection. So many people are ready to tell the truth, you have nowhere to hide anymore."

Pete slumped back down. "Haeley? Who's going to believe a tramp like that?"

"Nice try. You'd love to goad me into putting one in you,

wouldn't you? We've got all we need on you even without Haeley."

"Who've you got, Drake? Fox? He's damaged goods. Jazzy? Dead!"

"Yeah, you even got one of your plants at the safe house killed. You going to kill everybody, Pete?"

Wade blanched when his wife slipped in. "Yes, Peter, are you going to kill me, too? You've taken so much from me that you'll have to to keep me from telling everything I know."

"Thelma! What are you saying? You let them get to you?"

"Uncle Pete," Antoine said from the doorway, nearly in tears. "How could you?"

"You too? After all I've done for you? You turn on me?"

"Don't do this, Uncle Pete. I had no reason not to believe you. You were my hero, my role model. I bought everything you said."

"It was all true, Antoine! They're just pulling your chain now, trying to cover for themselves by blaming me!"

"Stop! I've seen the evidence. You can't fool me twice."

Jack came in, looking miserable, gazing sadly at Wade.

"I should have known you'd be behind all this, Keller," Pete said. "You've been jealous of me for so long."

"That's true," Jack said. "I never thought I could ever be the cop you were."

"Jack, it was Fox! He threatened me. He had the connections to the DiLoKi. I had no choice!"

But when Fletcher Galloway appeared, Pete fell silent. It was the end of a reputation, end of a career, end of life as Wade knew it. And Boone knew that if Wade still had his weapon, he would have shot them all or himself.

"You were one of my stars," Fletch said. "One of my boys."

Thelma burst into tears and Antoine led her out, Pete calling after them.

"It's just us now, Pete," Boone said. "Just our little team. When I joined the OCD, I thought I'd landed in paradise. What cop wouldn't have given everything he owned for a privilege like this? Look what you've done to us."

"I want a lawyer. I'm not saying any more."

"You don't need to," Fletch said. "Everything you've said since Drake got here is on the record."

"What can I do, Fletch? I'll do anything, give up anybody, everybody. I know I can't keep the job, but I can't go to jail. Please. For old time's sake."

The old man approached Pete's desk and leaned over it, palms flat on the top. "I liked you better when you weren't going to say any more."

"Fletch, please! We go way back. I'm going to need you in my corner."

"There's nobody in your corner, Pete," Fletch said. "Nobody who can help you. Word I get is that Fox is already singing, and you know the tune."

Pete's eyes darted between the three men and his chin began to quiver. "What have I done?" he said.

"What have you done?" Fletch said. "Violated your oath. Put a fellow officer's life in jeopardy. Tried to have a witness murdered. Falsely implicated a coworker. Lied. Extorted. Tampered with and destroyed evidence. Shall I go on?"

Pete buried his face in his hands.

"Worst of all," Fletch said, "you played me. There'll be no mercy."

"I'll kill myself. I will. I swear. You put me behind bars, you'll find me dead by dawn."

"That's on you," Fletch said. "But my guess is you won't be able to get that done either."

EPILOGUE

TUESDAY, MARCH 1

Boone Drake had never experienced anything like shoulder rehab. A young woman half his size manipulated and pulled and stretched his arm to where it was all he could do to keep from crying out. The pain meds barely kept up, and while he remained committed to returning to full strength as soon as possible, he could barely move the rebuilt ball-and-socket between therapy appointments.

Haeley visited him at his apartment every day, but Boone was also adamant about doing everything for himself. On the two occasions when Max was along, it was clear the boy had been warned to keep his distance. Boone looked forward to when Max could return to taking flying leaps at him.

Boone's mother had become so enamored of Max that she had prevailed upon Haeley to let him come downstate and spend a few days with "his future grandpa and grandma." Haeley told Boone she had left it up to Max, and when he had ecstatically agreed, "I asked Lucy not to talk as if our future was a foregone conclusion."

When Haeley arrived at Boone's around ten in the morning the first day of March, she had just taken a call from Max. "I needn't have worried about homesickness. He jabbered on about your dad's model planes and ships and trains and where they were going this afternoon—some indoor fair?"

Boone nodded. "Hope he likes the smell of manure."

Haeley peered out the window. "Your kind of a day."

"Is it?" Boone said, slipping behind her to see dark clouds roiling. "Oh, babe, we have to go out."

"You're not serious. What am I saying? You *are* serious. I thought our adventure today would be lunch at Carson's. Now I suppose you'll want a waterproof picnic."

"I'm all about compromise," Boone said. "If we can watch the storm from the beach, we can go to Carson's for lunch."

"I didn't bring a raincoat," Haeley said.

"You can wear my civvy. I'll wear my department-issue."

Twenty minutes later they pulled into the parking area near the Ohio Street Beach. Boone laid the two rain slickers and a blanket over his good arm while Haeley carried two lawn chairs from the trunk to one of several canvas, tentlike structures on the Lake Michigan sand.

"I don't want to rush you, Boone, but it'd be too ironic to lose you to lightning now."

He trudged along behind her as the wind whipped and the sky darkened. Whitecaps rose as waves crashed. They were unfolding the chairs just inside the flappy structure when the rain began. The temperature dropped quickly, so they donned their rain gear and sat close.

"Maybe we'll get to see lightning hit the Hancock," Boone said.

"That would make your day."

"It would. Ever seen that?"

She shook her head. "Lightning hit the ground a couple of blocks ahead of me when I was driving once. Scary."

"Cool. Wish I'd seen it."

"I know, Boone."

As the rain turned to hail, Boone rose and adjusted a flap on the tent so his view of the Hancock Center was unobstructed. "Would you ever testify against me, Hael?"

"Like Thelma's doing to Pete? That assumes you'd be guilty of something. I don't know I'd ever let it get that far."

"You'd mete out justice first, you mean?"

"Probably. You planning a crime, Boone?"

"Just wondering. That's got to be hard on them."

She shrugged. "She was able to cop a plea because of it. Three to five in Decatur? Could have been a lot worse."

"Pete tried everything to settle, but there's no plea-bargaining conspiracy to commit murder. Fritz says he'll get life."

Haeley shook her head. "And at Stateville. I'd rather get the chair."

They fell silent as the storm continued to rage. The hail stopped, the sky grew dark as night, and then the rain began again, huge drops becoming driving sheets as the wind challenged their tent on all sides. "This is living," Boone said.

"This is me loving you, Boone. You know I'd rather be curled up before a fireplace with a book."

Boone's phone chirped. It was Jack Keller. "We need to talk. You home?"

Boone suggested Jack meet him and Haeley at Carson's for lunch.

"Can't today, Boones, and this can't wait. Tell me where to find you."

When Boone told him, Jack said, "I'm in my dress blues, man. You want me sloshing through wet sand?"

"Wasn't my idea, boss. Third shelter from the left."

Half an hour later Jack slipped into the tent and immediately began wiping down his shoes.

"They'll just get messed up again on your way back," Boone said. "Forgot to tell you to bring your own chair."

Haeley immediately dropped to the blanket.

"I don't want to take yours," Jack said.

"Right," she said. "You're going to sit on the ground in your dress uni."

Jack shed his raincoat and hat, then sat and dug deep in the inside breast pocket of his uniform jacket for a manila file he had folded vertically.

"What was so important?" Boone said.

"For starters, Candelario has finished testifying. More record-setting indictments coming. He and his family will move out of the Wade condo and go into witness protection."

"What're they going to do, disguise him as a jockey?"

"Very funny. I have no idea where you hide a guy that size." Jack leafed through a few sheets. "Pete's sons are petitioning to try to get the condo. That's a long shot. I gotta think the court is going to want restitution for a lot of stuff. Feel sorry for Thelma's nephew, though."

"Yeah, what's happening with Antoine? You thought he was just used, right?"

Jack nodded. "Naive, but yes. Reprimanded for unapproved

activity outside his jurisdiction and on administrative proba-
tion pending review by Internal Affairs."

"Tough."

"A hard lesson. Hey, I tell you about Carl?"

"No."

"Going to get a medal of valor from the city, but get this:
he was fined forty dollars for unauthorized possession of a
deadly weapon."

Boone howled. "That could have been worse."

Keller folded his file and replaced it, eyes shifting.

"Out with it, Jack. You didn't come out into the weather
for just that."

"Well, I've got good news and bad news."

"About what?"

"About me."

"Start with the bad," Boone said.

"Margaret left me."

"Oh no!" Haeley said.

"I mean, she didn't *leave* me leave me. She still loves me
and all that, but she says we can't live together anymore, and
she won't see me unless I come to church with her."

"Wow," Boone said.

"She's going to your old church, Boones. Where Sosa is."

"Great church. You'd enjoy it."

"Haven't been there since, you know, the funeral."

"What're you gonna do, Jack?"

"Well, I don't think it's right to go to church just to keep
a woman. But I do love her. Respect her too. If this is that
important to her, I can check it out, I guess."

"Didn't matter that it was important to me? It's not like I never invited you."

Jack looked away and pressed his lips together, then smiled. "She has a little more hold on me, Boones."

"Time for the good news," Haeley said.

"I've been named acting chief of the OCD is all."

"Acting?" Boone said.

"It's just a timing thing. It'll happen."

"Congrats, Jack," Boone said. "Well deserved."

Haeley rose and embraced Keller. "So happy for you."

"There's good news for Boone too. That's really why I'm here. Downtown has authorized me to tell you that your petition for reinstatement has been accepted."

Boone pumped a fist. "Yes!"

"There's more. Funding for the Major Case Squad has been approved. They asked me about your suitability to head it up. I said there was nobody better. Next step is you officially applying."

"How do I do that?"

Jack dug out a business card. "Call this guy and tell him you want it. He'll tell you what to do next."

"And if I get it?"

"You'll get to staff it, and you'll be working out of the new offices at the 11th. There is a catch, though. You've got to pass a rigorous physical. This is management, but it's also street. You've got to be good to go."

"Just watch me."

On their way to Carson's, Boone insisted on driving. Haeley took a message on her phone and broke into giggles.

"From Dorothy Galloway," she said. "Inviting you and me and Jack and Margaret to a barbecue, listen to this, 'when the weather permits. And just so you know, I will be speaking to only the women.'"

As they were eating, Haeley's phone rang. "Yes, hi, Mr. Zappolo. . . . Yes, he's with me. . . . Okay." She glanced at Boone and whispered, "Wants me to put it on speaker."

She set the phone between them, and they leaned in to listen.

"You two free this afternoon?"

"We could be," Boone said. "What's up?"

"Well, first, you owe me five grand, Drake."

"Well aware."

"But maybe I can take it out of the settlement."

"Settlement?"

"The city wants to settle with Haeley quietly, avoid the courts and the press."

Haeley said, "I wouldn't—"

"They don't need to know what you would or wouldn't do, ma'am. They have a figure in mind and want to present it preemptively."

"Which means what?"

"Which means they bring a check, and when you sign it, it absolves them of all liability regarding your false arrest and imprisonment and everything that resulted from it."

"How much are we talking about, sir?"

"I'll tell you what they told me, Haeley. They said you would be very pleased. I said, 'Seven-figure pleased?' And they said, 'Oh yes.' You know what that means?"

"Of course I do, Mr. Zappolo. You get your boat."

TYNDALE HOUSE NOVELS
BY JERRY B. JENKINS

- *Riven*
- *Midnight Clear* (with Dallas Jenkins)
- *Soon*
- *Silenced*
- *Shadowed*
- *The Last Operative*
- *The Brotherhood*

THE LEFT BEHIND® SERIES *(with Tim LaHaye)*
Watch for the new look coming spring 2011

- *Left Behind®*
- *Tribulation Force*
- *Nicolae*
- *Soul Harvest*
- *Apollyon*
- *Assassins*
- *The Indwelling*
- *The Mark*

- *Desecration*
- *The Remnant*
- *Armageddon*
- *Glorious Appearing*
- *The Rising*
- *The Regime*
- *The Rapture*
- *Kingdom Come*

Left Behind Collectors Edition
- *Rapture's Witness* (books 1–3)
- *Deceiver's Game* (books 4–6)
- *Evil's Edge* (books 7–9)
- *World's End* (books 10–12)

For the latest information on Left Behind products, visit www.leftbehind.com.
For the latest information on Tyndale fiction, visit www.tyndalefiction.com.

CP0279

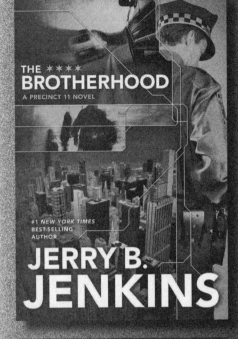

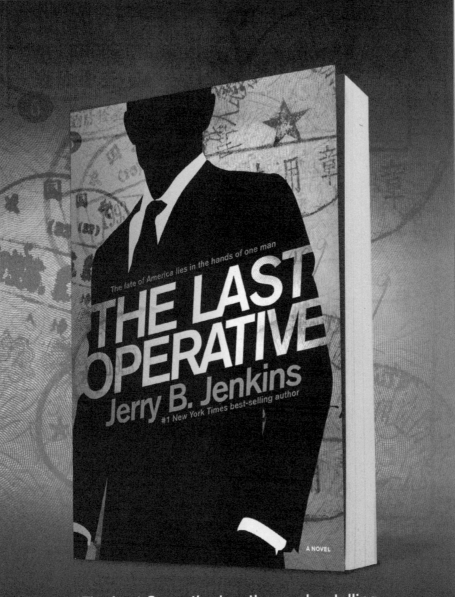

"*The Last Operative* is a thorough retelling of my very first standalone novel, which marked what I considered a major step in my writing journey. And of all my books, this has my favorite cover, hands down."

–Jerry B. Jenkins

From *New York Times* best-selling author
Jerry B. Jenkins

A condemned man with nothing to lose

meets one with nothing to gain,

and everyone washed

by the endless ripples

of that encounter

recalls the day

a bit of heaven

invaded

a lot of hell.

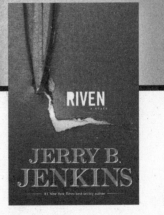

WHAT IF IT HAPPENED TODAY?

NEW LOOK! COMING SPRING 2011